Lazarus

3rd Edition

Also by this author

Assume Murder 2023

Lazarus 2024

Black Ice 2025

Contents

Acknowledgements

This story would not have been possible without the support and encouragement of my family and friends. I would like to acknowledge the support of the Thursday Night Writer's group at the Katharine Susannah Pritchard's Writer's Centre in Greenmount, Western Australia. A special mention should go to Jo, who, whilst listening to the first draft of the early chapters, encouraged me to introduce some romance, Clare for her sensitive guidance and Phil for his insensitive guidance.

I am also grateful for the information on the shipwrecks of the Abrolhos sourced *inter alia* from the Maritime Museum in Fremantle, my good friend Jeff Leach whom I have crewed for on many expeditions up to the Abrolhos, and a casual conversation I had many years ago with my mentor John Rothwell, concerning the lost treasure of the *Aagtekerke* which inspired this story.

For the avoidance of doubt, Jeff, whilst a very successful and extraordinarily generous businessman, is nothing like Lazarus!

I'd also like to recognise and thank Keith Richards, Barry Elswood and Mandy Bee for their priceless proof reading.

Disclaimer

This is a work of fiction. Names, characters, businesses, places, events, and incidents are either the products of the author's imagination or used fictitiously. Any resemblance to actual persons, living or dead, or actual events is purely coincidental All characters portrayed in this story are fictional although some share the names of my father, my friends, and my sisters (with their permission). The story itself, like all good yarns, interweaves historical facts with fiction. Interestingly, the stamp collection does exist.

Dedication

This book is dedicated to my wife Wendy and my son Jack who have supported and encouraged me to write when the storm clouds gathered, and to Jeff for his friendship and support.

To Mum and my late father, who gave me the self-confidence I have carried throughout my life and empowered me to do the impossible.

Cover image created with MS AI Designer Powered by DALL-E3
ISBN 978-0-6455678-3-0 Published by Black Ice Publishing 2025

Lazarus

Nigel M Barker

Part I

The Stamp Collection

Chapter 1 The Eulogy 1980

Gentle rain tapped against the windows, bringing to mind one of my dearly departed grandmother's sayings: 'Happy's the bride the sun shines on; blessed the corpse it rains upon.' My reflections were cut short as my older sister Karen spoke up.

"I just don't understand why he'd say that," she said as she pressed down his clothes into a cardboard box.

"Well, he's dead now, so you can't exactly ask him, can you? Maybe it's just how he'd like to be remembered?"

"Yeah, but no one would regard him as a keen fisherman, would they? Certainly, I can't remember him ever taking us fishing when we were kids, can you? I don't think he even owned a fishing rod. I mean, I haven't found any fishing gear, and I've gone through all his stuff; not even a fishing magazine."

"Well, maybe it was something he did when he was in the Navy before he met Mum? He never really spoke about that time, did he? He was quite secretive about it, as I recall."

"Well, he was a cryptographer! You can't get much more secretive than that, can you?"

"Yeah, you got that right. I remember when I was in hospital having my appendix out. I must have been about seven. He wrote a get-well message to me in code, and I had to decipher it.

"Who gives a seven-year-old boy a get-well card written in code? Jesus! It's a wonder I turned out as normal as I did!"

"There'd have been no point in giving that sort of thing to me or Judith. We wouldn't have had a clue at that age."

Kneeling on the mustard-coloured carpet in the lounge, we continued packing away his meagre possessions into the cardboard boxes we'd bought from the local storage company. I'd been staying at my sister's, and we'd travelled up to Dad's rented semi-detached property in Tonbridge from Eastbourne together to sort things out. The agent had insisted that we had to vacate the property at the end of the week.

Karen sighed as she packed away the last of his worldly possessions and sealed the box with a noisy application of sticky tape. She stood up and glanced around the room, devoid now of anything that might give evidence to the character of its former inhabitant. "You know he wrote his own eulogy," she said.

"Yes, I know. I don't think anyone's going to argue with a dead man, are they? If he wanted to be remembered as a keen fisherman, then so be it."

"It's sad, really," Karen said, "a modest man with a modest life who died practically penniless. At least he left you his stamp albums. Are you going to have them valued?"

"Nah, he told me he'd had them valued a year-or-so ago, and they weren't worth anything. I think it was just his way of travelling to those 'Far-away Places with Strange-sounding Names' when he was a kid; like the Bing Crosby song he used to sing to us when we were growing up."

"Yeah, I remember that. He was a good singer, too. Strange, it was the only gift he made explicit in his will. It seems odd that he'd specify that specifically, and then just leave the rest of his stuff to be divided between the three of us. Not that there's much left to argue about."

"Well, I guess it's all finalised now. I've no idea what I'll do with them.

"By the way, how's Judith coping?"

"Better now. She was always Dad's favourite. Struggled at school like me, but turned out alright."

Judith was the youngest of the three of us. We were each separated by two years.

"I'll pop in and see her before I fly back to Aus. What about Coco?"

"She'll be coming home with me," Karen said as the black and white cat sauntered into the room to see what was happening.

Karen drew a deep breath before changing the subject. "When d'you fly home back to Aus?"

"Next Sunday. I'm actually looking forward to it, after the trauma of sorting out the estate and everything.

"I tell you what, if I find a penny black or a fabulously valuable stamp in Dad's albums, I'll send you a postcard—from the Bahamas!"

* * *

It was some years later, around 1985, that I found myself at home in Perth, piling up books on the dining room table. I was deciding which to take to the op. shop and which to keep when I came upon Dad's old stamp albums. I don't think I'd opened them since returning to Australia. As often happens when I have a clean out, I got distracted by past images and other memorabilia. And so it was with Dad's albums.

What was I to do? I suppose I could have taken them to the local philatelist and see if they were interested in buying them. Dad had been quite insistent that I kept them when he was alive, but now they were just gathering dust. Then there was the question if I did decide to keep them, of who I'd leave them to, when I eventually fell off the perch myself.

Something made me open the first album. Its rough yellowing pages felt stiff and yet fragile in my fingers. The smell of gum Arabic reminded me of my youth, watching Dad with his tweezers and magnifying glass.

He'd sit for hours at the kitchen table telling us kids' stories behind a special stamp and tales of the exotic foreign land they had come from.

Dad was meticulous, that much was obvious. Every section was perfectly laid out by country. A place for every postage stamp, and every stamp in its place.

But then something caught my eye. An Australian fly fisherman twenty cent stamp in the UK section between two worthless stamps of King George V. I'd have easily passed over it, but as an old sergeant major once said when recruiting for the special forces, candidates that are going to make it, stand out like dog's balls. Could this be a hidden treasure waiting to be discovered? A quick check in Stanley Gibbons Stamp Catalogue, showed that the stamp in question was printed around 1979-81 and had a current value of $3.95. I guess he was right when he said that his collection wasn't worth anything.

I turned more pages and with a sad heart, acknowledged the countless hours my dad had spent in compiling the collection over his lifetime.

He'd left behind a legacy, and I felt his presence over my shoulder as I closed the last volume and stacked them on the table to be dealt with in the morning.

That night, I had a fitful sleep. I couldn't get the image of the Australian fly fisherman stamp from my mind. It was so out of place.

It was two o'clock in the morning when I gave up any pretence of sleep, and opened volume one, page twenty-eight, and looked at the stamp again. Was Dad sending a message from the grave?

That's just stupid, I thought.

I worked through the rest of volume one, and occasionally came upon a stamp that I thought might be worth something, only to be disappointed following a quick check in the catalogue. One thing was obvious; however, there was not a single other stamp out of place, not in volume one, and not in any of the other five volumes as far as I could see.

Turning back to the fisherman, I carefully lifted the stamp and found a small number twenty-eight written in pencil on the hinge behind.

Oh, Dad! What on earth are you playing at? I thought.

Chapter 2 Something Fishy

Over the five years that followed, I found myself returning to the albums from time to time, although with less frequency as the years rolled on. Whatever the message was, it was lost on me and probably for all time. Knowing Dad, it may well have been some witty remark like Spike Milligan had written on his tombstone. What was it now? Oh yes, 'I told you I was ill!' I smiled at the thought. Another red herring for me to follow.

One day, I thought enough was enough. It was with that thought in mind that I decided to take the albums down to the local philatelist at the weekend and take whatever I could get for them.

I retrieved the cardboard box from under my bed, emptied its contents on the kitchen table, and felt immediately guilty. Once again, I felt Dad's presence standing behind me. He was looking over my shoulder. I remember him emphasising just how important these albums were to him, and how they had been the only item in his will, which was specifically bequeathed to anyone. I could hear his voice in my head saying, 'Try harder'.

Closing the albums, I sighed and piled them back into their cardboard box. I struggled to carry it to the bedroom and slid it back under the bed. I'd take them to the shop another day, I thought.

The early hours of the morning have always been a good time for me. A time for clear thought, with no distractions.

Volume one, page twenty-eight.

It was quite deliberate. Of that much, I was sure. The stamp was printed before I had emigrated to Australia. Perhaps that's why Dad had chosen an Australian stamp so rudely inserted into the UK section of his album.

Dog's balls—I was meant to find it.

But what was the significance of the number twenty-eight? Or was it volume one page twenty-eight, twelve and 8 maybe? The twelve apostles sprang to mind. My middle name was Matthew. Was that connected? Perhaps it related to the twelve signs of the zodiac?

Fish represented Pisces. Could it have something to do with Jesus's five loaves and two fishes? Its face value was $0.20 so, how was twenty related to twelve or twenty-eight?

My little rental property in Perth was still and silent as I switched on the light over the dining room table and opened volume one. Sitting in my dressing gown, I started to jot down notes and quickly had more permutations than I could make sense of. There had to be another clue hiding in the album and then a key, a decoder, or a primer to make sense of it all.

I reached for volume two and painstakingly started to search each page. I almost missed it but there, on page 27, in the South African section, was a peculiar $0.50 stamp featuring a primitive coelacanth fish. This fish was believed to have been extinct for millions of years until scientists rediscovered it in 1938. It was hiding in plain sight and certainly not as obvious as the Australian stamp in the UK collection, but something about it caught my attention. I gently lifted the stamp on its hinge, and found another pencil mark, which read 27. So now I had four numerals. 2, 8, 2, and 7.

Well, it certainly wasn't a historical date, or a timestamp come to that. There was more to it than that, but what exactly, eluded me.

After several hours, the early morning sun shone through the curtains and I looked up at the clock. It was time to go to work and whatever hidden messages were waiting for me, had to wait a little longer.

A quick shower, three slices of toast, two with marmalade, one with vegemite and two cups of coffee later, I jumped into the car, checked the street directory and set off for my first meeting of the day.

I resolved to call Karen later that evening, to get her to email me a copy of Dad's eulogy that he had written. Perhaps there was a primer or more clues in that, which would unravel his final tease.

* * *

The call to my sister that evening was of no use, other than to assure her that I hadn't discovered a priceless stamp and fled to the Bahamas on the proceeds.

The thing was that there were literally thousands of stamps collected over his lifetime.

Volume three was, well, voluminous. Working through it I felt tired and conscious of starting to make mistakes when almost at the end of it I noticed a small stamp from France which featured another fish, a fresh-water pike.

I remembered the stamp from my youth. Pike in England were considered a coarse fish, but apparently the French ate them along with snails and other disgusting delights. I remember Dad laughing uproariously at how I turned my nose up at the thought of such a thing. Now I came to think about it, Dad had spent rather longer talking about that stamp and the coelacanth stamp than others in his collection, almost as though he was trying to imprint a memory in my mind.

Lifting the stamp revealed yet another number which matched the page number 30.

So now I had six numbers, two from each volume 282730. If I included the volume numbers, then that would take the total to 9, but something told me that they weren't part of the equation.

When I was in hospital, the coded get-well card from Dad was a simple transposition of numbers for letters where one represented the letter A, two the letter B, and so on. Here, it made no sense, no matter how I grouped the letters, no matter where I started the sequence. There had to be still more.

His sense of humour sprang to mind. There was definitely something fishy going on.

Something fishy! That was it! I raced through the other volumes and sure enough, I found three more stamps featuring fish, each with its own number pencilled behind it. I now had a set. twenty-eight, 27, 30, 113, 41 and 52.

Hours turned to days as I methodically examined every other stamp in the collection. There were no other hidden numbers, primers, or codes that I could see. I was definitely missing something.

The fish on the Australian stamp looked like a rainbow trout. Not exactly native to Australia. The second South African stamp featured a fish thought to have died out with the dinosaurs. The third French stamp featured a pike. The fourth an Indian stamp featured a dart, a prawn and something that looked like a pilchard. Then there was a Madagascan stamp featuring a hammerhead shark and finally, on the sixth stamp from Holland, a stylized red fish.

I wrote their concealed numbers down in my new notebook.

I also looked at my old notes from 1980. The more promising ideas that I had recorded at the time seemed less promising now, and I discarded them.

Interestingly, there was only one stamp in each album that featured a fish. Something fishy indeed! The only thing missing was a red herring! Oh dear! I thought. I am nothing if not my father's son.

Chapter 3 An Unexpected Journey

The numbers haunted me. They meant something, but what? Was there a hidden message in the names of the fish? Their Latin names, abbreviations, or countries of origin maybe?

A month later I am on the road again and I am thinking TGIF, Thank God It's Friday, as I drive to meet a client and an acquaintance at Fremantle Sailing Club. He was about to leave on an extended voyage around Southeast Asia and needed to set up some final authorities before he set sail.

Lazarus's yacht, '*Sea Dragon,*' was on the end of 'A' jetty, and I looked enviously at the boats penned alongside as I took the long walk out to the T.

The *Sea Dragon* was beautiful. A brand-new 50' Cruiser set up for solo handling. Lazarus had had her built especially in a three-cabin configuration and spent a small fortune prepping her for her voyage. First, up to Indonesia via the Abrolhos Islands, and then wherever the wind would take him.

I remember him saying, as far from his ex-wives as he could get. Rumour had it that he'd just got rid of number five from memory, although with Lazarus, you couldn't even be sure he had any.

"Michael, old boy! Come on! Lose the shoes and jump on board!"

I felt the warm teak decking beneath my feet as Lazarus's frying-pan-sized-hand engulfed my own with a bone crunching grasp.

"Come below. We can sign all the paperwork and have a drink to celebrate my imminent departure."

Lazarus, all 6'6" of him and not an ounce of fat, had perfected the look of an old sea dog with black wayward hair, an unkempt, full beard and a wild look in his eye. He had it off pat. However, beneath the crusty façade was a shrewd businessman who had made his fortune through inspirational investments and property development.

Inside, the cabin was surprisingly cool. The beautiful, lacquered teak cupboards and floor reflected the blue-and-white upholstery. Everything was perfect.

Lazarus's piercing blue eyes studied the documents I had brought over for him to sign, even though his own lawyers had already approved them. I was essentially just a delivery boy.

"So, when are you off?" I said, having placed the signed papers back into my attaché case.

"Tomorrow morning. Make the most of the Easterlies."

"I wish I was coming with you," I said wistfully.

Lazarus then surprised me when he said, "Come with me up to the Abrolhos. I know you've sailed up there a few times over the years. It'd be good to have someone else on board, initially at least. It's just a few days of sailing. Bit of a shakedown before the big trip really starts. What say you?!"

So, there are times in your life when opportunities present themselves. Places where you can choose to turn left or right in the fork of the road. My dad had said before he died that he had no regrets, and neither should I. If I had an opportunity for adventure, then I should take it. Here was an opportunity to have an adventure, albeit for only a few days. If not now, then when?

"Seriously?"

"Come on, don't be boring. Just do it."

To be honest, I didn't need much persuading. It was a long weekend and there was nothing at the office that couldn't wait for a few days, even if I didn't get back until the following Tuesday.

"Yes. Right. I mean, yes, I'd love to."

"Excellent. Get those papers back to the office, grab some gear and be back here by five.

"Five a.m.?"

Lazarus laughed. "We set sail at 5:30 a.m. but if you can, get back here by five this evening. We'll have a hearty meal and a gallon of rum at the clubhouse before we leave. It may be the last decent meal for a few days, and I have a rule that we'll need to be sober whilst underway, so it'll be the last drink for a few days as well."

At home I quickly stuffed a few items into my kit bag including my well-thumbed notebook which, incidentally, held all my ideas regarding Dad's cryptic messages although to be honest, I never imagined having much time to sit and ponder what they might mean.

A couple of hours later, I'd returned to FSC and stowed my gear in my cabin amidships. Lazarus and I strolled back down 'A' jetty to the clubhouse where we enjoyed a chicken parmigiana, washed down as promised, with copious quantities of booze.

Chapter 4 The Abrolhos

At 5:30 am, the sodium lights on the jetty were starting to lose their battle against the rising sun behind us.

Lazarus started the small diesel engine as I disconnected shore power and, with a nod from the skipper, cast off forward and let her bow swing out in the breeze. Lazarus leant over and cast off aft as I made my way back to the cockpit.

We motored through the heads and no sooner had we exited, than Lazarus hoisted the main and jib and swung her nose north as we passed the entrance to the Swan River.

As we sailed up the coast of Western Australia, the conditions could not have been better. A brisk twenty knot easterly off the land allowed us to put on a cracking pace, whilst the swell from the northwest was practically nothing. The sky was cloudless, and the yacht pierced through the water, its wake as straight as an arrow as the auto pilot held us steady. Lazarus turned to me and pointed to the brand-new state-of-the-art electronic chart plotter, the first of its kind, and zoomed in on the Abrolhos Islands to our north.

"I'll hold up in Turtle Bay for a couple of days, just behind East Wallabi Island. There's a choice of a few public moorings there, so I won't have to worry about dragging anchor at night. You'll be able to get a puddle jumper back to Geraldton from the Island and from there, a scheduled flight back to Perth."

Lazarus pulled up the chart on the screen. “Just put the co-ordinates into the auto pilot here, and it’ll do the rest.”

I’d flown back from East Wallabi on a previous occasion and delighted in telling my dad all about the dirt runway during one of my all too infrequent trips back to the UK. He seemed to know about the runway from a brief visit to the islands during his Navy days although as usual he was pretty tight-lipped about it.

“I’m not overly familiar with this new auto pilot. Can you show me how to do that?”

“OK, it’s quite simple, look. Here on the chart is where the moorings are. That’s my favourite one there.”

Lazarus moved the cursor on the screen and a set of numbers appeared; 28 degrees 25.44 minutes south and 113 degrees 42.21 minutes east. He confirmed it as our destination and pressed Enter.

It was such a moment of pure excitement and revelation that I gasped out loud.

“You’re an odd one, Michael,” Lazarus said, a quizzical expression across his face. “It wasn’t that exciting, was it?”

“No wait! Hang on a minute! Don’t go anywhere!”

“Where the bloody hell am I supposed to go out in the middle of the Indian Ocean?” he called out as I rushed below deck to my cabin. I grabbed my notebook, flicking the pages over and quickly found what I was looking for and returned to the cockpit.

“Here! 28, 27, 30, and 113, 41 and 52.”

“I don’t understand. What’s going on?”

I explained to Lazarus how I believed that my dad had left me a coded message in his old stamp collection, and the numbers just had to be longitude and latitude.

“Can you plot those on your new chart plotter and see where in the world they are?”

“No need, old boy. I can tell you that they point to a spot basically next door to where we’ll be mooring.”

“Humour me skipper, please?”

“OK, here we are.” Lazarus’s fingers moved deftly across the screen. He selected a ruler function and said, “There you go, a sandy patch on West Wallabi, 2.7 nautical miles as the crow flies Southwest of my favourite mooring. You might see some more detail on the paper charts below decks, but I doubt it. I'll drop you off in the tender and you can walk between the islands at low tide. You can go and have a look before you catch your puddle jumper back to Geraldton, but it doesn't look as though there's anything there. The islands are totally uninhabited.

"I tell you what, if you don't find buried treasure, you could always take a walk over to Wiebbe Hayes's Fort," Lazarus laughed. "You know, it's the first European structure built in Australia. Not much more than a pile of stones now, but it's still interesting."

"I might just do that," I said as I studied the chart.

* * *

That night, we continued our voyage up the coast of Western Australia. We planned to approach the Abrolhos from the east, soon after sunrise. This made spotting the treacherous reefs easier with the sun behind us.

We took turns holding watch and in between, Lazarus suggested that I read one of the books he had on board about the Abrolhos and the ill-fated Dutch East India ship, the *Batavia*, its passengers and crew. I was particularly interested to read about Wiebbe Hayes and his fort, since Lazarus had mentioned it.

Of course, the last stamp in volume six had been a Dutch stamp. The clue was there all along.

"You know the story of the *Batavia*, do you?" said Lazarus, as I climbed into the cockpit to take the next watch.

"Not really, but I'm learning fast. It's a pretty thick book!"

"Well, it's a fascinating story. The *Batavia* was the first recorded VOC, that's the Dutch East Indies Trading Company, shipwreck on the islands, carrying a fortune in silver coins. Something like thirty-five million dollars in today's money. Plus the passengers were carrying a personal fortune in gold."

"How come so much cash?"

"Ah well, me old mate. If you're sitting comfortably, then I'll begin," he said with the air of a lecturer about to serve up his pearls of wisdom to an attentive audience. "The reason they carried so much cash was to pay for spices, you know, nutmeg and the like. Worth more than their weight in gold when you got them back to Europe. You must remember that there were no refrigerators in those days, and people used spices not only to flavour meat but also to preserve it. A successful voyage could set you up for life!"

Lazarus was in his element. I was a captive audience.

"The *Batavia* was around 45 or 46 metres long. Pretty small by today's standards, but when she was built, she was the pride of the VOC, their flagship. What's more, she was on her maiden voyage when she was wrecked."

"Like the *Titanic*," I said, not wishing to appear a complete ignoramus.

Lazarus took out his pipe from his pocket and rubbed tobacco from the palm of his hand into the bowl.

He took his time striking a match and cupping it against the wind. The hollow flaring of the flame and the crackling of the Drum tobacco echoed in his hands.

The sweet aroma wafted briefly around us until it was whisked away in the breeze.

"Yes, like the Titanic. Anyway, after losing sight of her companion fleet, shortly after leaving the Cape of Good Hope, the *Batavia* ran into Morning Reef in the Abrolhos on the fourth of June 1629."

Lazarus turned to the chart plotter and pointed to the location. It was some way south of where we were heading.

"Like I said, she was the first VOC ship to be lost off the west coast of Australia but as it happened, not the last by a long chalk.

"Back then, of course, the world was a very different place and ignorance and superstition were constant companions of crew and passengers.

"Turns out that the ship's apothecary, Jeronimus Cornelisz, was a real psycho and was able to brainwash some of the ne're-do-wells on board, to do his evil bidding.

"Most of the 341 people on board actually survived the wreck, but only 92 of them survived their time on the islands. Cornelisz and his henchmen, murdered the rest."

"Shit! So many people on board such a small ship. Why would he want to murder the survivors?"

"Who knows? Maybe he was just insane. I think that historians have been asking that question since the story first broke. But the fact is that the events, if not the reasons, are well documented.

"Cornelisz took command of the survivors soon after the Commander Pelsaert took off in a longboat to find help from Batavia. That's what Jakarta used to be called. Not to be confused with the ship of the same name that was being pounded to oblivion on the reef!

"He took one of the more noble women on the ship, who had been treated badly by the crew, as his mistress. Her name was Lucretia and, well let's just say that she did what she had to do to survive.

"He then set about systematically murdering the remaining survivors, using henchmen loyal to him or sending them on treacherous missions in the hope that they'd never return.

"Now, this is where it gets interesting. There was one group of soldiers commanded by Wiebbe Hayes. Cornelisz had cleverly disarmed them before he sent them out to find water on East and West Wallabi Islands where we're heading. He was hoping that they too, would perish. However, Hayes was a great leader and he was lucky as well.

"He found water and sent a signal using bonfires to Cornelisz to join him and his troops.

"Turns out that Cornelisz had other ideas. Unbeknown to Hayes, he planned to capture any rescuer's ship and sail away to live the life of a pirate. Fearing that Hayes would warn approaching ships of his treachery, he set out to kill Hayes and his loyal band of soldiers.

"Hayes, who had built a crude fort on West Wallabi, managed to fight off the henchmen. He learned of Cornelisz's plans and warned the rescue ship, just as it was dropping anchor.

"The original Commander of the *Batavia*, Pelsaert, who had made the perilous journey to get help, was on board the rescue ship. He quickly captured Cornelisz and his mutineers and put them to death on Long Island, right in sight of the reef where the *Batavia* had floundered. Cut their hands off and hanged them, one after the other!"

"Shit!"

Lazarus paused and looked at me as the gruesome images flashed across my mind.

"Interestingly, it was many years later that the graves of Cornelisz's victims were uncovered by modern day cray fishermen. The wreck of the *Batavia* was partially recovered in the 1970s and put on display in Fremantle Museum."

"What of *Batavia*'s treasure?"

"Sorry Michael, me old mate, practically all of *Batavia*'s cargo and riches were recovered by Pelsaert and sent to Batavia. All that is, bar one chest of silver which was spilled and lost to the ocean. So, whatever your dad is trying to lead you to, it certainly isn't buried treasure from the *Batavia*."

"Quite the tourist attraction!" I said to Lazarus. "I can't believe that the VOC actually had the power of life and death, over its employees in the 17th century."

"Yeah. It's all been downhill since then, if you ask me. Unions would never allow it these days."

I laughed.

Lazarus gave up on his pipe and tapped the ash overboard. Placing it back in his pocket he said, "You know, today we have pretty accurate satellite navigation, right? But back in the 1600s, whilst latitude was relatively easy to calculate using astronomy, longitude was much more of a guessing game. In the absence of accurate timepieces, a lot of navigation was basically done by dead reckoning. A ship could be a hundred miles or more away from its actual position."

"So the *Batavia* didn't really know how far east it had travelled since leaving the Cape?"

"Yeah, that's right.

"At one time, ships from Europe would sail southwest to South America, then across the Atlantic to the Cape of Good Hope, making use of the trade winds. Then they'd turn north and follow the east coast of Africa before travelling around India to reach the rich spice islands of the Dutch East Indies.

"Then one bright spark decided that he could sail due east from Cape town and, after some dead reckoning, could turn north before he hit the coast of Australia and cut a considerable amount of time off the journey. I think it was about a month.

"The only problem was if you didn't turn north soon enough, you stood a good chance of crashing into Australia at night, or if you turned north a little too late, then you'd run into the Abrolhos and that, me old mate, is exactly what happened to your *Batavia*, not to mention several other ships, some of which have never been found.

"Did you find out anything else about Wiebbe Hayes's fort in that book?" Lazarus had clearly been thinking of my dad's coordinates.

"No, not really. The archaeologists from the maritime museum found a few relics there, clay pipe fragments together with the odd button but no buried treasure unfortunately. Looks like it's been visited a fair few times over the years, so anything that was there, would be long gone."

"Ah, perhaps your dad found the lost silver and squirreled it away before the archaeologists did their work!"

"I doubt that very much," I said, smiling, but not wholly convincing myself nor it would appear, Lazarus.

Chapter 5 Flaming Red

Arriving at Turtle Bay shortly before noon, the wind dropped and the ocean glassed off. We picked up Lazarus's favourite mooring not far from a beautiful little bommie which provided a feast of fresh lobsters, washed down with copious quantities of wine, now that we were no longer underway.

"This is beautiful, isn't it?" Lazarus pondered, as the sun started to set over the island.

"Perfect."

We sat in silence for a while, relaxing in the knowledge that we were safely moored, taking in the beauty of the turquoise water and white sandy bottom.

After the sun had set, we made our way below decks where I prepared dinner and Lazarus selected and poured the wine.

Sitting back in our seats, our bellies full and our minds relaxed, I asked Lazarus, "How long are you going to hold up here?"

Lazarus paused as he took another sip of an exquisite vintage port he had selected.

"Weather's closing in a bit up north the day after tomorrow, so I'll let that pass before taking her up to Bali. Have you booked your flight on the puddle jumper yet?"

"Nah, I'll radio them in the morning if that's OK?"

"You're welcome to stay on board for a couple of nights if you want to go exploring your dad's co-ordinates. There's a sextant and a nautical almanac in the cupboard over there, if you want to use it."

"That'd be great but I have to admit I'm a bit rusty on navigation with a sextant. Couldn't give me a refresher course, could you?"

Lazarus smiled, half anticipating the question. "No worries. It's not nearly as complicated as it looks," he said.

He opened a brass-inlaid teak box and carefully lifted out the delicate precision instrument.

After going over all its features and controls he summarised, "OK, once you've recorded all the information you need, you'll need to consult this nautical almanac. You'll need to correct for refraction, semi-diameter, index error, and dip. Make a parallax correction using the table on page A2 and calculate your latitude. Simple really."

I looked at him as he tried desperately to keep a straight face before he cracked into a broad smile and laughter.

"Seriously, Michael, if you take your time, it's still one of the most accurate navigational tools ever invented."

* * *

We were the only boat in the bay and in the morning a gentle easterly, meant that we could get to shore easily in the tender without the threat of waves swamping us on the beach.

"Are you coming with me?" I asked, as we lowered the tender into the water using the davit.

"Nah, you go have fun. I'll catch you later. Come and get me if you want a hand carrying the treasure chest back. More importantly, make sure you flip the outboard before you beach her. I don't want to have to swim ashore to replace the prop!"

"Yes, Dad!" I groaned.

Lazarus smiled and waved me off as I pulled the ripcord and the outboard sprang to life.

The white coral sand was scorching beneath my feet, and I soon retrieved my thongs, dusted the sand off my feet and slipped them on. Sitting on a small rock above the high-water mark I pondered the azure sea, white sand, red earth and blue cloudless sky. It must have been pretty much the same when Dad was here in the 1940s. Actually, come to think of it, it must have been pretty much the same in 1629.

I startled a pair of tammar wallabies which hopped away through the low scrub as I lifted my small spade and a water bottle over my shoulder. I climbed up a low hill following an animal track to the end of the red-earth airstrip and recalled that Wiebbe Hayes's men had supplemented their sea food diet with wallaby which they referred to as a type of indigenous cat. Clearly enough of these 'cats' had survived to maintain the population since the 17th century. Amazing.

Even though it was early, the sun was beating down relentlessly, and I was grateful for the sunscreen and broad-brimmed-hat that I had donned before leaving the yacht.

After half an hour stroll I reached the narrow divide between East and West Wallabi Islands and waded across. The water, waist deep, was far too shallow to navigate for all but the smallest of craft used by the cray fishermen who lived on the neighbouring islands during the season. Even then, the uncharted bommies would make short work of the boat's hulls and props. It was an area that was mostly avoided, even by the most skilful skippers.

Climbing the low rise on West Wallabi, I recognised what Hayes had described as the cliff-top from where he and his men had repelled Cornelisz's attack. Having no weapons of their own they had thrown rocks into the sea, splashing water onto the flintlocks of the assailants, soaking the gun powder and making them useless. Talk about keeping your powder dry, I thought.

I pulled out the sextant and Almanac and soon tracked to the position represented by my dad's coordinates. Lazarus had been right. It was a sandy patch with no identifying features. No cairn, no trees, no nothing. I looked around for a bit and thought, oh well, I may as well have a scrape with my spade.

I was kneeling in my excavation which was about a foot deep and at least a yard wide, when the blinding sun was blocked out by the silhouette of a figure which looked like a character out of the 'Mad Max' movie. Feet spread wide, hands on hips, face covered with a bandanna, a broad-brimmed hat pulled low over dark glasses.

"Who the fuck are you?" the female voice came as a surprise. I staggered to my feet and stepped to one side to get a better view of this stranger on what was supposed to be an uninhabited island. The only thing I could think of saying was "I'm Michael. Who the fuck are you?"

They say there's no such thing as love at first sight and if I was going to fall in love I doubted very much it would be with someone dressed in a shapeless khaki boiler suit with kneepads and an obscured face. But then, with a sweep of her hand, she removed her hat and let her titian hair fall over her shoulders, wiping her brow with her sleeve.

Pulling down her bandanna, she smiled and said, "I'm Kate, that's who the fuck I am," and held out her gloved hand.

Until that point in my life I had never pondered what a deer caught in the headlights of a car would feel like, but well, that's exactly how I felt. I was frozen to the spot, unable to speak.

"What are you doing? That's a pretty big hole if you're thinking of taking a crap. Where have you come from?" she said scouring the horizon.

I quickly regained some composure and managed to stutter out, "We're moored in Turtle Bay. I'm just digging for buried treasure."

"Yeah right. Seriously though, you know you can't go around fucking up the environment here. This is a site of special scientific and archaeological interest. Hell, you're only a few hundred yards from Wiebbe Hayes's fort, the first European structure to be built in the whole of Australia. Did you know that?"

It was then that I noticed the embroidered patch on her boiler suit. 'Museum of Western Australia.'

"Are you with the Museum then?"

"No flies on you, are there?"

"Ah, it's just on your um…" I pointed to her left breast and immediately regretted my decision.

"I've just finished up a quick survey of Hayes's fort, seeing how much damage has been done over the past decade by idiots like you, souvenir hunters. We need to protect the site, you know. There's been an increase in the number of visitors to the islands and people have no idea that even just walking around here can cause so much erosion and damage, let alone digging bloody great holes."

It was then that I cast my eyes down into my excavation and noticed the tip of what appeared to be a large cigar-tube poking out of the side of the hole where the bone-dry sand, had fallen away.

Kate noticed it, too.

"Jesus Christ! Would you look at that! Some idiot has even been smoking out here. Can you imagine the environmental disaster a fire would have on this island?"

I knelt down and retrieved the tube which was still sealed with a screw cap and what looked to be red paint around the thread.

"What the fuck?"

"Kate, I wasn't kidding when I said I was digging for buried treasure."

"What is this? Some sort of game?"

"No."

"Then, what?"

I slipped the cigar-tube into my pocket.

"I tell you what Kate, come over to the yacht this afternoon and we'll open it together. I'll tell you all about it. I'll even give you an ice-cold beer."

Kate looked at me suspiciously, but curiosity overcame her natural caution and to my delight she said, "OK, but you'd better fill that hole in before you go."

Chapter 6 The Cigar Case

Lazarus laughed uproariously as we all sat in the open cockpit of the *Sea Dragon*, sipping on ice-cold beers.

"Only Michael could be dropped off on an uninhabited island in the middle of bloody nowhere and bring back a beautiful young woman!"

"Why, Mr Lazarus! You are a flatterer."

Did she bat her eyelids when she said that? This was not going well. It was me who was supposed to be wooing Kate the archaeologist, not my old friend, lecherous Lazarus.

I gave Lazarus what I hoped was my strongest 'back off mate' stare and asked, "I wonder what is it that women see in this crusty, old multi-millionaire?"

Lazarus and Kate both laughed. They were getting on far too well.

"Come on Michael, let's open your buried treasure."

"Yes," said Kate, "but not here. Let's do it down below, out of the wind. I'd hate for whatever's inside to blow away.

"When I was visiting Mawson's hut on a field trip to the Antarctic for the Museum, I opened a tobacco-tin outside. It had a piece of paper in it, and I spent hours chasing it across the ice before I caught it and then realised that it was nothing more than packaging for the tobacco that was once inside."

"Ah, a true explorer! Perhaps my dear, we could sail down there together one day?"

"Mr Lazarus, you are incorrigible! Come on Michael, let's get below."

After nearly 40 years, the seal around the screw cap had become brittle and crumbled as soon as I applied pressure to it. The roll of paper secreted inside however, looked as though it had been placed there yesterday.

"A cigar tube is actually a pretty good choice if you want to keep something well preserved, you know," Kate said, "better than a bottle with a cork in any case. Termites love corks. The fact that the Abrolhos Islands don't get a lot of rain hasn't hurt either."

I unrolled the paper delicately and was confronted with a series of widely spaced lines of dots and dashes.

"Bloody hell, Dad! Couldn't you have just drawn a map?" I said out loud.

"Read Morse code, either of you?" Lazarus said, as he sat back in his chair. I wanted to wipe the grin off his face with a wet mullet.

"I remember dot dot dot, dash dash dash, dot dot dot, as being Morse for SOS and that's about it, I'm afraid. My dad tried to teach me as a kid. He used to say it was easier to remember if you matched syllables to the dots and dashes like bumble bee .... Dash, dot, dot. Ha! there we are, we now have three letters!" I took another a swig from my can.

Kate picked up the paper and carefully examined it under the cabin's light.

"There's something odd about this paper, Michael."

"What do you mean?"

"The discoloration along these two edges, but nowhere else."

"Well, it's over 30 years old."

"OK you two, I can't keep this up any longer. I have no idea what you'd do without me."

"What?" Kate and I turned to see Lazarus who was twisting around to retrieve an old hard-backed book bound in a faded and stained orange-canvas cover from the shelf behind him. 'The nautical almanac 1977."

"Turn to the back, detectives. There's a Morse Code alphabet there."

* * *

It took an hour and a bottle of Lazarus's Shiraz, with three of us working on different sections to decipher the letter.

"This is pretty personal stuff, Michael, perhaps you'd better keep it to yourself," Lazarus said.

"It's OK. Dad's been gone for a few years now so there's nothing that will hurt him or his memory."

I compiled the three transcripts and started to read the letter out loud.

> *"It's July 1949, and I have to say it's very odd sitting here in the radio room of HMS Renown, writing a letter in Morse to the son that I hope to have one day.*
>
> *Time is short as we sail for Singapore tomorrow and I have to get back to shore to carefully conceal this letter on the island of ghosts in a place where only you will be able to find it, my son, most likely long after I am dead and gone.*
>
> *If you do ever find this, I hope that I have convinced a future wife to call you Michael for reasons that will soon become obvious, as what I am about to tell you is my own dark secret that I may well have taken to my grave by the time you read this.*
>
> *There is, of course, a reward for you but also a great curse in knowing the truth. How you reconcile these two is up to you, but I hope that you are able to do so and live an exciting life with no regrets.*

You see Michael, I have two secrets which I cannot share with this world until I am no longer part of it.

The first is easy. I have discovered a treasure on a reef not far from here. It's likely that no one will ever find it as it is too shallow for boats and so remote that no one would ever visit it. I have recovered a very small part of it, something which I believe has great value, and concealed it. I want it to be yours. Use the wealth it will bring to enrich your life and the lives of others. Do good, for no one will remember you for the fancy objects you buy but for your deeds.

You see, I cannot disclose the whereabouts of this treasure to the Navy, for my reward would be a small piece of tin on a ribbon if I am lucky. If I am unlucky, then a swift trip to Davy Jones's locker!

The second secret is harder as it deals with love, and that, my son, is something you will learn is a cruel mistress."

I looked up at Kate and Lazarus who sat silently, their eyes were locked in deep concentration on my own. The gentle lapping of the waves and creaking of the rigging were the only sounds to be heard.

I continued to read the letter written by someone who was so familiar to me and yet, it was almost as though it had been written by a total stranger.

"As you grow, I will teach you all you need to know to decipher this message.

I hope that in time it will make sense to you and that you and your mother will find it in your hearts to forgive me the great deception.

If the finder of this letter is not my son, then it is perhaps for the best and I implore you to let sleeping dogs lie.

Your loving dad to be, Kenneth".

After a moment of silence, Lazarus and Kate both said in unison, "That's it?"

Chapter 7 Of Lobsters and Lemons

I turned over the original paper and looked for other clues. There was nothing.

"Well, it's got me stumped. I think we need more thinking juice!" Lazarus said as he stood to pull out another bottle from the drinks' cabinet.

"Oh no, not tonight, thank you Mr Lazarus. I need to get back to my campsite, and there is no way I am going to let one of you scoundrels steer me back in the tender whilst full of 'thinking juice.'"

"Kate, it's getting late, the wind'll be up soon. We've plenty of room and you can have a cabin all to yourself and…" Kate was already standing to leave "…we have a water maker on board which means you can even have a long, hot, luxurious, freshwater shower, without ever worrying about running out."

"Oh, my God! Do you ever know the way to a woman's heart, Mr Lazarus. I've been on that island for over a week, making do with salt-water soap and the ocean."

"In which case, Michael, you're on kitchen duties. Let's cook up that big boy we caught, and there's still fresh salad in the fridge which needs finishing off. I'll take care of the refreshments and show the lovely lady to her cabin."

I was a little wary of letting 'lecherous Lazarus' alone with Kate but figured she could take care of herself.

"Kate, the shower is self-draining so you don't need to pump out the grey water. There's a towelling robe in the closet there; might be a bit big for you, but it's new, and it's soft. There's a bar of shampoo soap and conditioner in the drawer and a hair dryer somewhere. If you need anything else, just holler and I'll come rushing in."

"Anyone would think you were expecting company, Mr Lazarus. As for rushing in where angels fear to tread, let me assure you I eat angels for breakfast."

"Ah! All my dreams come true."

* * *

Lazarus retreated to his favourite spot in the lounge as I busied myself in the galley.

"I say old boy, she's a bit of a wild one!" he said, looking over the table to me.

I looked at Lazarus and digested his comment.

"I like her," I said. "I like her a lot."

"I know what you mean. Do you think that a young woman like that and an old sea dog like me, could ever…"

"No, I don't. Never. No, no, not ever," I answered a little too quickly.

After a while, the door to the cabin opened and Kate stood there in her towelling robe, her open features a picture of softness and beauty.

We both just stood and stared, mouths open and gormless.

"I hope you don't mind; I found the washing machine. I couldn't bear to get back into my grubby old work clothes. I put them in on a quick wash. I hope that's OK?"

"Of course, my dear, stupid of me not to think of it myself. Please take a seat. Michael has worked his magic. Would you look at that lobster? We've even got fresh lemon juice to drizzle over it and a homemade thousand island dressing. Tuck in!"

Lazarus poured a generous measure of a perfectly chilled unwooded chardonnay into three heavy glasses without asking.

"Cheers ma dears!"

Kate and I let the cold white wine caress our tastebuds and perfectly complement the fine taste of the crayfish drizzled in lemon juice, and dipped into homemade thousand island dressing.

"Oh, my God! You have no idea how delicious that tastes after living on prepacked, rehydrated rations for a week."

"Well, my dear, we need to combat scurvy on these long ocean voyages."

We finished our meal and started to talk about the letter from Dad and what it could mean.

Kate was feeling more relaxed and occasionally her robe would fall forward, revealing her soft décolletage beneath a blushing, wind burnt V neck. A point that neither Lazarus nor I missed, but were, of course, far too polite to mention.

"The letter has four components," Kate said, slurring her words slightly.

"Firstly, your dad has revealed he has two secrets. The first one is simple. The existence of the treasure which for some reason, he was never able to retrieve for himself. The second secret is more obscure, although it has something to do with love. Maybe you have brothers or sisters you're unaware of? Maybe your dad had a girl in every port?"

I shook my head.

"No? OK then. That leads us to the third component which he is either ashamed of, or at least is seeking forgiveness for? And finally, something that only you would know from your youth to help you decipher the rest of the message. Let's face it, without your knowledge, the letter's a dead-end. What was it that he taught you when you were growing up, that only you would know?"

We pondered the question until we felt that we could go on no longer and retired to our respective cabins, none the wiser.

Even through my stupor, I felt an uneasiness in letting Kate stay on board, in such close 'proximity' to Lazarus. As the minutes turned to hours, I sobered up and went up on deck to clear my head and drink a pint of water.

The sky was full of stars and in the water, St. Elmore's fire danced with shades of green in the wake caused by the gentle movement of the tide against the hull. The anchor light cast a soft glow across the deck.

My silent reverie was broken as Kate joined me.

"Couldn't sleep either?" I asked.

"No, I heard you walking on the deck. My cabin's just beneath us."

"I'm sorry. I didn't mean to wake you."

"That's OK."

"You have beautiful eyes, Kate."

"Ha! wait until you see them in the morning!"

"Sorry. I'm not very good at this." I fumbled with my glass of water.

"You're doing just fine."

"I am?"

"Yes. Just don't rush it."

Although we sat there in silence, my mind was racing. 'Just fine,' she said. Hmm.

"What are you smiling at?"

"Nothing really. Well, perhaps the thought of being on a luxury yacht, with a beautiful woman in the middle of nowhere and the promise of finding buried treasure in the morning, has something to do with it."

Kate laughed and as she did, her eyes lit up and what was left of my heart melted.

"Have you thought of anything that your dad taught you that may have relevance to the letter?"

"I can't think of anything. I looked at the words, the punctuation, the length of sentences and no, nothing. There has to be a key, a primer somewhere."

“Well, if you fail as a treasure hunter, you could always make it as a chef. That lobster was to die for, the way in which the lemon juice lifted the flavours rather than overpowered them, was a stroke of genius.”

Mmm, I thought, she liked my cooking.

I looked into her beautiful green eyes, and then it hit me.

“Fuck! Lemon juice!”

“What?”

“No. I mean lemon juice.” Kate looked at me quizzically. “As a child growing up, Dad showed me how to write invisible letters using lemon juice as ink. It’d dry invisible, then you’d heat the paper up over a candle to reveal the secret text.

“When my sisters were old enough, I taught them to do the same. We would always play games like that. The spacing of the lines, the discoloration around two edges. There has to be another message embedded in the first letter.”

“Or a treasure map!” a voice bellowed from behind us.

“How long have you been standing there, Lazarus?”

“Long enough to protect the lady’s virtue if needed,” he replied.

Chapter 8 Hidden Messages

There was a glint in Lazarus's eye.

"The hairdryer's in my bathroom. Let's go below and check out your theory," he said.

We practically tripped over each other in our haste to re-examine Dad's letter.

Sitting around the table, Lazarus plugged the hairdryer into an inverter socket and passed it to Kate.

"Here, you had better do the honours. You'd be more experienced in dealing with artifacts than me and I don't want to be blamed for sending the whole bloody thing up in smoke, but be careful, that thing gets really hot up close."

Kate looked at Lazarus as if to say, 'Do you really think I've never used a hair dryer before,' but chose to keep such comments to herself.

"We could always take this back to the museum and look at it there. I have a full lab at my disposal. It'd be a lot safer and avoid any risk of damaging the document."

"Kate, it might be nothing. Just my dad playing one of his silly games. Let's just try."

"OK, but on your own head be it," she said.

Kate tested the heat from the hair drier on several sheets of scrap paper until she was confident that she knew its limitations, including sending one piece up in smoke. Fortunately, Lazarus had the foresight to have a bucket of water to hand to drop it into.

Now reasonably confident to give Dad's letter a go, she carefully passed the hot air backwards and forwards, to reveal yet more Morse Code written in between the original lines of text.

"Michael, you're not nearly as stupid as you look!" Lazarus said.

"Thanks 'Dad'," I groaned.

As Kate continued the passes, she became more excited. "Take a look at this," she said. "It looks like a drawing of a sundial or something."

"It's a picture of an Alberti cypher disk," I said in surprise.

"A what?" they both said in unison.

I laughed again. "Are you two going to talk in synchrony all evening?

"God! My dad and I would spend hours making those when I was a teenager. Then we'd write and decode secret messages. Yes, I know, I should have got out more but hey, I thought it was normal at the time. After all, Dad was a cryptographer."

"So, how does it work?" Kate asked.

"OK, well, you can see that it consists of two circular disks, a small one that sits on top of the big one and spins. I know the image isn't very clear, but it doesn't have to be. I know what it is and how to make one.

"Both disks have all the letters of the alphabet around their periphery. Once you have the primer or key, you can spin the smaller disk to align say the letter N to the letter Q in the cypher and create a coded message.

"If you want to get really clever, you can change the primer several times in the message and send that series of primers in another coded letter to the recipient.

"I think we'll find that the hidden Morse Code message will need to be deciphered using Alberti's cypher disk."

"The first line here. What does that say?" Lazarus asked as he pointed his finger at the letter.

Kate read out the Morse and quickly translated it. "G for A".

"OK, assuming that's the primer, all we need to do now is create the Alberti cypher wheel."

"Simpler just to draw up two columns?" said Lazarus.

"Yeah, assuming Dad didn't go all polyalphabetic on me!"

In a few minutes Lazarus had drawn up the columns, and we were able to decipher the first word and spelt it out.

"A A G T E K E R K E. What sort of word is that? It doesn't make any sense. Are you sure you got the letters right? You must have fucked it up," Lazarus said accusingly.

"Of course, I bloody well got it right. Look, you can check it yourself!" I said, stabbing the paper with my finger.

Kate sat silently staring at the paper, seemingly oblivious to the increasingly heated discussion I was having with Lazarus.

"Guys!" she shouted, forcing us to be silent.

"Guys! Michael. Your dad may have just stumbled on one of the greatest maritime mysteries of the century, the fabled wreck of the *Aagtekerke*."

"The what?" said Lazarus as he struggled with the pronunciation. "Shit. Couldn't it have been called the Black Swan or something? How the fuck do you pronounce that again?" Lazarus was calming down and getting down to business.

"It's Dutch. Ignore the spelling. Just try 'argex tee ker kee,'" Kate said. "That's not quite right, but it's close enough."

"Bloody clever, these foreigners," Lazarus laughed. Turning to Kate he said, "What do you know about this sea turkey?"

Kate looked up. "The *Aagtekerke* vanished in 1726. It was on a similar route to that taken by your beloved Hayes on the *Batavia*, almost a hundred years earlier. Like the *Batavia* she was carrying a rich cargo. Silver, gold and ivory from Africa, bound for the markets in China but unlike the *Batavia*, she was lost with all hands. Her cargo was never recovered."

Kate continued, "The location of the wreck itself has always been a subject of debate. Many believe that it shares the same site as another shipwreck called the *Zeewijk* which foundered on the 9th of June 1727, almost exactly a year to the day later. You'd have to consider that a massive co-incidence, but I have to say that there's compelling evidence to support the theory."

"How much treasure was she carrying, Kate?" Lazarus was ever the mercenary.

"I don't know for sure; some say over a billion dollars in today's money, but I'd have to check."

It took us until dawn to translate and decipher the rest of Dad's message which related solely to the shipwreck and his discovery of a small fortune in silver and gold coins, and a golden brooch which he had buried on West Wallabi. There was still more to translate but we'd deciphered enough to find the treasure, if indeed it really did exist.

Kate was stubbornly insistent that the site—when we found it—be preserved and properly excavated by marine archaeologists from the museum. But Lazarus somehow managed to convince her that a guy burying a box of coins and a trinket in 1949 did not constitute an archaeological site, and there might be nothing there in any case.

We agreed that we'd go ashore in the morning and see if we could find anything.

"Even if you do find something, you can't keep it," she said.

"What do you mean?" Lazarus said.

"Under the Historic Shipwrecks Act of 1976, and the Maritime and Archaeology Act of 1973, wrecks and their contents belong to the Federal Government."

"Fuck them! This isn't a wreck, is it?"

I let Lazarus and Kate fight their war of words and went to lie down in my cabin, holding Dad's letter in my hand.

We had all been so fixated on the lure of buried treasure that we had forgotten about his dark secret that dealt with love.

I held it up and studied it against the light above my bed. I flicked the light to red to prepare for a few hours' sleep and noticed a faint watermark. It was a second primer; 443.

Four, four, three; no, four for three. I aligned the fourth letter of the alphabet D with the third C on a hurriedly constructed cypher wheel.

I translated the remainder of the message, letter by letter, word by word, and at long last sat back and read it in its entirety:

"My son, this is the hardest thing I have ever had to write. If my secret is discovered before I die, I may well end up in prison and you my son, may never be born. You see, I had a love. A love like no other that permeated my very soul, but it was a forbidden love, for it was a love I shared with another man.

Michael was lost in a tragic accident at sea, just a few months ago. I feel that my heart may never truly heal. I was not allowed to grieve his passing in the way that I needed to, for fear of disclosing our closely held secret. But I played my role. I took part in the pomp and ceremony of his burial at sea as a mannequin might. Face devoid of emotion, stiff upper lip and all that.

I hope that one day things will be different, and men such as I can live in freedom openly without shame, persecution or discrimination, but I fear that the world is not yet ready for that and may never be.

I hope you found the treasure and that it will bring you happiness, adventure and fortune. I am sure that I will offer you many words of advice as you are growing up. However, the only advice I can give you now is to quote the words of the poet Alfred Lord Tennyson "It is better to have loved and lost than never to have loved at all."

I hope that one day if you truly find love, you will grasp it with all your heart and soul, no matter the cost, and will also find it in your heart to forgive my great deception.

All my love, Dad."

Chapter 9 Penny for Your Thoughts

Kate quietly entered my cabin a couple of hours later.

"Penny for your thoughts?" she said.

"Kate, aren't you meant to be getting some rest before we venture forth on our treasure hunt?"

There was a moment's silence whilst Kate's eyes made contact with mine and she saw through the veneer that hid the sadness beneath.

"You deciphered the rest of your dad's letter, didn't you?"

"Yeah."

"Wanna talk about it?"

Kate squeezed up next to me on the bunk. I felt her breast pressing hard against my arm, which suddenly sought to release itself and seemingly manoeuvred of its own accord around her shoulders.

"You know, you think you know someone. I mean, like really know someone, like your parents, but then you discover something about them that completely and utterly shatters all of your preconceptions and beliefs."

"So, your dad was gay?"

"Fuck! How did you reach that conclusion?"

"You're too close to it, Michael. I think it was pretty obvious. Homosexuals were still being incarcerated in the 50s. I don't think homosexuality was actually decriminalised until the late 60s.

"It was common practice for homosexual men to marry and have children in an attempt to deny their sexual orientation, as much to themselves as to others."

I felt tears well in my eyes as I realised that in many ways, Dad had lived a lie all those years. How different the world was today to that of the 1940s, when he was in the Navy.

He'd named me Michael after the one true love of his life. I had no idea. I felt torn between anger and sadness. How could he do such a thing? But then, he had loved me as only a father can love a son. I realised that I must have been both a joyous and painful reminder for him, every day of his life.

Kate's soft hand wiped away my tears, and I felt her lips brush against me. In a moment, we were locked in a soft embrace as she moved her leg over mine. I wanted this woman there and then, but a noisy clunk interrupted us as we heard Lazarus prepping the tender against the side of the hull.

"Shit, it's that time already," I said.

"Well, maybe we can continue this at a later date." Her eyes fell to below my belt. "I take it that homosexuality doesn't run in the family?"

Kate smiled and wriggled off me. I hurriedly rearranged myself and appeared on deck, feeling like a guilty teenager.

"Nice of you to join us, lover boy!" Lazarus's none too subtle jibe found its mark.

We loaded a shovel into the tender, and Lazarus insisted on bringing a stick of dynamite. Where he got that from, I have no idea. I didn't even know if it was real, but knowing Lazarus, it probably was.

"What on earth is that?!" Kate said, pointing to the dynamite, "If you think for one moment, you're going to use explosives to excavate a site of scientific interest… Not only is that unnecessary, but it's also illegal!"

"It's only illegal if you get caught. Come on, you'll get over it," he said, stuffing the stick down the front of his trousers like a phallus.

Clearly, there was no point in arguing.

We motored in the tender around East Wallabi to a small bay on the northern side of West Wallabi, called Horseyard Bay, and—reaching the shore—we dragged the tender above the high-water mark.

We walked a short distance to the new location and found, to our delight, a small cairn of no more than a dozen stones exactly where they were supposed to be. It was so small that a casual visitor would not have noticed them at all, let alone an aerial survey plane. Satellites were non-existent in the 1940s and, even though modern geo-mapping satellites have discovered many natural and archaeological sites, they would never have registered a small pile of stones on West Wallabi.

Lazarus stood with his hands on his hips, apparently ready to deploy his dynamite as Kate held out her arms, preventing either of us from immediately excavating the site.

"We should document this. Photographically at least," she said.

"Well, I didn't bring my SLR," I said, "so we have a choice, excavate or emigrate!"

"No, Michael, on second thoughts, I think we should stop."

"Kate, we've been through this a thousand times. It's my dad. Please, let me look?"

Kate turned to Lazarus looking for support, but he disappointed her by saying, "Fuck photography, let's blow the bastard up!"

"OK, OK. No one is going to blow up anything! Michael, have a scrape and see if there's anything there."

I used my hands to carefully scrape away a foot or so of soft sand and coral debris, and eventually reached for my spade. My heel pushed hard on the spade's step, and half a blade deep, it hit a solid surface. It felt - and sounded - like metal on metal.

Kate and Lazarus both leaped forward to see what it was.

"Stop!" yelled Kate as she knelt down next to me and threw my spade to one side. She used her hands to gently reveal an old and rusty ammunition box.

Carefully excavating the sand around the box, it practically fell apart. A river of tarnished silver and gleaming gold coins from the Dutch East India ship *Aagtekerke* cascaded down into the sand in a seemingly never-ending flow. Riding atop the wave of gold and silver was a huge, golden, jewel-encrusted brooch, which gleamed in the early morning light. Although only a small fraction of the treasure that the *Aagtekerke* would have been carrying, it must have been worth a fortune.

We all looked upon the treasure, agog. Kate picked up the beautiful brooch which was studded with diamonds, rubies, sapphires and emeralds. Fire danced in their facets and reflected in her eyes.

Unlike silver, gold doesn't tarnish and once the white sand had fallen away, it looked pretty much the same as it had the day it was made. I imagined that Howard Carter must have felt exactly like this when he first spied the treasures of Tutankhamun through a small peephole in the door of the treasury room in 1922.

A sickening thud broke my reverie as the spade that Kate had thrown to one side suddenly impacted on her head, sending her crashing face first into the shallow excavation.

I looked up and my world, too, turned black.

Chapter 10 All Good Things

The voice appeared to be coming from somewhere else.

"Michael, wake up!

"Michael, are you OK?" The question came with increased panic. A shadowy figure was hovering over me, blocking out the unbearably bright, mid-day sun.

I tried to sit up, only to feel as though I had hit my head on a low ceiling.

"Don't try to move too fast. You've a very nasty gash to your head."

As my blurred vision started to clear, I saw Kate's face staring down at me. Her hair was matted with dried blood.

"Kate, are you OK? Where's Lazarus? What happened?"

"He's gone, Michael, and taken the treasure with him. Bastard took us both by surprise. I think he must have thought that he'd killed us both. It'd have taken a good few trips to load the tender, and the bastard left us for dead!"

"We have to go after him." I tried sitting up, saw double, and passed out again.

It must have been late afternoon by the time I was able to stand up, walk anywhere near normally, and properly check on Kate.

'Pretty thick skulls in our family,' she'd said, claiming that she'd really just received a glancing blow—whereas I appeared to have copped the full force of Lazarus's spade.

Even though we were in no condition to do so, I insisted that we traipse back to Turtle Bay to board the yacht somehow and teach the bastard a lesson he'd never forget.

We staggered along the soft white sand of the northern beach of Horseyard Bay until we reached the narrow strip of shallow water, which divided West and East Wallabi Islands. The cool water served to revive us somewhat and we were able to wash some of the dried blood from our faces.

Traversing East Wallabi and mounting the low rise at the end of the airstrip, we looked out on the beautiful turquoise waters of Turtle Bay and its empty moorings.

Lazarus and his yacht, *Sea Dragon*, were gone.

* * *

That was the last time we saw Lazarus or his yacht, although rumours would occasionally surface about a mad Aussie who had married a Filipino woman—or two—in order to buy a private island somewhere in the South China Sea. Our paths seemed destined never to cross again.

As for Kate and me, well, let's just say that not all treasure can be counted. I believe that we have fulfilled my dad's hopes and dreams and together we have found true love.

Kate's research is being funded by a wealthy philanthropist of Dutch extraction, to confirm the location of the *Aagtekerke*. They have a firm plan and funding in place to recover the bulk of the treasures she was carrying.

Me? I'm decorating the nursery for our firstborn.

Kate wants to call the baby Lucretia if it's to be a girl, and Wiebbe if it's to be a boy. I think there'll be some discussion to be had before we make a final decision.

In the meantime Dad's secrets and Lazarus's crimes remain buried. Kate and I did go back to West Wallabi and discover a handful of coins that Lazarus had left behind in his haste to escape. These eventually paid the deposit on a modest house in Fremantle but that, as they say, is another story.

Part II

Nazi Gold

Chapter 11 Dead Man's Tales

The chorus of 'Happy birthday, dear Wiebbe,' rang out across the table of the Little Creatures pub in Fremantle as boisterous friends, family and strangers celebrated Wiebbe's 21st birthday.

The longer-serving bar-staff appeared to turn a blind-eye to the fact that my son Wiebbe and I, had been drinking there regularly for at least five years.

A cake arrived at our long table and Kate made a big fuss of making sure that Wiebbe was the one to blow out the candles and make the first incision.

She was still the most beautiful woman in that massive barn of a room, even though we were both in our 40s. I had eyes for no one else. Her flaming red hair and strength of spirit meant that I had been fighting a losing battle when it came to naming our son.

Wiebbe Hayes had been a soldier on the Dutch East India Ship, the *Batavia,* when it had floundered on the Abrolhos Islands back in the 17th century. He had been a hero in caring for his men and suppressing, and eventually orchestrating, the capture of the mutineers.

It was the Abrolhos Islands where Kate and I had first met, and Wiebbe was somewhat of an historical hero to Kate—so when all was said and done, our first born carried his name.

I have to admit it did suit him, even though neither of us had any Dutch heritage in our blood. At six foot two, a ready smile and startling green eyes, inherited from his mother, Wiebbe was strong of spirit, powerful of body, fearless, reckless and a champion of the underdog. Wiebbe was everything a father could wish for in a son and everything he wouldn't, all rolled up into one.

Wiebbe could be bold, brash, overconfident and a bit of a prick. Yep, he was my son alright. No doubt about that.

The small treasure that Kate and I had recovered from West Wallabi—well, the bit that Lazarus had left behind for us when he had betrayed us on the island all those years ago—had given us a head start in life. We had climbed the property ladder and found ourselves in a 'comfortable' situation through a combination of good luck and hard work.

Wiebbe had somehow followed a path of recklessness which had miraculously (no, make that unbelievably) paid off.

Leaving school with nothing more than a bad reputation, he had chased the dollar and caught it. Firstly, as a commercial diver and secondly, off-shore where some idiots reckoned that he was worth an hourly rate greater than that earned by both his mother and father combined.

Now a 21-year-old with money burning a hole in his pocket, he was definitely in his element.

As the celebrations turned up a notch, I turned to Kate and smiled. "Yes," she nodded as the unspoken words between us said, that we should leave them to it.

Kate and I sauntered back to our now more substantial property in Freo, arm in arm.

"I love you, Kate Hawkins," I said without so much of a thought.

"I love you too, Michael. Do you think we should have stayed?"

"Christ no. I expect they'll be off to some rowdy night club soon where you won't be able to hear yourself speak," I replied.

"I guess you're right."

Approaching our home Kate checked the mailbox, pulling out a solitary letter. As I continued to walk up the driveway, I noticed that the envelope bore a stamp from the Solomon Islands.

I sensed, rather than heard, Kate's reaction.

Turning, I saw her beautiful complexion turn a lighter shade of pale.

"What is it?"

Kate just said, "It's a letter from a dead man."

"What are you talking about, Kate?" I said, walking a little unsteadily back down the driveway as the Little Creatures' Pale Ale had found its way into my system.

"Look, it's from your old mate, lecherous Lazarus."

"Now that's a name I never thought I'd hear again. It's been over twenty years since he had betrayed us and gave us up for dead on West Wallabi. Why would he be contacting us now?

The brief covering letter was from a law firm in Honiara which simply stated that they should forward the sealed envelope to our address in the event of their client, Mr Lazarus's death.

"Let's go up to the house and read it," I said.

"Coffee?"

"Yeah. I think I'll need to sober up to read this," I replied.

I laid the contents of the envelope out on the table in our country kitchen and, cupping a hot mug of sobering caffeine in my hands, read it out loud.

> *"Dear Michael, Kate and Wiebbe, it may come as a surprise to you to learn of my demise.*
>
> *It may also come as a surprise to you to find out that I know of your circumstance and the name of your son, Wiebbe. Such an illustrious name!*
>
> *But for an old sea dog like me, it hasn't been so hard to keep track of your careers and success, especially since the advent of social media.*
>
> *As soon as I saw you together, I knew you were meant for each other and I must apologise to you, Michael, for the awful teasing I subjected you to, although part of me says you deserved it!*
>
> *I see that you have both been successful in your chosen careers, not that I ever had a doubt, and you*

really didn't need the few gold coins I left for you in the pit on West Wallabi.

But as Pauline Hanson infamously once said, 'If you are seeing this, then I am dead.' The only difference is that I probably am. That's providing my moronic lawyers in Honiara have done their jobs.

But I digress.

I have lived with the guilt of abandoning you on West Wallabi and cannot put into words my relief when I discovered that you had both survived, seemingly none the worse for wear. Not only that, but I saw that you had married and started a family."

"What a bastard!" Kate exclaimed. "Is he really seeking absolution from beyond the grave?!"

"Hang on a minute, there's quite a bit more here." I continued to read out loud.

"I want to make things right.

And that is why, like your dad, Michael, I want to share a secret with you. But don't worry, it's not about sexual orientation of which there can be no doubt, but another treasure I have found in the hulk of a small Japanese freighter sunk by the Americans in WWII near Iron Bottom Sound.

It's deep. Just over 100m. One hundred and five at high tide, to be precise. It's deep but not impossibly deep, like most of the wrecks in the sound.

Too deep for recreational divers for sure and so far, tech divers know not of its location, although for how long that will continue, I don't know.

There is a fortune in gold bullion to be had. I want you to have it. Some years ago I retrieved one bar from this freighter but, in doing so, I stuffed up and suffered a terrible diving injury which effectively put an end to my diving days.

As the years have passed, I now feel that my days are numbered and I want to do something right by you two and Wiebbe.

The gold is still there, Michael.

I have left an encrypted message for you with my lawyers in Honiara together with evidence of my discovery. Only you will be able to decipher the message. (I thought that would make you smile.) It will give you the location of the wreck and the bullion within it. You will have to overcome certain technical challenges in retrieving the treasure and even greater ones in repatriating it to Aus. But that, as they say, is not my problem.

Act swiftly.

Your old friend Lazarus"

"Old friend! Who's he kidding?! That bastard left us for dead on West Wallabi," Kate said, as she struggled with her emotions. "And what's he been doing? Spying on us all these years?"

The fire in her eyes was palpable.

The door opened and Wiebbe walked into the firestorm.

I looked up surprised and asked, "What are you doing back here? I thought you'd be going clubbing with your mates."

"Nah, getting too old for that and besides, I've got a cash diving job to do tomorrow at the sailing club."

Sensing all was not right, he looked at us and said, "Mum? Dad? What's up? Is everything OK?"

Kate stood up and stormed out of the kitchen, throwing the letter onto the table. Wiebbe picked it up and read it.

Looking up at me, he smiled and said, "This is so cool! When do we leave?"

Chapter 12 Honiara

After a short flight from Brisbane, arriving at Honiara Airport was like stepping into a different world.

A cacophony of sound and smells assaulted our senses as we rolled our heavy dive bags through the crowded concourse. As we emerged into the hot and humid air, it was like walking into an invisible wall. We found the taxi rank across a field of broken floor tiles and puddles of milky water. Before we even reached our destination we were hustled by a dozen noisy islanders, all keen to grab our business.

A persistent toothless driver, with dark skin like crumpled parchment, won the battle and we were soon loading our bags into the back of his rusty ute, which may well have started its life white but now was a patchwork of red-lead and rust. Wiebbe was told by the driver in Pidgin, "You should sit in the stret long taim to stop local thieves stealing your bags. You should hold on tight. Yes? OK?"

The driver's advice seemed appropriate, as several attempts were made by street urchins to snatch the bags from the back of the tray, as we made our way slowly through the heavy traffic to our hotel.

The Solomon Island Travel Advisory issued by the Australian Government had not prepared us for this anarchy. Kate and I were appalled but Wiebbe took it in his stride, sitting unrestrained in the back of the ute. He laughingly kicked away the hands of the would-be thieves who seemed to think of it as a huge game.

In contrast to our taxi journey, the hotel was an oasis of calm, cool marble, and air conditioning.

After checking in and getting cleaned up, we agreed to meet in reception where we asked the concierge to arrange a driver to take us to Lazarus's lawyers office.

I had contacted their offices a few weeks earlier from Perth. I had spoken to Mr Bosa, the senior and seemingly sole partner of the firm. Mr Bosa had struggled to refrain from slipping into his native Pidgin English during our conversation. Nevertheless, I was reasonably confident that he was expecting us.

The receptionist greeted us like long lost family. "Ah! Mr Hawkins, karamapim tok Mrs Hawkins, karamapim tok Master Wiebbe! So lovely to meet you ami last. Mr Bosa is expecting you, please man bilong nambis this way!"

It took a while, but I was slowly getting the hang of the Pidgin English and we followed her down a short corridor to Mr Bosa's office, where she knocked on the door softly.

"Man bilong nambis in!" The gruff voice came from the other side of the door.

The receptionist opened the door and Mr Bosa stood up from behind his desk. Facing us, a broad grin spread across his face, exposing the gold fillings in his two front teeth. Making his way around to the front of his desk, he held out both arms and greeted us with warm affection.

Rotund with slicked-back black hair, his facial features betrayed an ancestry of Spanish and Islander heritage. His grey silk suit was crumpled. It looked to be one size too small for him and, if it had had a brain, I was sure that it would be wishing that it could be somewhere else.

"Please take a seat," he said, motioning to four chairs around a small conference table. After an exchange of pleasantries and offers of tea and ice-cold water, Mr Bosa began to address us formally.

"Firstly, please accept my sincere condolences on the death of your friend. He had left our firm with instructions to send you the letter you received in the event of his death and to pass to you in person this small attaché case which, as you can see, still bears Mr Lazarus's sealing wax seal. I assume you have the combination?"

The case looked battered, and the locks looked as though several attempts had been made to crack the combination but the red seal was intact.

"I'm sure we'll figure it out," I said as I reached forward to take possession of the case.

Mr Bosa pulled it back, out of my reach.

"It's rather embarrassing bamim. I am sure that you will understand that Mr let bilong karapela Lazarus has left one or two small invoices to be paid," he said, slipping back into Pidgin.

"How much?" I asked.

Bosa looked at me and glanced slightly to his upper right and said, "$1,200 US Dollars… cash."

The amount seemed to have come out of thin air, Bosa making a judgement on our capacity to pay from his first impression of us.

There was a silence around the room until Wiebbe stood up and menacingly leaned over the table, his green eyes staring unblinkingly into Bosa's. "What say I take the case and I don't break both your arms?"

Bosa blanched visibly and stuttered, "Of course. A small misunderstanding, but you will understand that our firm will need to recover the amount of unpaid invoices from Mr Lazarus's estate. I just thought it might be quicker this way if there is anything of value in the attaché case..."

"Thank you, Mr Bosa," Wiebbe said as he grasped the case in one hand. "It's been a pleasure doing business with you."

Wiebbe led us to the door. Kate and I hurriedly followed him out.

Getting into the hotel taxi, Kate found her voice. "Oh my God, Wiebbe! You even scared me in there! And I'm your mum! That poor Mr Bosa, he looked frightened beyond his wits!"

"Don't worry about him, Mum. He'll get over it. I've dealt with worse off-shore. It's all huff and puff. There was never any twelve-hundred-dollar debt. He just wanted some cash for handing over the case."

"OK," I said as I turned the case over in my hands, "it looks as though Mr Bosa has tried and failed to open it without breaking the seal. Fortunately, I have the combination back at the hotel."

Kate and Wiebbe looked at me in disbelief.

Back in our room, I took my large titanium dive knife from my dive bag and violently popped both locks.

Chapter 13 An Uninvited Guest

Upon opening the case we were presented with a gleaming bar of gold, embedded in a grey foam insert. It was emblazoned with an Imperial Eagle perched on a wreath which encircled a swastika. Approximately 10cm long by about 4 or 5cm wide and about 13mm thick. It was imprinted with the lettering Deutsche Reichsbank 1 Kilo Feingold 999.9.

"What the fuck?" Wiebbe said before his sentence was cut short by a cuff around his head from his mum.

"I've told you not to use that language, Wiebbe." Talk about the pot calling the kettle black, I thought.

"Sorry, Mum. I just don't understand what a bar of Nazi gold was doing on a Japanese freighter sunk by the Americans in the Solomons."

"That's if it was," Kate replied. "Something you should know about the lecherous Lazarus is that he is, or at least was, a liar, a thief, a philanderer and a bastard that could not be trusted in life and I doubt very much, can be trusted in death either!"

"Oh, come on Mum, why don't you say how you really feel?"

Wiebbe's sense of humour seemed to calm Kate down a bit as I lifted the heavy bar from its recess and passed it to her, revealing an envelope beneath its foam recess.

Lifting the envelope out, I turned to Wiebbe and said, "What you have to remember, Wiebbe, is that in WWII, Japan and Nazi Germany were allies. It's entirely possible that some high-ranking Nazi sent gold to Japan in the later stages of the war, as Nazi Germany was losing. He probably thought he could retire there, to a life of luxury amongst friends."

"I thought that all the high-ranking Nazis fled to South America?" he said.

"Well, who knows?" said Kate. "What we do know for sure is that right now we have one gold bar here and an envelope."

"Hardly original," I said as I opened it and extracted an Alberti disk and a page of seemingly random letters.

"Look at the back of the ingot, Michael," Kate said as she turned it over in her hands.

There was what appeared to be a serial number stamped into the soft yellow metal.

282711341-443.

Kate smiled, and we both started to laugh.

"WTF? Mum, Dad, what are you two laughing at?"

Kate turned to Wiebbe and explained, "28 degrees, 27 minutes and 113 degrees 41 minutes is the approximate longitude and latitude of the wild goose chase that your grandad sent your dad on before you were born. West Wallabi Island in the Abrolhos. It's where we first met.

"The 443 was the primer to the Alberti disk, which enabled your dad to decipher the hidden message in your grandad's letter, which eventually led to the wreck of the *Aagtekerke*. I think that if we interpret that as four for three, we should be able to decipher the letter in the attaché case."

Kate and I had kept a lot of the detail of our adventure in the Abrolhos secret from Wiebbe. Until we received the letter from Lazarus he had been deliberately kept in the dark about Lazarus's treachery and the gold coins we had concealed from the authorities and eventually sold on-line over a period of a year or so, so as not to attract attention. It was that small collection that had given us a deposit on our first home in Freo. All he knew was that his mum had spent her entire career working on the famous wreck and assisted in recovering millions of dollars of treasure and artifacts for the Museum.

"Do you think he used lemon juice as well?" I said as I held up the letter to the light.

"I doubt it. I doubt that he'd have had the patience."

An hour later and we had deciphered the letter and had all the information we needed, to locate the sunken Japanese freighter and the location of the treasure, if indeed it really did exist.

Wiebbe turned the small gold bar over in his hands. "You reckon this is real, Dad?"

"Nineteen times the weight of water, Wiebbe," I said. "If you like, you can put it in a glass of water and calculate the displacement for volume and figure it out. It's how the old prospectors used to calculate the purity of their gold nuggets in Kalgoorlie. But it feels pretty close to a kilo to me."

Wiebbe took my dive knife and scratched the soft metal looking for a lead core, but the scratches revealed yet more of the yellow metal.

"I wonder how many there are down there?" he said. "Lazarus just said several cases split open. I mean, is that like 10 bars, or a hundred, or a thousand? How many bars to a case? Is it like what one or two men could carry? What's that? 50 kilogram? Or 25 kilogram each? How much is this worth in any case?"

Kate was on her laptop. "At today's price of around US $696 a Troy ounce, and 32 Troy ounces to the kilo, that little bar you are holding is the better part of US $22,000 or 25,000 Aussie dollars."

"Shit!" we both said in unison.

"Wiebbe! Michael!"

"Sorry, Mum," Wiebbe said. I just smiled.

"Kate, Wiebbe, we need to think seriously about this. If that gold exists where Lazarus said it does, then it's not a simple recreational dive to get to it. You can bet your bottom dollar that if we involve the local dive operators, we'll be lucky to get out of the Solomons alive, let alone get any of the gold out."

Wiebbe asked,"I don't see how we are going to get to it without a lot of local support. I mean, we'd be there supposedly on a diving holiday, but we'd need specialised salvage gear. Plus, it's a technical decompression dive, way beyond recreational SCUBA limits. How would we get the operator to take us to this site and let us dive without him suspecting we're up to something?"

"Well, let's go diving," I said. "After a few days, we can make a judgement call and might be able to convince our guide to let us do some tech diving on the wreck. That way we can at least have a look. Just a bounce dive. I doubt that any of his young dive masters or trainees will be qualified to 100 metres, so they won't go to that depth and certainly won't see anything, but they'll be good as safety divers as we come up and get shallow."

* * *

"Absolutely not, Boss! Are you crazy?" John Manu, the local dive operator, said as he unconsciously took a step backwards. "Look, I know you're good divers. I can see as soon as you get in the water, that you know what you're doing. I've seen your tech cert cards and Wiebbe's commercial diving ADAS certs, but I am just not covered for anything like that. I could lose my business licence, and my insurance would never cover me. The nearest decompression chamber is in Honiara but there's no chamber anywhere close to the location you want to dive; another reason no one dives there. In any case there are so many more accessible wrecks closer-by that will give you everything you want.

"You get bent at that site and you die. Simple."

"We won't get the bends, my friend, but we want to go off-piste, you know. Do something no one has done before. Off the beaten track." Wiebbe put his arm across our guide John Manu's shoulders as he spoke.

"No, Boss."

"We can make it worth your while," Kate said, using her most disarming smile.

"Not for all the tea in China, missy."

I pressed a little harder, "It's OK, John. It's just that you have everything we need on your boat, such a great boat, plenty of space, twin sets, plenty of cylinders, and you're not such a bad diver yourself! It'd be pretty essential to have someone up top that knows what they are doing when Wiebbe and I go deep. Your dive master can be our safety diver. Come and keep an eye on us when we ascend to say 20 metres and Kate will be our surface marshal. Make sure that everything is tickety-boo."

"Boss, I just won't do it."

Kate leapt into the conversation before Wiebbe and I, applied too much pressure. "No worries, John. Where are we going to dive tomorrow?"

John instantly relaxed his shoulders and promised enthusiastically to take us to a huge Japanese oil tanker wreck, whose cavernous holds were—he assured us—like diving through the nave of a vast cathedral, with shafts of light filtering through holes in the deck above.

* * *

Back at the hotel, Kate, Wiebbe and I sat together in the restaurant away from prying eyes and ears.

"Everyone has a price, Dad. You're a good judge of character. What do you reckon we cut John Manu in on a deal? Do you think he can be trusted? He seems like a pretty straight shooter to me."

"I think Wiebbe's right, Michael," Kate said.

"Ah, Mr Hawkins!" a gruff voice called out from across the room. I turned to see a smiling Mr Bosa making his way across the floor.

"Mr Bosa. What a pleasant surprise to see you here," Kate said as he pulled up a chair and sat down uninvited at our table, keeping as far away from Wiebbe as he could.

"I see you've been making the most of our Solomon Islands hospitality. Are you enjoying the diving?"

Kate responded, "Well Mr Bosa, you know we love to dive, Wiebbe and Michael more so than me and, as we had to come to Honiara in any case, we thought what a wonderful opportunity to mix a little business with pleasure. Michael and Wiebbe were hoping to get a tech dive in on one of the less well-known wrecks."

"How did you know we were diving?" Wiebbe asked, eyeing Bosa suspiciously.

"Oh Mr Wiebbe, Honiara is a small place. There are no secrets here and I happen to be what you might call a silent partner in John Manu's dive operation!"

"Fingers in many pies, Mr Bosa!" I said, although I was probably thinking 'pockets' rather than 'pies' at the time.

"It is the way of the Islands, Mr Hawkins. I want our tourism to thrive, so I make sure that my friends are very well taken care of—and kept safe."

Chapter 14 Innocents Abroad

I wasn't sure what Mr Bosa meant when he said, 'well taken care of'. Honiara is a challenging place for 'innocents abroad' but were we receiving special attention and his personal protection? Or were we being spied upon?

Bosa continued, "John told me that you want to dive a very dangerous deep site away from the major tourist wrecks. I don't suppose that has anything to do with the contents of Mr Lazarus's attaché case, does it?"

The directness of the question floored me for a moment. My hesitation was evidently enough to confirm, at least in Mr Bosa's mind, that the answer was yes although Kate chirped in quickly with an, "Oh no, not at all."

"You may not know it, Mr Bosa, but Mr Lazarus was actually instrumental in Michael and me first meeting each other over twenty years ago on his yacht.

"Over the years we lost touch with him as he went off on his travels, but it was lovely to hear from him and look through the old photos and letters he had saved in his battered old attaché case," Kate said, trying to deflect the conversation.

"It was a very heavy case for such documents," Bosa's eyes were darting around as the words spilled from his still smiling mouth.

"There were a lot of photos," Kate said, returning his smile.

"I see." Bosa paused and stared into Kate's eyes, looking for a hint of deception. An experienced lawyer, he reckoned that he could tell when a person was being less than truthful.

"I tell you what. I will tell John Manu to take you to your dive site if you really want to go. But you will have to sign a waiver. I'll draw it up and arrange to have it dropped off at the hotel in the morning."

"Mr Bosa! Thank you so much. That really does mean a lot to us, especially as I think that we may have got off on the wrong foot when we first met," Kate glanced at Wiebbe but quickly returned her gaze to Bosa. She was doing her best to be gracious but I noticed Wiebbe sitting in stony silence as the pantomime played out.

"In that case, I will bid you good evening and please, enjoy a bottle of champagne on the house to accompany your meal."

I looked quizzically at him, to which he responded with, "I also have an interest in the hotel."

Shortly after Bosa's departure, the waitress arrived with a bottle of champagne, three flutes and an ice bucket. A waiter opened the champagne and filled our glasses. "Compliments of the house, sir," he said as he poured.

"Well, that changes things," Wiebbe said as the waiter and waitress both moved out of earshot. "We can't possibly take John into our confidence now."

"I agree," Kate said, sipping her champagne. "Also, did you notice how his English improved? Not a single word in Pidgin."

I thought that perhaps it was to put us off our guard as he played the role of a simple islander. As our food arrived, we ate largely in silence.

"OK, we'll plan the dive and talk with John tomorrow about our requirements," I said. "We've got a few days left and we'll need to get the gear and gases, mixed well in advance.

"Did you bring the oxygen and helium sensors in your dive bag, Wiebbe?"

"Yes, I did, but that's assuming we can get helium in Honiara. If so, I'd want us to mix it myself as I wouldn't trust the local operator."

What a lot of people wouldn't know is that, whilst oxygen is vital for life, at high pressure it becomes toxic and it needs to be diluted to breathe it at depth. We use a rare gas called helium in place of some of the nitrogen and oxygen naturally occurring in the air we breathe. Being less soluble in tissues, it reduces the risk of the bends and decreases the time spent in decompression when surfacing from a deep dive.

"Mum, we'll label the spare cylinders, but you'll need to watch John on board, to double check what he's doing whilst Dad and I are deep. If we need more air to gas off near the surface, you'll need to make sure the safety diver brings the right mix to us. We can't just pop to the surface to help out."

Kate looked a little concerned but I said, "From my observations he's pretty good so there shouldn't be a problem, but two sets of eyes are always better than one, especially as I have no idea who he'll bring along as his DM to help out on the day."

Wiebbe was all business. His training as a commercial diver and his technical diving experience was going to be invaluable as we checked our calculations against each other's, making doubly sure.

Wiebbe continued, "Once we are down there, we'll plan for no more than 10 minutes bottom time so it will really be little more than a bounce dive, a reconnaissance dive if you like. If we do find anything, then we'll have to figure out another way of getting it to the surface undetected."

"I may have an idea about that," I said as I wiped my mouth with my napkin.

Chapter 15 Plan the Dive, Dive the Plan

A day later, we had consulted with John regarding our needs and signed our liability waivers. Wiebbe and I were sitting at our table back in the hotel room as Kate fussed around making cups of tea. We'd be diving open circuit SCUBA, which made things a little more complicated.

Wiebbe was clearly in charge as he went over the plan again on a piece of paper. "So, the plan is to dive to an absolute max of 110 metres. That should give us a margin for error and safety. Lazarus's depth gauge may not have been as accurate as ours. Also, we'll plan to dive at slack tide. No point in using our travel mix to fight a current. I know we're both pretty good with our air so I'm not terribly worried about consumption, but we'll play it safe.

"We'll use a descent line which we'll drop as close as possible to the location that Lazarus gave us. We'll have a pretty good grappling hook on the end to snag the wreck.

"Once the line is secure, the DM, who will be our safety diver, will drop in and attach two spare cylinders at 30 metres using pre-tied alpine hitches and karabiners with a 30:20 Triox mix, and two additional ones at 15 metres with 60% O2 just in case. He'll charge the hoses, test them, then close the cylinder valves.

Remember to open them again if you need them, or you'll only get a couple of breaths.

"Yes, son," I said sarcastically but, in truth, I was grateful for revising the plan in such detail.

"Having said that, we shouldn't need them as we'll be diving with twins and three separate twelve litre cylinders with all the mixes we'll need.

"We'll follow the line past the cylinders all the way down to the bottom. We don't want to waste time looking for the wreck once we get to depth. The viz should be great, but we're not going to see anything until we hit around 70 metres. Also, watch your descent rate. We shouldn't have to worry about narcosis using these mixes, but you never know. Keep an eye on me and I'll keep an eye on you. If either of us start to do somersaults or tell dad jokes, then we abort the dive and follow the safety stops or deco stops on the most conservative of our two dive computers."

"I always tell dad jokes. I'm a dad and it's expected."

"Believe me, he can talk underwater, Wiebbe," Kate said as she placed two hot mugs of tea next to us.

Wiebbe sighed.

It had been a while since I had done any decompression diving, but it soon came back to me like riding a bike. Looking at Wiebbe's sheet of paper, I said, "We should have a descent time of just over 6 minutes to 110 metres, Wiebbe, but maybe we can cut that down a bit without using too much travel gas. What do you think?"

"We'll be fast and accelerating, Dad. We'll be overweighted, too." There was a pause as Wiebbe let that information sink in. "It's easy to lose control in a rapid descent, so concentrate. Equalise on the surface and obviously all the way down, even if you don't feel the need to. Things are going to happen really fast and you don't want to burst an eardrum.

"So, we'll both be carrying a total of five twelve litre bottles. One twin set on our backs, and three which our safety diver will attach to us once we get in the water." Wiebbe checked himself,

"Oh Lord! Did I just say bottle? Forgive me Father, for I have sinned!"

"Converted to the dark side more like," Kate said.

It had been a long-standing joke in our family that as a commercial diver, Wiebbe had never referred to SCUBA cylinders as bottles or tanks.

"OK, each **cylinder**," he said, emphasising the word**,** "will have its own first and second stage and be clearly labelled with the gas mix inside. We'll turn them on when we're on the surface and leave them on. Check for free flowing from all the regs throughout the dive. It should be pretty obvious, but even a small trickle can quickly deplete gas at the depth we're diving at."

"I didn't think you could get trimix in Honiara," Kate said.

"You can't, Mum, but you can get balloon gas."

"I don't think I want to hear any more," Kate said as she stood up to leave the table.

"It's OK, Mum, please sit down. I spoke to some mates back home and they said it was fine, around 95% pure, and I need you to understand everything that's going on when you're topside. I'll analyse it and adjust our mixes to allow for the 5% but really, it's not going to make a huge difference.

"We obviously can't dive air at that depth. At that pressure, oxygen becomes toxic and we'd likely fit and drown before we were halfway through the dive. I suspect Lazarus was just lucky in that respect but I also suspect he got bent as he surfaced too quickly. My guess is that he was probably running out of air on his deco stop and thought that the laws of physics didn't apply to him!"

"Yeah, that'd be right! He always said, 'It was only illegal if you got caught.'" The edge to Kate's voice betrayed a contempt for the man that had tried to kill her on West Wallabi two decades ago.

"We'll use the descent line for ascending and watch each other for any signs of trouble. After 10 minutes bottom time, it's going to take us nearly an hour-and-a-half to reach the surface.

"John'll remain on the boat and his DM/safety diver will drop in half an hour after we go down. We'll be well on our way up by then and should be at around 30 metres. He'll do a quick visual check on us."

"At least we won't run out of air, although we may die of boredom," I said.

"John'll have a trapeze set up with rungs at nine, six and three metres from the surface. It'll make things easier for our final stops. Even with trimix, we'll still be spending over half an hour gassing off on the trapeze."

"Have you met the DM? Do they know what they're doing?" Kate asked Wiebbe.

"No, Mum. It won't be the one that's been diving with us so far as they've had to go back to their families for some reason but John said not to worry, he has a handful of young DMs that work for him as casuals. Apparently, they're all pretty experienced with recreational divers and are used to dealing with panicked Japanese tourists. Shouldn't be a problem for us. I told John to tell him not to touch any of our gear."

It was an unwritten rule that when tech divers are on board a vessel, no one ever touches their gear without a specific request from the diver. A lot of dive master trainees (DMTs) learned the hard way when they went to check air and gear, only to receive a sharp "fuck off!" or in some cases worse!

This was tech diving at its best and I could already feel the excitement building in my chest as we both looked over and triple checked our calculations.

It was late in the day and the dive was planned for two days' time. That gave us a full day for gas mixing and checking.

That night I had vivid dreams of Lazarus and woke with a start as he once again brought down the spade on the back of Kate's head on West Wallabi Island.

* * *

Wiebbe and I prepped all the gear the next day and personally loaded it into the back of John's pickup at the dive shop.

There was the usual fun to be had with the balloon gas in the shop as the staff inhaled it and spoke in high-pitched voices to raucous laughter. But this was a serious business and Wiebbe and I, were not easily distracted.

On the morning of the dive, daylight was already shining through the gap in the curtains and I roused Kate with a gentle kiss on her cheek.

"Up for an adventure?" I asked.

Chapter 16 Dive Master's Dilemma

We had agreed to meet John Manu at the now familiar dive boat, a 12 metre plate aluminium cuddy cabin that had seen better days. It had a rusty davit on the transom. The SCUBA cylinders were already unloaded from the back of his truck and lined up on the jetty.

A beautiful young girl, barely larger than the cylinders themselves, was busy checking their contents with a couple of gas analysers, even though we'd brought our own.

"Well, that's a good start," I said to Wiebbe. At least she's doing the right thing. I wonder where the Dive Master is?"

She looked up and set her eyes on Wiebbe.

She had a light brown complexion that hinted at her mixed heritage, Spanish maybe with some Islander girl thrown into the mix. Her long, black, softly curled hair hung 20cm below her shoulders and framed her beautiful face. Her wide, intelligent eyes were so dark that it was difficult to distinguish where her pupils stopped, and her irises began. Her high cheekbones and open smile made her look as though she had just stepped out of a magazine shoot.

I remember wondering at the time how someone would be blessed with such perfect teeth so far from western dentistry. I know it was an odd thought to have but, having grown up in

England with a high-sugar diet, my teeth had been the subject of frequent fillings and crowns and it's something I notice about people even today.

Her orange and white bikini, modest by today's standards, clung to her perfectly toned body in a way that exuded fun and self-confidence.

"Well, don't just stand there like a stunned mullet, Wiebbe. Give her a hand!"

"Let me introduce you," John said as he emerged from the cabin of the dive boat, wiping his hands on an oily rag. "This is Rose. She'll be your DM for today."

"Hi, Rose," Kate said as she stepped in front of her gobsmacked son.

"Hi, Mrs Hawkins," Rose said in perfect English as she held out her hand.

"Please, call me Kate."

Both Kate and I were surprised at the strength of her grip as we exchanged welcomes.

Wiebbe, all fingers and thumbs, ended up grabbing the tips of her fingers in a ballsed up handshake and immediately started to help load the cylinders into the boat.

"Your English is perfect, Rose; did you study abroad?" Kate asked.

"Actually, I'm reading Law at UWA in Perth in Western Australia. This is my summer vacation job."

"Really! That's brilliant! That's where we're from," Wiebbe stepped in. "Yes, brilliant, excellent, good."

"You don't look old enough," Kate said with a disarming smile, attempting to save her son from further embarrassment.

"Actually, I'm in my final year. I want to come back to Honiara to practise, eventually. There's so much that needs to be done here, as I'm sure you can imagine. In the meantime, diving is my passion. Oh, and don't be shy, you can ask. I am a fully qualified DM and insured. I have my PADI Instructor exams next week and, unlike a lot of DMs, I actually have over 3,000 logged recreational dives and, although I have not done any technical diving, I'm dead keen to learn."

It was often an awkward discussion to have with new DMs or DM Trainees. The PADI system was designed to churn out DMs for a price. It would attract young people who sacrificed just about everything in their lives in order to get to dive for free in exotic locations around the world. 'Living the dream', they called it. Consequently, you'd often find open water divers with more dives under their belts than the DMs or DMTs who were supposed to be looking after them. That certainly wasn't the case with Rose.

"OK," Rose said, "you'll need to re-check all of your cylinders yourselves. John said you had your own helium and oxygen analysers but you can use mine as well if you'd like, to speed things up. Once you're happy, please re-initial on the gaffer tape showing the mix in that bottle if it agrees with your reading and sign it. No one will remove or modify that tape but you."

It was probably an unnecessary check as we'd already marked up the cylinders in the dive shop, but you never know if some joker interfered with the cylinders or their labelling when they were out of our sight. As it turned out, all was fine.

Rose looked at Wiebbe. "Oh dear, did I just call them bottles?"

Wiebbe babbled out the words, "That's fine. I call them bottles all the time. Interchangeable terms really. Bottles, cylinders, tanks, call 'em what you will. It's all fine by me,"

Kate and I exchanged a glance of disbelief but chose to remain silent.

"It'll take us a couple of hours to get to your dive site, Mr Hawkins," John said, as the last of the gear was loaded and stowed. "The weather's looking good so far but come late this afternoon we may have to make a dash for it as it looks as though it might get a bit choppy. Nothing serious but probably a few squalls associated with the afternoon thunderstorms. The good news is you should both be out of the water well before then, provided we get a move on now."

"Looks great," I said. "I don't think I've ever seen the sea so flat."

"OK, jump on board. Let's go!"

Rose cast off, skipping over the boat with surprising agility and the soft footfalls of a ballet dancer.

After an hour we had set up, checked and double checked our gear and gone over the dive plan with Rose, John and Kate.

"It's a good plan," John said. "I think you've covered all contingencies, but it's the ones that you don't think of that are going to kill you. Do me a favour please and go over it one more time with Rose."

"I'll do it, Dad," Wiebbe said, and sat with her in the small cuddy cabin in the front of the boat.

The dive site was surprisingly close to the shore of a small uninhabited island in the Bay's southeast. We could have easily swum to it. Kate observed that the drop-off must be almost vertical for us to be sitting in 100 metres of water this close in.

Rose let out the anchor rope which was tied to a large grappling iron designed to snag the wreck below. Its tines were made from 10 mm rebar designed to hold and yet straighten when excessive force was applied.

The rope went slack, then taut, and Rose declared success in snagging the wreck.

"Feels good and strong, John, metal on metal."

"Let's hope we can retrieve it later!"

"A man of your skill and seamanship? Never a doubt in my mind," she said cheekily.

Rose kitted up in her snug wetsuit, with a rather over-attentive Wiebbe completing her buddy checks which she was gracious enough to allow.

Over the course of the next half an hour, Rose and John set up our emergency reserve tanks and the trapeze off the back of the boat.

Once back on board, Rose was happy to help us get our gear on but refrained from any action until invited to do so by Wiebbe.

Satisfied that everything was OK, Rose, Wiebbe and I fell backwards over the gunwale into the refreshing waters of the sound. We already had the twin sets on our backs and John passed Rose our separate cylinders containing the different mixes we needed to make the decompression stops on the way back up to the surface. There were three each which she attached to our Buoyancy Control Device vests in the order and in the positions which we had requested whilst on board. Satisfied that all was well, we deflated our BCDs and began our rapid descent to the depths below.

At 40 metres, our dive torches stared down the descent line into oblivion. Then, as if appearing out of nowhere, the soft dark outline of a ship's hulk started to appear. It's always a moment of excitement when diving a wreck for the first time as its ghostly image materialises before your eyes.

The ship was sitting almost perfectly upright. The beams from our torches started to penetrate and illuminate the upper superstructure as we got closer.

We saw where the grappling iron had snagged the wreck and briefly checked it before venturing further.

Checking our dive computers, we saw that we had made the descent in five minutes exactly.

As we made our way up towards the bow, we could see the dark hole Lazarus had described in his letter where a torpedo had clearly smashed into her.

* * *

"So, what made you want to study law, Rose? And why at UWA?" Kate said, as they completed the tidy up on board John's boat.

"Well, I've always had an interest in social justice, especially for the under-privileged, you know. Here in the Solomon Islands there's a massive divide between the haves and the have-nots. I know that there are a lot of reasons for that and well, clearly, I'd be regarded as one of the haves, but that doesn't mean it's fair.

"I believe that with power, wealth and privilege, comes responsibility.

"I chose UWA because it's got a good reputation and I think my dad knew the head of the law school or studied with him at some time or something.

"I know," she said, "it's not what you know but who you know. But believe me, I worked hard and got good grades, good enough to get there on my own merit."

Rose smiled, slightly embarrassed at her disclosure, and her face lit up. Kate could definitely see how this girl had already melted Wiebbe's heart.

"You sound like me when I was your age," Kate smiled, "full of righteous idealism and indignation."

"I guess so and of course, my dad's a lawyer. So that didn't hurt either. He practises here in Honiara: Joe Bosa."

Chapter 17 Too Much Gold, Too Little Time

Arriving at the gaping hole in the ship's hull, the beams of our torches reflected off what appeared to be dozens of gold bars identical to the one Lazarus had left us, spilling out over the ocean floor.

The funny thing about gold is that it's totally inert. It doesn't tarnish and even a small movement of water will keep it gleaming like new.

Wiebbe swam quickly over to the cache and picked up two bars, wide-eyed and grinning like a Cheshire cat—until the wrinkles in his cheeks flooded his mask, which he quickly cleared. I checked my dive computer: we'd been at 100 metres for 6 minutes. We had four left before we had to begin our ascent.

I swam up to Wiebbe and pulled out the left integrated weight pocket from his BCD. Tearing back the Velcro pouch, I let the lead it contained fall to the bottom. I took five of the gold bars and pushed them inside, clipping the pouch back into place, then repeated the exercise with the right-hand pouch and Wiebbe did likewise with me.

We had been careful to shield from the view of Rose and John, the amount of weight we were putting into our weight pockets in our BCDs when we were prepping our gear. We wanted a quick descent, but we had other plans too, in the event that we found something.

We both normally dived light. In warm tropical waters with thin wet suits, we'd rarely dive with more than 6kg of lead. Wiebbe would often make do with 3kg or less. DMs tended to load up their students with up to 15kg to help them with their buoyancy control at shallower depths, so there was always plenty of spare lead on board. On this dive we both carried around 13kg.

After we had each swapped 10kg of lead for 10kg of gold, the temptation to pick up just one more was almost irresistible, but we had planned this as a reconnaissance dive and couldn't take the risk of over-staying our welcome or compromising our ascent. Plan the dive and dive the plan.

I glanced at my dive computer and noted 10 minutes of bottom time had elapsed.

I indicated to Wiebbe that it was time to leave. We began to make our way back to the ascent line, rising slowly in the water column as we went. Wiebbe turned and glanced at the treasure we were leaving behind. At least another twenty bars were visible, with unopened cases just inside the wreck.

I grabbed the back of his BCD and pulled him to me. Turning, I saw the torment in his mind but then the surrender on his face as he realised that all the gold in the world was no good to you if you were dead. Is that what happened to Lazarus, I wondered? The dive hadn't killed him, but it had so affected his health that he never dived again.

On our descent we had swapped our travel gas mix at 50 metres, to a lower concentration of oxygen to reduce the risk of oxygen toxicity. Now, after ascending 50 metres from the ocean floor, we swapped back.

We hovered at 30 metres and waited for Rose to come and check on us. After a couple of minutes when she hadn't shown, we made our way up slowly to our 15 metres stop where we swapped to our final mix. We would use this mix all the way to the surface, although it would take us another 41 minutes to travel that last 15 metres safely.

It was then that we noticed, with some consternation on my part, not one but two boats rafted up above us. The new arrival was a sister to our dive boat, but a clean hull indicated a higher level of maintenance if not a much later model.

We waited again for Rose to come down and check us, expecting to see her splash, but it was another 10 minutes before the water above our heads parted as a stranger wearing board shorts and a Hawaiian shirt under his BCD dropped in. By this time, we had ascended to 9 metres and were hanging off the bottom of John's trapeze.

The unfamiliar face peered into my eyes and gave the universal dive signal for OK. I returned the signal and tried to ask, "Where's Rose?" but failed to make myself clear. The stranger checked my air and turned to find Wiebbe.

Wiebbe was gone.

Chapter 18 Wiebbe's Gone

A moment's panic grabbed me as I looked beneath me, imagining that Wiebbe had gone back down to grab another gold bar. I then glanced quickly up to the surface, looking to see if he had experienced an uncontrolled ascent.

I twirled around until eventually I bumped into the back of the stranger who had dropped in to check on us. He indicated to me to go up which I declined, pointing to my dive computer and indicating that I still had nearly 30 minutes of staged decompression to complete.

He looked at me and eventually headed for the surface.

Shit, Wiebbe, what on earth are you playing at? I thought, as I continued to scan my surroundings.

What was going on up top? It was only metres above me but to all intents and purposes, it could have been on the other side of the moon. I was stuck here for at least 25 minutes before I could make a safe ascent without risking the bends.

My mind started to play tricks on me. Were we being boarded by pirates? Had Wiebbe done a runner? Was he OK? Had the uninvited guests pulled him out of the water and laid him on the deck as his body convulsed with the agony of the bends?

I forced myself to work the problem. Having excluded all irrational explanations, I decided that Wiebbe had exercised discretion and left the area until he could figure out exactly what was going on.

At nine metres, Wiebbe could comfortably stay submerged for over an hour on one twelve litre cylinder, so I wasn't awfully concerned about that. He had more than enough gas to complete his deco.

Mid-water safety stops were sometimes challenging for beginners, but that was something we both had plenty of experience with. I looked up to see if I could see any deployment of a Surface Marker Buoy but then thought, if Wiebbe didn't want to be found, it's the last thing he'd set off. The only difficulty was, if you had no reference points and started to drift in a current, you could end up literally miles away from your boat.

I suddenly realised that Wiebbe must be making his way to the island's drop-off and be planning to complete his deco there.

I peered to the south—the direction of the drop-off—and saw a flash from his torch.

Was my mind playing tricks on me? Surely, he'd have turned it off when he realised all was not well. No—he was signalling me to follow.

* * *

"They'll be another half an hour at least, Dad," Rose said as her father, Joe Bosa, eased his bulk into the helm seat of the newly arrived vessel. He swivelled around to face his daughter, John and Kate, all of whom were sitting uncomfortably on our dive boat.

The skipper of their boat leaned over the side as his crewman surfaced and swore some unintelligible oath in a local dialect.

The smallest of movements in Rose's lips betrayed the fact that she had heard and understood what he had said.

"What do you mean, you lost one?" Bosa's captain said before the crewman could get into the boat.

Bosa looked over in alarm.

"Where's the other one?" he said, his voice sounding increasingly anxious.

The crewman was now on the swim platform at the back of the newly arrived boat, taking off his mask and holding fins in his hand. “He says he’s got another half an hour to go—gassing off.”

“You lost one, and you left the other one down there to his own devices?! What the fuck! Get back down there now and stay with him until he surfaces. I don’t care how you do it—but don’t let him out of your sight.”

The crewman, realising his error, immediately donned his fins and mask and fell backwards into the sea.

I heard, rather than saw, the splash. Sound travels faster in water than it does in air. Something to do with the density of molecules. The problem is that it’s difficult to pinpoint the direction that sound is coming from in water as it reaches both ears at effectively the same time, whereas in air there is a miniscule difference in the time it takes to reach one ear over the other. The human body has learned to use this miniscule difference to pinpoint sounds. On this occasion, however, I knew instinctively that the sound of his entry was at least 50 metres behind me, as I swam with powerful regular fin strokes in the direction of Wiebbe’s torch. I knew that even with 25 metres of visibility, my strange diving companion would not be able to hear or see me.

I hesitated for a moment and thought of Kate and Rose, but there was no way she’d come to harm.

There was something fishy going on and I didn’t want Wiebbe and myself, to climb on board with half a million Aussie dollars’ worth of gold bars in our pockets.

To my immense relief—and not a little amusement—I caught up with Wiebbe on the drop-off and settled down next to a large brain-coral bommie, about five metres beneath the surface. Our deco was going well enough, but we’d be tight on air, having exerted ourselves in our swim to the island. Fortunately, we had planned to give ourselves a little more than we needed.

* * *

On our ascent, Wiebbe had seen the new arrival before me and had already devised a plan of action. By the time we had reached 18 metres, the wind had come in a little earlier than John had predicted, creating a messy chop with a few white horses on the surface. Wiebbe had rightly deduced that it was sufficient to camouflage our bubbles as we swam towards the drop-off.

We now swam back to the boats at a depth of five metres and broke the surface of the water alongside. Our arrival came as a bit of a surprise to everyone—not to mention relief—to the stranger who had lost us.

"Where have you two been?" Kate said as we climbed on board.

"Sorry sweetheart, the trapeze was getting a bit bouncy in the chop, so we went forward to the anchor line." I don't think that I was fooling anybody, but the stranger let it go for fear of being further disciplined.

"Mr Bosa, well, this is a surprise," I said as I looked into the other boat.

Bosa's diver who had climbed aboard our boat, pulled the weight pockets from our BCDs and two small lead weights fell out of them, one landing noisily on the aluminium deck, the other on his bare foot. He let out a satisfying yelp, followed by a string of profanities in his local dialect.

"Careful. You might hurt yourself. Now, would someone tell me just what's going on?" Turning to Bosa I said, "This gorilla of yours scared the shit out of me and Wiebbe. We thought we were being boarded by pirates!"

"Don't mess with me, Mr Hawkins. What did you find down there? Where's the gold?"

"Gold! Mr Bosa, I think you've been reading too many crime novels."

"There's nothing here, Mr Bosa," the gorilla said, looking up pleadingly into his boss' eyes, a trickle of blood flowing from his big toe.

"Look again."

"I'm telling you, there's nothing."

"Dad! I told you."

I looked at Kate in shock as Rose addressed her father. Kate just shrugged and half smiled as if to say, 'What can I say?'

Bosa turned puce with anger and disappeared back into the cabin of his boat, whilst his captain instructed his crewman to cast off.

The wind was getting up, and we had a long journey home.

"I'm sorry about that. My dad. He means well, but he can be such an arse sometimes.

"Ever since he met your friend Mr Lazarus, he's been fantasising about finding a hidden treasure in one of the wrecks in the sound.

"You see, Mr Lazarus was never short of gold to trade and, well, my dad thought it had come from a wreck somewhere here, even though the gold Lazarus traded seemed to be of Dutch origin. I saw some of his gold coins once.

"I think that it was because Mr Lazarus had been diving in the sound and got terribly bent that my dad put two and two together—and came up with five.

"How was your dive, anyway? Did you get to see much of the wreck?"

It appeared that Rose was oblivious to her father's plans for that day, and totally trusting of our explanations. She stooped down to pick up the lead weights, but Wiebbe beat her to it and threw them into the steel bucket with the rest of the weights on board.

"You dive light," she said, "I thought you'd be heavier than that but then again, I guess you're both pretty experienced. Me, I love to dive with no weights at all, if I can. It just gives me such a sense of freedom in the water."

"Yeah, I know what you mean," said Wiebbe, "I'm exactly the same. But with the amount of gear we were carrying, I'm surprised we needed any lead at all. Do you free dive?"

"Rarely, but I really enjoy it. I'm getting better at holding my breath too, almost four minutes now. I'd like to add it to my skill set for teaching, once I pass my PADI instructor exams."

“That's great! We must go over to Rottnest Island when you get back to Perth. There are some fantastic free diving spots over there and if we're lucky, we might even get a feed of lobsters.”

“Yeah? I’d like that, I’d like that a lot,” Rose said with an open smile.

Back at the hotel, we closed the bedroom door.

“So, what’s the story?” Kate said.

I held my finger up to my lips, not sure if our room had been bugged, and said in a somewhat louder voice than usual, “It’s a wild goose chase—there’s nothing there. But the wreck was interesting. You could see where a torpedo had blown a big hole in the hull.

“It’s a pity we couldn’t extend our bottom time, but it was great to do some tech stuff before we fly home in a couple of days’ time.”

“No more diving then?”

“No. All sun, sea, sand and sex for a couple of days,” I said with a cheeky grin. “I think we should visit some of the islands, don’t you? Do the touristy thing. A picnic lunch on the beach, wine and a dip in the sea. Just the tonic before we go home.”

“What about Wiebbe?” Kate said.

“Oh, I think he'll find his own entertainment. He seemed pretty keen on Rose, don't you think?”

“Yes, there’s definitely a spark there. What a pity that her dad is such a prick,” Kate emphasised the word ‘prick’ a little too loudly. There was no point in riling him if in fact he was listening.

“Yeah, I know what you mean but it's not a perfect world, is it? Rose says he’s a good dad,” I said hoping to deflect some of Kate’s criticism.

Kate picked up on my caution immediately and, changing the subject, asked, “Talking of perfect worlds, where would you like to have our romantic picnic?”

“I do have somewhere in mind as it happens, but let’s leave that as a surprise for you.”

Chapter 19 A Golden Sunset

Kate and I lay on our hotel towels on the sand of a secluded, uninhabited island in a remote southeast corner of the Sound.

We had hired a boat for the day, under the watchful eye of Mr Bosa's gorilla, who failed miserably to conceal himself as he tailed us on the short walk from the hotel to the dock.

We thought about trying to lose him but decided against it. We made sure that our boat was empty of dive gear to avoid suspicion. We made light of the two beach bags we were carrying, stuffed with our picnic, snorkels, face masks and fins under our towels.

On the beach of the deserted island, Kate leaned towards me and kissed me deeply, sandwiching twenty gold bars between us.

Wiebbe and I had emptied the gold bars from our integrated weight pockets and concealed them in a small nook on the seaward side of the large coral bommie at a depth of just 5 metres.

We had taken our non-dumpable weights from the backs of our BCDs and placed them in the front weight pockets to avoid suspicion. It was an easy duck dive to retrieve them two at a time and make the short swim back to shore.

"I guess we'd better get going," Kate said as she smoothed my fringe from my forehead.

"I guess you're right," I said.

"Do you think Gorilla man will be waiting for us at the dock?"

"Undoubtedly. Are you still OK with our plan?"
"Yes, of course."

* * *

It came as a bit of a surprise to see Gorilla man standing between the shoulders of two armed police officers on the dock. We weren't expecting that.

The officers took our bags roughly from us and emptied their contents on the dock, spilling out the remnants of our picnic, some plastic wine glasses and an empty wine bottle.

"Nothing here, Boss," Gorilla man was on his mobile. He looked up and instructed one of the officers to conduct a search of the boat, having clearly received further instructions.

After half an hour's delay, the police officer that searched our hire boat emerged to say that there was nothing on board.

Gorilla man and the officers thanked us for our co-operation, muttering something about a trade in illicit drugs, using tourists as mules, and subsequently left. Their story fooled no one.

* * *

The previous day, Kate and I had left Wiebbe and Rose, to their own devices. They were walking along the harbour wall, hand in hand. Wiebbe turned to Rose and said, "Rose, there's something I have to tell you."

For some reason, Wiebbe had been terrified that disclosing his deception would end whatever chance he had of forming a lasting relationship with this girl of his dreams. However, he had come to the rapid conclusion that honesty was the best policy. As it turned out, Rose was at least one step ahead of him, if not two.

She stopped and, grabbing both of his elbows, she turned him towards her. Looking up into his eyes she smiled and said, "So what did you do with the gold you found?"

Wiebbe was stunned and his jaw literally dropped and then bounced with no words coming out.

Rose laughed and held up her finger to press his chin closed.

"I um, well, what I mean is... oh fuck…"

"Let me help you, shall I?"

"No wait, I…"

"You found some gold and stashed it somewhere safe and tomorrow Michael and Kate will retrieve it."

"How did you know?"

"Oh Wiebbe! Do you really think I'm that silly?"

Wiebbe was exposed, but Rose was still there—smiling and clearly wanting to be part of the great adventure.

"So, the problem as I see it isn't so much getting your hands on it and keeping it secret, but actually liquidating it—and that means getting it out of the Solomons. If you tried to sell it in Honiara, the secret would be out quicker than you can say Adolf Hitler, and we'd all be lucky to get out of this alive!

"Fortunately for you, I have a plan. Now, how many bars did you find?"

"Twenty, but there's many, many more down there, Rose. It was incredible. I wish you could've seen it for yourself," he gushed. The flood gates were open now and it was pointless trying to hold anything back as he went into great detail of the dive and subsequent deception.

"Twenty kilograms. That'll work. Michael and Kate mustn't bring it back to the harbour tomorrow. We'll have to meet them offshore and smuggle it ashore ourselves. I'll borrow my dad's boat. No one's going to search that."

"OK, I'll have to tell Mum and Dad where to meet," Wiebbe said.

"Of course."

"What's your plan?"

"In a few days' time I'll be shipping my huge trunk over to Perth for my final year. Another twenty kilos isn't going to make any difference. With thousands of overseas students arriving for the start of the new semester, customs won't be looking too closely at my trunk."

"So, your dad will be paying to ship our gold to your flat in Perth without knowing anything about it?" Wiebbe was beside himself with laughter. "The irony of it!"

Kate and I had stopped off on our way back to the dock, to meet up with Rose and Wiebbe on a remote beach. They took the gold to Rose's house and concealed 18 bars in the large trunk that was destined for her digs in Perth.

Rose would use the two bars she kept, as payment for her help. She would use the proceeds to fund the orphanage. She'd make sure that it was done piecemeal by shaving off an ounce at a time and trading it with the same jeweller that Lazarus had used to trade-in his ill-gotten Dutch coins. She knew she wouldn't get full market price for it but it was still worth a fortune and would—in her mind at least—transform evil into goodness.

Wiebbe had tried to convince her to take more but she had insisted that she had more than enough to change the lives of so many.

* * *

Mr Luke the jeweller knew better than to ask where Rose had got her ounce of fine gold from, but curiosity got the better of him.

"There's a lot of wastage if you are going to hacksaw a gold ingot into little pieces, Miss Rose. Why not bring it all to me and we can sort out a price for you?"

Rose had been taken by surprise and initially tried to feign ignorance, but to no avail. She reasoned that it would be in the corrupt jeweller's own interest to keep his mouth shut and so had agreed to bring the rest of the bar to his place of work unannounced. She didn't want anyone else surprising her.

After a few days, she took the remnants of the bar she had been shaving to Mr Luke. Time was running out, as the beginning of the new semester was approaching, and she'd soon be returning to Perth. Cargo tracking showed that her trunk had already arrived at her digs without incident—and was waiting for her.

The shaved gold bar now sat on a black felt cloth, on a desk in the back office of Mr Luke's jeweller's shop.

"50 cents in the dollar is the best I can do," he said leaning back in his chair.

"But you gave me 90 cents for the ounce I brought in," Rose complained.

"Miss Rose, that was before I realised that this is Nazi gold. It could be traced. Even when it's melted down, it still carries its own fingerprint.

"The mint in Perth developed a technology for this. You should visit the mint when you return. You'll see I'm not lying."

The fact that Luke was lying wasn't worth arguing with. Rose had been to Perth Mint and understood that the fingerprinting technology related to the origin of the gold mined, not its ownership. "Maybe I'll find someone else," she said as she reached to grab back the shaved bar.

"Let's not be hasty, Miss. Have you got any more of these trinkets?"

"No."

Rose wasn't sure if the jeweller could see through her deception but she wasn't game to trade both her bars for half their value.

Rose's fingers wrapped around the bar but Mr Luke gently grabbed her wrist.

"Miss Rose, I could go to 75 cents if you might be able to secure more of these trinkets for me."

"90 cents or the deal is off."

"Ah, you're your father's daughter I see. I assume he knows nothing of your … ahem, transactions?"

"No, and if he did, it's you, not me, that'd be taking a swim with some concrete shoes."

Luke's features blanched a little as the words sank in.

"85 cents? I have expenses to cover and a family to feed. My wife is not well and treatment is expensive."

"Mr Luke, I know for a fact that you're a confirmed bachelor so don't fuck me about."

The use of the F word from such a small and apparently delicate young girl shook him more than he cared to admit.

"85 cents doesn't give me the margin I need, Miss," he continued.

Rose grabbed the bar, twisted her arm, and released herself from his grip. As she stood and turned to walk out of his office, he called after her, "90 cents!"

Completing the transaction, Rose slipped out of the shop and made her way home.

Mr Luke sat staring at the gold bar on his desk—and smiled.

He picked up the phone and dialled a number he had, long ago, committed to memory.

Chapter 20 International Direct Dial

A series of tones echoed in the 'phone's handpiece as the call he had placed was automatically diverted to an international number.

"You said I should call you if ever I came across a gold bar bearing the mark of an eagle on a wreath encircling a swastika."

Luke sat waiting for a reply, visibly nervous and perspiring. He felt that he was in a conversation with the devil himself.

"A small amount appears to have been cut off but the bar is essentially complete."

He took a deep breath and forced out, "There will, of course, be a small premium for such a treasure. A modest 150% of the bullion price should cover the considerable expenses I have had to incur to obtain this specimen and naturally, a very, very small profit for myself. I'm sure that you would understand that such transactions do not come cheaply. There are many mouths to feed along the way."

There was silence on the other end of the phone and, as nature abhors a vacuum, Luke continued, "Also, the bar comes with information which I am sure that you'd be interested in."

Luke paused again, forcing himself to be silent.

"100%."

"I'll take it," he said, groaning as he replaced the receiver. It wasn't such a bad deal. Almost $2,500 profit for half an hour's work.

He would never have accepted such a small margin normally but his deep-seated fear of the mysterious contact, and a deeply held suspicion that there was a lot more to come, had forced his hand.

* * *

Rose had a feeling that she was being followed to the airport and was surprised at the thoroughness of the customs officials in searching her carry-on, prior to departure.

Landing at Perth International airport, she was thrilled to be greeted by Wiebbe who grabbed her in a warm, smothering embrace.

"Did you have any trouble getting through?" he asked.

"No, everything went as planned and you can pick up your gold as soon as we get to my place, once you have properly welcomed me back to Perth."

Chapter 21 A Deal with The Devil

It was some months later that Wiebbe, Kate, Rose and I were sitting around our country kitchen table in Fremantle. The small pile of gold bars in front of us was nothing like the big ingots you see in the movies, but it was still worth nearly half a million dollars.

"There's a lot more where that came from," I said, "but the problem is getting it in the first place and getting it out of the Solomons in the second place."

I had been working hard on a strategy to convert our bullion to cash and had called a family meeting to discuss our options.

Rose now I considered to be part of our family and we had all fallen in love with her—none more so than Wiebbe.

Their relationship had blossomed into a full-on romance and, to be honest, Kate and I couldn't be happier. She was everything he needed; challenging, smart, resourceful, strong willed, and beautiful to boot. She also, ironically, had a calming influence on Wiebbe. Just what the doctor ordered.

"What are you going to do with this lot?" Rose asked.

"Well, that's simple. We've bought a small lease up around Leonora so we are officially gold prospectors now. There's four years to run on the lease and another four after that if we renew. We'll melt it down into smaller ingots and sell it piecemeal to the gold traders in Kalgoorlie. We'll salt it with a little copper or silver to match the purity of the gold we find on the lease, but we should be able to move half this year and half next without raising too much suspicion."

"Isn't that illegal?" Rose said.

"Only if we get caught!" we answered in unison.

After a moment of reflection, Wiebbe leant back in his chair and said, "The problem is that smuggling out 18 small one kilogram bars was one thing, but another hundred or so, is quite a different proposition. We'd have to have a local partner."

Kate piped up, "What about Rose?"

"No," I said, "we need someone who's on the ground, well connected with the local authorities, and knows how things work. Someone to grease the wheels of industry if need be."

"I can talk to my dad, if you like."

We all sat there incredulous, gawping open mouthed at the beautiful Rose. Eventually I broke the silence. "What are you talking about, Rose? Your dad would kill you if he knew you'd hoodwinked him."

Rose laughed. "Actually, I would put money on it that he'd be quite proud of me, especially if I offered to cut him in on a deal. Look, you said yourself that we were lucky to get away with it first time around, and if we're going to go back for a second bite at the cherry, then you're going to need a lot more support than subterfuge, and a lot more security.

"Dad could provide you with all of that. He'd also be able to help convert the bullion to cash."

"For a hefty fee, of course!" Wiebbe interjected.

"You know Wiebbe—it's the way of the Islands," Rose said, parroting the phrase so often used by her father, while reaching over to touch Wiebbe's now bearded face. "And besides, is he really going to try to screw over a member of his own family?"

The irony of Rose's comment hit me, but I decided to keep my mouth shut for a change.

"What about cutting a deal with the government?" Kate asked. "At least then it would all be above board."

Rose took a deep breath and interlaced her hands on the table in front of her. "Sadly, that's probably the worst choice. We'd be lucky to walk away with our expenses covered.

"It's still like the Wild West out there, and rumours abound about Nazi gold and sunken treasure. People live in fear of their lives for just talking about such things. People think you know something and the next thing that happens is you disappear. Then there's the possibility of ownership claims or disputes from insurance companies or government lawyers. No, you'd be tied up in the courts for years and end up with nothing.

"The governments of all these countries, Solomons, Japan, Germany, they have more lawyers than brains and everyone, and I do mean everyone, will want to take a slice."

There was no denying the fact that we needed in-country support and using Rose's father, one of the major players in Honiara's high society, made sense.

Whether he could contain the operation and prevent his network from leaking like a sieve was another matter. But if we were going to be successful, it was clear that that was exactly what he had to do.

I realised that Kate, Rose and Wiebbe had all stopped talking and were looking at me.

"How will you tell him?" I asked.

* * *

Bosa sat alone staring wide-eyed, as Rose—on her end-of-term break—walked into his office and without a single word of warning, dropped a one-kilogram bar of Nazi gold on his desk in front of him.

It wasn't often that her father was speechless, so she was really enjoying the moment.

Bosa picked up the bar and held it in his hands. Its polished surface reflected fading sunlight from the window across his features.

Eventually he looked up, rocked back in his chair and laughed so loud and so long that Rose thought he might have a heart attack on the spot.

"I should have you shot! You little minx!" he said as he wiped tears from his eyes. "My own flesh and blood! Lord save me! I have spawned a monster child who has deceived her own father!"

Rose stood with her hands on her hips, a look of defiance on her face. "That one is mine. If you want it, you can buy it off me," she said.

"Of course, my dear, and what sort of price would you be looking at for a kilogram of fine Nazi gold?"

"$25,000 Australian dollars. It's a fair price, but the real value lies in knowing where the rest are and how you are going to help recover them for an even bigger share in the spoils."

"Oh, my word! My own daughter has me over a barrel and is torturing me with a smile and soft words!" He continued to play out his role as the injured party, pouting his bottom lip before getting down to business.

"Who knows about this, Rose?"

"The Hawkins, of course, and the jeweller, Mr Luke, has an idea that there may be more to come."

"John Manu?"

"No, he doesn't have the slightest inkling."

"Good. Let's keep it that way for the time being.

"Luke may be a problem, but he knows when to keep his mouth shut. Still, it might be worth Sol paying him a visit to put the fear of God in him." There was an edge to Bosa's voice that sent a cold shiver down Rose's spine.

"I don't want anyone hurt, Dad."

"Don't worry, if we are going to move the rest of this bullion, we're going to need him in any case. Now, where were we? Ah yes, about to negotiate?"

"No Dad, no negotiation but you can draw up a cheque now for $25,000 made payable to the orphanage trust and once it clears, you can claim your tax deduction and spruik your charitable credentials around the whole of Honiara."

Bosa's mind was racing, but he quickly embraced the idea. "You don't have to wait for it to clear, my dear. Don't you trust your old dad?" He stuck out his bottom lip and presented what he hoped was his best puppy dog expression.

"Just about as far as I can throw you Dad, and, looking at your waistline, that's not going to be very far anytime soon!"

Bosa relented and drew up a cheque but insisted that they go to the hotel to sit in a private booth and have a sumptuous dinner to celebrate Rose's return to Honiara. He also insisted that Rose tell him the full story of how he had been so wonderfully hoodwinked. Was it her idea? How much gold had been recovered and how much more was there still to be had!

He was also keen to come up with a way that would ensure the secrecy and security of the operation he was about to embark upon and needed the devious mind of his daughter, not to mention her relationship with Wiebbe, to plan it.

* * *

"I'm fine, really," Rose said down the line to Wiebbe. "You should have seen his face when I dropped that bar on his desk. I'm sure he was just expecting me to say, 'Hi Dad I'm home and I'm broke!'

"Of course, he had suspected all along that you and your dad had recovered something but had no idea what it was, how much it was worth, how you managed to conceal it and get it out of the country. I think he was actually quite proud of me."

Wiebbe and Rose chatted for a while about sweet nothings before things returned to business.

"Dad's totally in. He wants to keep the number of people involved in the salvage operation to a minimum. He'll need John Manu, of course, but John owes Dad big time, and he'll be happy to take cash or, knowing Dad, full ownership of his own business in return for his help.

"He'll use Mr Luke to shift some of the bullion over time and make sure that we all get a reasonable price for our efforts. He said he'd talk with John in a few days' time and tell him to advertise that he was now taking tech divers to some of the more popular sites, given the success of your latest exploits, but leave your site alone. That way we won't be arousing too much suspicion when we arrive.

"There are plenty of deep sites in the Sound and once the word spreads amongst the tech diving community, he's bound to have a waiting list soon enough.

"Then next year we'll be ready to salvage the loot!"

"Why wait until next year?" Wiebbe said. "What if Manu gets suspicious and takes tech divers to our site?"

"Don't worry, Wiebbe, my dad will ensure his co-operation and John Manu, well, he knows the way of the Islands."

Chapter 22 The Operation

It was mid-April when we next arrived in Honiara but unlike our previous arrival, we were met on the wrong side of immigration by Mr Bosa's gorilla, who we later learned was called Sol, which we assumed was short for Solomon. He took our passports and told us to follow him to the VIP channel.

Having whisked us through customs at breakneck speed, much to the consternation of our fellow passengers, we climbed into the back of a limo which made its way to our hotel in record time, horn blaring and narrowly missing at least a dozen pedestrians on the way.

"Low profile?" I said to Kate who was sitting next to me in the back seat.

Wiebbe turned around in the front passenger seat with a huge grin spread across his face and said, "I could get used to this!"

Rose had arrived a few days before us and was naturally staying in her family home, a luxury villa surrounded by high walls crowned with rusty barbed wire and broken bottles. Security was something Bosa took very seriously and as a practicing lawyer he always had in the back of his mind a list of people that would do him harm if they could.

Wiebbe and I had talked about upgrading our dive gear to closed circuit re-breathers but decided to stick with open circuit because of the lack of in-country support. Keep it simple stupid.

Even though Rose had said that she would not greet us at the airport, I think that Wiebbe was a little disappointed that she hadn't made a surprise entrance. She had reasoned that the less locals knew of their relationship, the safer it would be for the both of them.

I thought that was a bit of an over-kill, but we agreed to go along with it.

"Me pick up 7pm," Sol said as he deposited both ourselves and our heavy bags at the hotel reception, making sure that we had been upgraded to the best suite available. "You not be late."

Apparently, we were expected to dine with Mr Bosa at his family home that evening, and a polite apology was clearly not an option.

* * *

Passing through the heavy gates of Bosa's residence, Sol pulled up at the front door and before Wiebbe was fully out of the car, he was tackled by Rose who launched herself at him, squeezing the air out of his lungs.

Bosa stood in the doorway broadly grinning, his arms opened wide. "It is the way of the Islands! Welcome, welcome, welcome to my humble abode!"

Kate had slipped on a beautiful cocktail dress for the occasion, whilst Wiebbe and I opted for the cool, casual look of crisp white open-necked shirts, slacks, and deck shoes. I also carried a linen jacket—just to be on the safe side. I needn't have worried. Bosa was in a very loud Hawaiian shirt, tented over his rotund belly, with dress shorts, tall socks, and sandals, whilst Rose herself was dressed in a smart T-shirt and jeans.

Rose was still smothering Wiebbe with kisses as Bosa led us into the entrance hall. "Don't be too long, you two!" he called back to them.

* * *

We discovered that Mrs Bosa would not be joining us and didn't find out immediately whether she was away, dead or divorced and it seemed impolite to ask. It transpired later that Ellie Bosa was Rose's step mum. Her birth mother had sadly passed away when Rose was just five years old. Ellie was in New York on business which apparently consisted mostly of shopping, much to Bosa's dismay.

The table was set for five with fine linen and rather over-the-top gold cutlery and gold trimmed plates. The décor was Italian renaissance meets Jackson Pollock, neither of which seemed to work very well together, but the chairs were comfortable, and the food served by his private chef was superb, even if the selection of wine was a little unusual.

"I knew it!" Bosa yelled enthusiastically as we came clean about our little deception. "I knew it, I knew it, I knew it! You can't kid a kidder, you know. I just couldn't understand how you did it and poor old Sol, well let's face it he's not the shiniest tool in the tool shed. He thought that there was sorcery and witchcraft involved in the skulduggery. It was as much as I could do to get him to pick you up at the airport today."

Bosa leaned forward with his elbows on the table, his demeanour now all business and glanced around furtively to make sure that no one was eavesdropping. "So how many bars did you leave behind? Rose said at least twenty but hinted that there may be more."

He was practically salivating awaiting our response.

I put down my napkin and sat back in my chair. "We collected twenty and gave Rose two. She could have had more but said that two was more than enough."

You could see Bosa's perplexity but he remained silent. We knew that Rose had told him how many bars we had salvaged, so it was important to keep our stories the same.

"We had a very short time on the bottom and will have limited time again when we return for technical reasons. When we left the bottom, there were at least another twenty bars that had spilled from the broken crate we collected ours from.

"I reckon that crate probably held fifty bars—that's fifty kilograms of fine gold per crate, or around $1.25 million Australian in today's money. Fifty kilos is about as much as you can expect one man to carry. I remember, in my youth, we used to haul fifty-kilo bags of cement on our shoulders. Probably explains why my back's so bad now. But each case would've had two rope handles—a two-man lift, I reckon."

"How many crates did you see?"

This was something that we hadn't discussed with Rose and were uncertain about ourselves. Bosa, however, clearly wanted to do the math.

"To be honest, Mr Bosa, we didn't stop to count them. I think there were more than three, maybe as many as ten, but that was just what we could see from outside the hull. We didn't venture inside for more than a metre."

"Ten crates —1.25m in each. Twelve and a half million Aussie dollars!" Bosa whispered in a soft voice.

I didn't want Bosa to get ahead of himself. Gold can do that to a person. It's true what they say about gold fever and it was important that he remained focussed on the job. I had to manage his expectations.

"I don't think you should get your hopes up but I reckon that we can count on at least another $2m if the wreck hasn't moved or been covered."

My comments sent Bosa into a mild panic. The thought that the ship could move, or the gold be buried by nature, was something he clearly hadn't considered.

"I hope your delay hasn't cost us our prize!" he said accusingly to Rose.

"Dad! It was your idea to wait."

Bosa glared at his daughter, then calmed down.

"Michael, I don't understand. Tell me, how can a shipwreck that's been down there for over 60 years suddenly move? Surely, you're not suggesting that it will float away after 60 years on the bottom?"

"No, the wreck's sitting upright, but it's on a ledge on a steep drop-off, about 100 metres beneath the surface."

"Yes, yes I know all that: Rose explained that it's very deep."

"Well, that slope below the ledge, just keeps on going another kilometre down, far beyond any technical diving limits. If there was an earthquake, it's not inconceivable that she could be buried under millions of tons of rocks and mud or simply slide off the ledge and disappear into the abyss, lost for ever." Bosa's complexion turned pale. "Wrecks can move," I continued. "The *SS President Coolidge* in Vanuatu slipped 20 metres down a slope in one earthquake and you can bet your bottom dollar that it **will** happen again."

"Earthquakes. We get tremors all the time." Bosa was starting to take on the look of a desperate man. I have to admit; I was quite enjoying his discomfort.

"Dad, we haven't had a biggie for ages. I'm sure everything will be just how Michael and Wiebbe left it, plus a few lead weights, of course..."

We all laughed, but Bosa's laughter was strained, and his laughter didn't quite reach his eyes. "I think we should accelerate the programme," he said eventually. "Make the dive tomorrow and grab what we can."

"That's not going to happen, Dad," Rose came to our rescue.

I continued, "There is a lot of preparation to do, checking and planning. We plan to do a couple of shakedown dives first in any case, with a day off afterwards to let our bodies recover." I turned to Rose and asked, "Have you spoken to John Manu about our plans?"

"No, not yet," Rose said, "he knows you're here, of course, and is looking forward to taking you out to some deep wrecks. He's got plenty of balloon gas for you. I said that you'd want to go back to your special wreck at some point, but that's all he knows for now."

"Good. We'll need him to modify his davit. Wiebbe will help. It needs to be able to accommodate 150 metres of 4 mm Dyneema rope. We brought two lots with us as we didn't think we'd get it in Honiara and besides, we didn't want to raise suspicions.

"It's incredibly strong for its diameter with a breaking strength of over two tonnes. That's more than enough to bring up all the gold in one hit, but I doubt the davit will be able to handle more than half a tonne in one load. We'll know more tomorrow.

"Once we've loaded the last of the bars into the basket, we can begin our ascent."

"Forgive me. I had no idea that this was going to be so involved," Bosa said as he stood up.

It was clear that the evening was over. He called Sol to take us back to the hotel.

"I'll catch the next limo back if that's OK with you, Mr Bosa," Wiebbe said.

"Very well. Sol will take your parents back to the hotel and return in one hour."

Rose took Wiebbe's arm and they wandered out onto the patio through the French windows into the balmy evening air.

Bosa turned to Kate and me and somewhat surprisingly smiled broadly and said, "Ah, the wonders of young love. It is the way of the Islands!"

Chapter 23 Loose Lips Sink Ships

Wiebbe and I were greeted like old friends when we turned up at the dive shop, and shook hands with John Manu.

The shop itself was within its own walled compound, surrounded by a mismatched collection of high Colorbond fence panels. Entrance was via two tall, spiked security gates.

Sol parked the car by the air intake for the compressor and was about to sit there with the engine running, spewing out exhaust, until I made him move. Breathing in carbon monoxide from our cylinders was never a good idea.

The short, crushed road base driveway led to a tin roofed building on stilts, which housed the accommodation for John Manu, his family and visiting DMs. Under the accommodation was the 'shop', housing the compressors, gas mixing panel and hire equipment. The walls were mostly wire mesh, allowing for free air flow with some colorbond panels shielding more valuable items from thieving eyes.

Like many operators I have dived with in the tropics, the climate and scarcity of spare parts take its toll on gear. The absence of occupational health and safety we take for granted in Australia, means that it pays to at least observe procedures and gently intervene where we see potential problems arising.

John seemed genuinely pleased to see us. His wiry frame was all sinew and muscle. Bare foot and wearing a grubby singlet and shorts, he was keen to show off his new red baseball cap sporting a Nike logo. A small treasure that he had been given by an American tourist recently.

John had lived and grown up in Honiara for all of his 50 years. Unlike many full blood Islanders he had succeeded where others had failed; thanks in no small part to the financial support of Joe Bosa. Joe, for all his failings, had seen in John a hard and loyal worker, and had wanted to support him—knowing full well that he'd die on the job rather than let him down.

"I'd like to thank you for helping me expand my business, Mr Hawkins. I have a long waiting list of tech divers that want to dive the Iron Bottom Sound, but for you there will always be space."

"Thank you, John, we've got a few weeks here so there's no rush but we'd like to do a couple of shakedown dives first, no deco, just shallow stuff, you know."

We were keen to get back on board the dive boat and inspect the davit. When we did see it, the news wasn't good. It had definitely seen better days and had stopped working all together at some point.

"I'm afraid I'm not much use when it comes to things electrical. It's been like that for a year or more. I get by, but I do miss not having it."

"Wiebbe, you've had a bit of experience in fixing up those things, haven't you? Why don't you take a look at it for John and see if you can fix it?"

"No problem, Dad."

John was taken aback and said that he had a full tool kit at his disposal.

It didn't take Wiebbe long to find the problem, which was a corroded wire, but he stripped it down in any case and regreased the gears and added the new rope.

"Are we going fishing?" John said when he saw the thin Dyneema rope.

"No mate, over two tonnes breaking strength. This is Dyneema winch rope, not your Chinese rubbish. She's as good as new John, good for lifting at least 550 kilograms, maybe more once we have the rope bedded down."

"How come you brought this wonderful rope with you to Honiara?" John said as he eyed it suspiciously, rolling it between the fingers of his gnarled hands, trying to gauge its strength.

Wiebbe laughed, "OK John, you got me," he said, "I'll come clean. I saw the crappy wire rope you had on your davit last year, and thought I'd bring you a present," he lied. "I just didn't realise that the davit itself was also in need of repairs!"

"Mr Wiebbe, you are too kind." John was still not convinced but was also reluctant to look a gift horse in the mouth. After all, anything would be an improvement over a non-functioning davit on the back of his boat.

"Not at all, John. I tell you what, we'll test it all out tomorrow. I assume you have a steel basket we can use?"

"Yes, of course, Mr Wiebbe."

"Once we have the rope bedded down, we can look at its safe working load—back at the dock with some known weights—to make sure you don't exceed that."

"I thought you said it was two and a half tons?"

"That's the breaking strength of the rope, John. If we put two and a half tons of weight on your rusty old davit, she'll fold, rip out your transom and disappear into the deep!"

John shook his head but then looked up and said, "Mr Wiebbe, your kindness is unbelievable, great! What time do you want to go tomorrow? Do you want to dive air or your special party gas?"

"Air is fine, John. Take us somewhere nice, no deeper than 40 metres. Let's see some coral before we dive the wrecks."

"You have a deal!" he said, as he continued to finger the rope suspiciously.

* * *

"The davit is working perfectly, Dad. The good news is it's got a really large cable capacity, which can easily accommodate the new rope. But the bad news is—I have no idea what its Safe Working Load is.

"We'll test it tomorrow, but a retrieval speed of around 10 metres a minute, means that we'll only have time to make one lift. If there's anything left after the first lift, it'll mean a second dive another day—and, after the first dive and salvage, the chances are the cat will be well and truly out of the bag by then."

"It'll be pretty tight, Wiebbe. We need to think about our contingencies and see about stretching bottom time on the gas we have."

"I think that's a non-starter, Dad. I really don't want to cut it any finer than it is already."

Of course, Wiebbe was right. All the gold in the world was useless if you weren't alive to spend it. "You're right, Wiebbe. Is Rose going to be our DM tomorrow?"

"I wouldn't have anyone else, Dad," Wiebbe smiled.

* * *

A young islander man dressed in a filthy T-shirt, oil-stained jeans and thongs had been hanging around the docks all day. He was now talking on his mobile phone as he walked along the street, away from the hotel towards the town.

"So, the son was working on John Manu's davit?" the shadowy voice on the other end of the phone asked.

"Yes, but it looked like he put some thick fishing line on it. Maybe they are going trawling for a nice fat tuna or mackerel?" he said enthusiastically.

"Yes, maybe they are. Keep your eyes and ears open and call me as soon as you have any further information. I want to know what's going on and when it's happening. Where are the Hawkins now?"

"I followed the son back at the hotel, Boss, but I can't go in there. You know how it is—they take one look at me, and I won't make it past the front door."

"I understand." There was a slight pause. "Your sister is a chamber maid there, isn't she?"

"Yes, Boss."

"Talk to her and ask her to find out what they're up to. It'll be worth your while and your sister's if she gets the right information."

"Yes, Boss. Uh, what shall I tell her?"

"Tell her to look around their room for any paperwork, maps, calculations and the like. Bring them to me."

"Boss! She'll get fired if she takes anything from their room. She won't do it."

"Well, it looks as though they are going out for the whole day tomorrow, so she can take photos on her phone—make copies.

"There's $50 US for each of you if you bring me something worthwhile."

"Yes, Boss!" There was a moment's hesitation before he said, "Assuming we find something, where shall I bring it?"

"I'm Stateside now, but I'll be back in Honiara in a couple of days. Don't worry, I'll find you."

The young man had a spring in his step and made a beeline for his home. He hoped that his sister would find something. He had already convinced himself that it wasn't stealing just to take copies and felt it would be easy enough to convince his sister too. He'd give her $25 US and pocket the balance. More than enough for making some copies, he reasoned.

As the line went dead, the mysterious caller immediately regretted disclosing his location even to an imbecile. It was unlike him to be so careless. However, his mind was elsewhere as he replaced the receiver and walked from the lounge of his hotel suite to the bedroom overlooking Central Park.

"More champagne, my dear?" he said to the Rubenesque woman in his bed.

"Oh! Mr Lazarus, you are a charmer!"

Chapter 24 Hell Hath No Fury Like a Woman Scorned

He sat on the edge of the bed and filled her glass to the brim. It was just past midnight and the evening had already been filled with fine dining and energetic sex.

She had propped herself up on a pile of pillows, luxuriating in the pristine white linen sheets which contrasted beautifully against her dusky, ample breasts.

"He has no idea?" Lazarus asked as he admired the view.

"None at all," she said, "far too busy with his scheming and deal making to notice me. He only pays me any attention when he gets my credit card bill. He's so stingy, unlike certain other gentlemen I could mention." She employed what she believed was her most seductive smile.

Even given the large gap between their ages, she had found Lazarus attractive. He was in good shape apart from the slight paralysis of his left arm which had done nothing to diminish the energy of his love making.

Then there was the obvious wealth. Yes, Lazarus was a very wealthy man—but unlike her fat slob of a husband, he had both breeding and taste. Then there was the additional bonus: she was sure to outlive him and inherit his fortune, if she played her cards right. Not that that had ever really entered her mind, she kidded herself.

"Now, how about we consummate this partnership one more time before we have to get up for breakfast?" she said.

"Why, Mrs Bosa, I thought you'd never ask."

* * *

Life is a lottery, Ellie thought as she lay there half asleep. She was not one for self-reflection, but on this rare occasion she let her mind drift.

She could have been born in the United States or England. How different would her life have been then? For some reason she ended up being born in Honiara. She had been cursed with poverty, but blessed with a sharp mind and a determination of spirit that would see her climb out of that mire of despair, no matter what the cost.

Ellie recalled the endless hours she would spend as a young girl, looking at the glossy magazines which she had retrieved from the rubbish skips behind the hotels. She also recalled the beating she had got on one occasion, when she'd been caught rummaging through them by hotel staff.

Here were beautiful people who wanted for nothing. Perfect lives, showcased for the world to see. She wanted more than anything to be one of them. She wanted it so badly, that she was prepared to do almost anything to get there. What had they done to achieve such perfect lives? Was it the lottery of birth—or was there a magic formula, a secret society that, once entered into, would protect its own?

'Fake it 'til you make it', people used to say. She thought she could write a book about that, but doing so would reveal her humble beginnings to the world and that was a secret she chose to hide in the deepest corners of her mind. A woman of mystery is better than a guttersnipe made good. Even though in recent years, stories of rags-to-riches became fashionable, but she had far too many skeletons in her closet.

She thought that Peter Sarstedt's song, *Where Do You Go To* (my lovely), could have been written for her. She both loved it and hated it at the same time.

Growing up, she and her younger brother Jimmy had survived on the streets of Honiara as their parents had eked out a living doing whatever they could. They had a small unpowered plot of land on the outskirts of the growing town. This provided them with a ramshackle shelter, a well—with cool clean water, space to grow some vegetables and keep a few chickens. Harvesting fruits from the forest when they came into season, supplemented their diet and would also be sold on the roadside to get cash for kerosene and matches. There was never any spare money, and clothes—although always clean and fresh—were almost always hand-me-downs, skilfully patched and resized.

Early one morning, her dad had returned from the forest with three large breadfruits, which he'd been keeping his eye on over the past month as they ripened. He placed them on the shaded trestle by the roadside and gave Ellie—who was nine at the time—strict instructions on their sale price, and not to let them go for any less.

Passersby were few and far between that day. As the day began to heat up, her thin printed cotton dress started sticking to her as she took the last swig of water from her recycled Coca-Cola bottle.

Sitting on the bench behind the trestle, her bare feet kicked up the dust making patterns with her toes. She heard her brother playing by the well and called over to him, "Hey Jimmy! Bring me some water please, would you?"

Fate, however, was about to intervene and within a few short moments, her life would change for ever.

A well-dressed young man of around 14 or 15 years old, approached and offered to buy one of her breadfruits, just as her brother came over.

He was tall for his age and good-looking. He wore soft leather shoes, and his cream trousers and white open-necked shirt looked as though they'd been tailored for him. He sported a thin gold chain around his neck in an opulent—if ultimately risky—display of his wealth.

"Pretty shitty breadfruit, girl," he'd said, smiling as he poked the fruit none too gently. "How about you give me one for free?"

"Hey, don't poke my fruit if you got no money," she'd replied cheekily.

It was clear that no one spoke to him like that where he came from—and rather than laugh it off, he chose to take offence, seizing the opportunity to exercise his power and authority over this hapless lowlife.

"Shit breadfruit!" he said as he threw it on the ground, smashing it to pieces.

Jimmy was outraged and even though only half the size of this stranger, he leaped towards him with flailing fists.

It was not the aggression but the casualness of the backhand that sent Jimmy crashing to the ground which had really shocked Ellie. His head had connected with a sickening crunch to the only rock that was sticking out of the soil for as far as the eye could see.

The young man who was subsequently identified as Charles Edgar II, son of a successful businessman in Honiara, cursed at the dirty mark that Jimmy's fist had left on his sleeve and walked away.

Ellie dropped to her knees in the dirt and cradled Jimmy's head, as a small trickle of scarlet blood ran down from his nose and across his lips.

Jimmy never regained consciousness. He survived for nearly two whole days, laying in the ramshackle house with his mother and his sister Ellie at his side, taking turns to dab his head with cool water from the well. Eventually, the swelling of his brain took his life. All for one lousy breadfruit.

Of course, there had been an enquiry but the well-connected family had convinced the police that it was a tragic accident. Jimmy had been running towards his sister bringing her a fresh bottle of water and had slipped and fallen. Charles Edgar II had heroically reached out to arrest Jimmy's fall, dropping the breadfruit in the process (for which he had offered to pay). But Jimmy had slipped from his grasp and fallen backwards, cracking his skull on a rock which his father should have cleared long ago. The coroner attested that Jimmy's poor diet and upbringing had resulted in his somewhat stunted development and thin and fragile bones.

Ellie was outraged. They were blaming Jimmy for being poor and Charles Edgar II was not only getting away with murder but was being made out to be some kind of hero.

Finally, the police had maintained that the testament of a nine-year-old-girl, traumatised by the event, could not be relied upon.

Justice, it appeared was the preserve of the rich.

Even at just nine years of age, Ellie knew it was wrong and refused to accept the ruling. She retreated into her own world of make believe and silently set about planning her revenge, although it would be another decade before she would extract it.

Over the years, Ellie worked hard to perfect her seamstress skills and delighted in rescuing wonderful fabrics from clothes discarded by rich visitors to the islands. She would skilfully create the latest fashions using little more than photographs from glossy magazines and sell these on to the girls that worked in the local bars. The girls were never short of money for a pretty dress, and soon her reputation spread so that her work was always in high demand. The very best work, however, she kept for herself.

Ellie grew into a beautiful woman and learned the art of subtle makeup to emphasise her beauty. Far too many girls didn't understand just how *less was more*, she thought.

Then all of a sudden, the time had come.

There was the annual gala charity night to be held at the Plaza Hotel in Honiara and everyone who was anyone was going to be there. It was invitation only, however, with the right attitude and presentation, she was confident that she would have no trouble attending. What's more, she was going to meet Charles Edgar II, Honiara's most eligible bachelor and make him pay for killing Jimmy.

Ellie's friend Sally had practised for months on perfecting a hairstyle for her, which was simple but stylish. It was all about the cut.

Ellie felt that the person she had created, the person she was fast becoming, wasn't so much a deception but who she really was. She had no intention of going in any kind of low-key disguise. She wanted to stand out, to be seen, to be unapproachable by security. She wanted every head in the room to turn towards her when she walked in—every red-blooded male to admire her, and every woman to covet her.

Her beautiful full length red dress was a simple classic Balmain design, exquisitely cut to emphasise her smooth lines and full breasts. She had resisted temptation and opted for the classic look over more contemporary styles. It was complemented by elbow length white satin evening gloves and a black clutch. Her shoes were four-inch red patent leather, which gave her a height designed to intimidate men shorter than her. Charles Edgar was over six feet.

Over the last decade, Ellie had spent lazy days in the ocean. Often, she would gather shellfish to supplement the family's diet. During those days, she would sometimes find an oyster containing a South Sea Island pearl. She could have sold it, course—however, she wanted to create a pearl necklace like the ones the beautiful people in *Tatler* magazine would wear. And so it was that she accessorised her ensemble with a single strand necklace and matching pearl bracelet which had been expertly strung for free by a local jeweller. The jeweller, young Mr Luke, had even included 9ct solid gold clasps free of charge, on the understanding that he would be given an opportunity to purchase them once she had finished with them. The natural pearls, to his eye, were of unusually high quality, far superior to the cultured pearls entering the market from Japan and he planned to make a tidy profit on the transaction.

She'd practised walking in her heels for months, perfecting the elegant movements of her hips with a casual air of sophistication that appeared to come naturally to Hollywood film stars.

Her timing had to be perfect. Not too early to be left awkwardly standing, and not too late to be lost in the crowd. She wanted an audience.

Passing the security was far simpler than she had imagined. She simply strode confidently in. The main reception area was already bustling with excitement as she made her entrance.

It was like the ocean parting before her, she recalled, as her eyes met with Charles'. He was standing chatting to an elderly couple in the middle of the room. He immediately—and somewhat rudely—turned away from them and stared at Ellie, as she stood at the top of the stairs leading down into the room.

Ignoring the elderly couple, he strode towards her.

"May I?" he said, as he held out his arm to assist her descent.

He had spent most of the evening with her, talking about himself and she was keen to let him do so. The less she told him of herself, the safer she felt.

She had used her auntie's name to introduce herself and was bemused to see how Charles was wracking his mind to place it amongst Honiara's elite.

She wove a web of lies about how she had recently arrived in Honiara and was expecting her luggage to arrive soon, but the shipping company had lost it, and she was reduced to wearing last year's fashions, a point that she made sure was overheard by several ladies at the gala event.

At one point in the evening, she had been introduced to a Mr Bosa, a young lawyer who had tragically recently lost his wife to cancer. Just how profound that meeting was to be, only became apparent in the year that followed.

As the evening wore on, Charles appeared only slightly worse for wear when he suggested that they move out onto the terrace to take in the evening air and partake in some cocaine.

Ellie had heard all about Charles's predilection for the party drug and had come well prepared.

Inside her clutch bag was a cocktail of cocaine and strychnine. Moving to the terrace, which was largely deserted, Charles had taken a small compact bearing his moniker from his pocket and placed it on the low wall.

Ellie faked a stumble in her heels and knocked the compact onto the tiled floor, spilling its contents over the ground. Charles was quick to anger and turned to see the smiling Ellie waving her bag in front of him.

"Lucky for us I have some more," she slurred.

Charles snatched the clutch from her and roughly opened it, retrieving the white crystalline powder and emptied its entire contents into his compact.

Placing a large quantity of the powder on the back of his hand, he inhaled it deeply and Ellie laughed as she took a serviette and wiped away the tell-tale marks left around his nostrils.

The effect of the high was almost immediate. Charles felt on top of the world. Tonight was going to be great, and he would crown it off by giving this belle of the ball, the fucking of her life.

Ellie laughed, slipped off her shoes and led him around the terrace in circles, teasing and embracing him for all the world to see. After about 15 minutes they slumped down on an iron filigree bench overlooking the gardens.

"You don't remember me, Charles, do you?" Ellie said as she turned to face him.

Charles was beginning to feel a little restless.

"Of course, I remember you. Didn't we meet at last year's gala?"

"No Charles. We met a long time ago."

Charles' stomach twinged and he grabbed at his side.

"Bloody caterers," he complained. "Please, would you excuse me for a moment?"

"Please, don't go. Please stay here with me. I'm sure it will pass."

Charles took a deep breath, not wanting to lose the moment or the promise of a shag.

"You see, it was ten years ago that we met. I was selling breadfruit by the side of the road…"

"You!" he gasped.

Charles doubled over as his body went into spasm, pivoted on the seat until his head fell to rest in Ellie's lap. He looked up at her with bloodshot eyes and realised with startling concern, that he could no longer move his limbs.

"Yes, I know it's painful, Charles. It's strychnine. Rat poison. Freely available and you don't even have to sign for it," she said as she cradled his head and smoothed his fringe, in much the same way as she had cradled Jimmy's head, all those years ago.

Charles tried in vain to stand up, to call out, to fall off the bench, anything to attract attention but to no avail. He was aware of what was going on, totally lucid and yet unable to do a damn thing about it. He was terrified.

Ellie continued, "Firstly, you get the spasms—they're terribly painful, Charles. But not nearly as painful as the hurt you and your lying family, imposed on mine. Especially when you tried to blame me for Jimmy's death. Why would you do that to a nine-year-old girl, Charles?"

"You've already lost the use of your arms and legs, haven't you? Don't worry now, it won't be too long. I'll be here. I'm not going to leave you to die alone.

"Soon your diaphragm will give up, and you'll suffocate to death."

Joe Bosa called from the entrance to the terrace as people were filtering out into the cool night air. "Is everything OK over there?"

"Oh yes, thank you Mr Bosa," Ellie said with a disarming smile, "we're just taking a little breather." Ellie turned her attention to the increasingly vulnerable person in her lap.

"You see, Charles, no one really cares about you. Your playboy drug taking reputation will be seen as the cause of your death, a warning to others that might follow in your footsteps.

"I've done my homework and apparently, it's not uncommon for cocaine to be laced with strychnine. It's just a pity that whoever supplied your last fix got the mix wrong and, well, accidents do happen, don't they?"

Ellie watched the life drain from Charles' eyes as she continued to stroke his hair. She moved her hand down around his collar and felt for a pulse. There was none. She continued to sit cradling his head for another ten minutes, whispering sweet nothings for all the world to see, then stood up screaming as he fell to the floor.

The police and subsequent coroner's investigation determined death by misadventure. His personal compact had been found to contain a lethal mix of cocaine and strychnine which, although present in unusually high quantities, was not unheard of.

Ellie was never a serious suspect and had received several generous offers of help and support from those who had witnessed her distress at the event, not least of all from Joe Bosa.

She was careful how she proceeded, not wishing to appear desperate or move too quickly. Her first priority was to accept the friendship of several women that had been at the gala. Through those friendships and the lies about losing her wardrobe in a shipping mishap, she acquired the clothes that she needed to maintain her façade. Items that had long gone out of fashion or were hopelessly ill fitting, were donated to her to get her by, until her cargo turned up. These were transformed into garments of such elegance that their original owners never recognised them.

Having ingratiated herself into Honiara's elite society, all that remained was to make sure that Joe Bosa seduced her.

For Ellie, like Lazarus, her talisman was money.

* * *

In New York Lazarus was pondering his situation. He accepted that he found all women irresistible but had always married for purpose rather than love. He was pretty sure that love existed, but he saw it as a weakness to be exploited for gain if he could. He would manipulate people for his own benefit or sometimes just for his own amusement. People were so gullible and trusting. It was easy.

He wasn't a bad man, he told himself. He could be spontaneously philanthropic. He just couldn't help himself. He was a loveable rogue. Yes, that was it, a loveable rogue.

He was going to use Ellie Bosa in the way that he had used countless women before. In a way, she deserved no better. Cheating on her husband and sleeping with him would come at a cost but for him it was a bonus. What he really wanted was to hedge his bets just in case things didn't work out the way he had planned.

It was clear to Lazarus that the Hawkins were planning to retrieve the rest of the gold, and he planned to take possession of it as soon as they did. The challenge now was knowing exactly when that would happen and when to pounce.

They ordered room service for breakfast at Lazarus's insistence and sat by the large window overlooking Central Park. He didn't want to be seen in public with Ellie any more than necessary.

"When's your flight back to Honiara?" she asked as she helped herself to another croissant smothered in butter and jam.

"This afternoon. I have to be at the airport at 3pm. What about yourself?"

"Tomorrow."

"Good. It wouldn't do to be seen travelling together. Well, not at this stage in any case."

Chapter 25 Sharing A Confidence

It was almost a week later that we told John Manu of our plans to dive our special wreck. We had decided to leave it until the last minute—so that he had little or no opportunity to betray our confidence. We also decided that Joe Bosa needed to be present when we talked with John, to ensure that there was no doubt in his mind: that there would be serious consequences for him if he told anyone what we were up to.

It was unusual for Bosa to invite John to his home but, having talked with Bosa and explained our concerns, he embraced the idea.

When John arrived, it was clear he had done his best to look presentable. He had smoothed down his wayward hair, and the wrinkles in his ankle-length chinos and short-sleeved shirt.

Bosa opened the door himself. "John! Welcome, welcome, welcome. Come inside! There was really no need to dress up!" he said as he cast an eye over his junior business partner. He tried not to linger his gaze on the filthy trainers that he was wearing. John was clearly uncomfortable in such opulent surroundings and wasn't sure if he should remove his shoes before entering. The fact that he wasn't wearing socks made the decision a *fait accompli* and he shuffled in as humbly as he could.

Sol stood a foot taller than John and looked down on him with an intimidating stare that would have *frozen the fires of hell*, as Joe led him to the lounge room where Rose, Wiebbe, Kate and I were already seated.

We stood up briefly as Bosa and John walked in, followed by Sol, and offered our welcomes before sitting back down.

Bosa was in his element as ring master—strutting about the room, exerting his authority over John, and ensuring that the opulence of the setting was on full display.

"Thank you so much for coming to my humble abode. You're probably wondering why I have invited you here today, but what I have to tell you—you must swear on the lives of all those you hold dear—that you will keep this secret and take it with you to your grave. Do I make myself clear?"

John sat tensely on the edge of the sofa in Bosa's lounge, a low coffee table before him, its glass of water still untouched. He twisted and turned, trying to follow Bosa as he strutted around the room.

"Mr Bosa, you know you can trust me with your life."

Bosa glanced up at Sol—who moved imperceptibly closer to John. The movement was not lost on him, and he stiffened at the implied threat.

Kate, Wiebbe and I were seated on the sofa opposite.

"Sit down, Bosa," Wiebbe said, with a terseness of tone that did not invite dissent, "you're making me dizzy."

Rose looked at Wiebbe with quiet admiration. Until then, she had been the only one to speak to her father like that and get away with it.

If Bosa was angered by Wiebbe's comments he didn't show it and he sat down on an elaborately carved high-backed chair which actually had a gilt crown on the top back rail.

The Court was clearly in session.

"John, you will recall that last year you took Mr and Mrs Hawkins and Wiebbe here, out to dive a deep wreck in the southeast of the Sound. Their special wreck, yes?"

The question was rhetorical and Bosa was enjoying his moment in the sun.

"Since then, you have kept the site secret and not ventured back there, correct?"

John nodded quickly, "Yes, Mr Bosa, like we agreed. No one has been back."

"The fact is that when Mr Hawkins and Wiebbe dived on the wreck, they thought that they saw something that may be of value, and I want to recover this."

There it was. The belief of sunken treasure was one that was commonly held amongst islanders. John's eyes widened as words tumbled out of Joe's mouth.

"Oh, Mr Bosa, is it true? You have found the sunken treasure of Iron Bottom Sound!"

John Manu had conveniently forgotten that it was Wiebbe and me who'd found the treasure—and deferred humbly to the omnipotent Bosa.

Bosa nodded to Sol, who turned to the drinks cabinet and poured him a large scotch.

Taking his drink from Sol, Bosa continued, "Let's not get ahead of ourselves, John. It may be nothing but six of the seven people in this room have kept this secret for over a year and will take this secret to their graves. If I hear any murmur of this conversation outside of this room, I will know that it is you who has betrayed us."

Bosa let the words sink in as John's mind was flitting between excitement and fear.

"John!" Bosa shattered his reverie.

"Yes, Mr Bosa, sorry, Mr Bosa. It all makes sense. The new rope for the davit, the ban on taking other tech divers to the site, the … Tortorri!" he said, slipping back into his native Pidgin.

Bosa leant back in his throne and chuckled. "Mr Hawkins, please would you care to fill in John on our plans for the salvage?"

I leaned forward and explained our plans in detail, pretty much along the same lines as the dive we had done previously, only this time, Bosa would come out in convoy on his own boat and raft up alongside as he had done a year ago.

Eventually, John looked at Bosa and plucked up the courage to ask, “What about the captain’s share?”

It was a question that Bosa had anticipated. “John, there may be nothing but if there is something, I want to give you my word that you will be very well taken care of.”

John was immediately suspicious. He wanted some assurance. “Equal shares all around then?”

“John, you make me laugh. I am the one taking all the risks here.”

Wiebbe was about to speak up, but a quick glance from Kate silenced him.

“But you need me, right?”

“John, don’t get greedy.”

Sol moved half a step closer.

“I want to know what’s in it for me. It’s only fair.”

Bosa’s eyes alighted on his daughter Rose.

“John,” she said, “you know there may be nothing there. So how about we cut a deal—one percent of anything we find, or, alternatively, my father gifts you his share in your business now, and you get nothing else?”

“What! That’s outrageous! That dive business is a cash cow for me—and you know it, Rose!”

It was difficult not to laugh at Bosa’s feigned indignation.

There was no doubt that Bosa’s return on his investment at Manu’s dive shop was a massive drain on the business. John often felt that he was doing all the hard work and only just scraping a living for himself once all the bills were paid. To own 100% of the business now, as opposed to perhaps 1% of nothing, was hugely attractive.

John countered, “Five percent of anything we find plus I get 100% of your interest in my dive operation now, irrespective.”

“I won’t do it! It’s daylight robbery! Rose! How could you suggest such a thing? The deal is off. I don’t know how you have the gall to sit in my house, enjoying my hospitality, and then try to steal my interest in your business plus 5%!"

John looked very nervous in his seat as he saw the deal-of-a-lifetime slipping from his grasp.

"OK, I'm sorry Mr Bosa, I meant no offence. Maybe we could agree on one percent of anything we find, plus I get to own 100% of my dive operation, now."

"John, you are trying my patience, not to mention my civility."

Bosa glanced at Sol who was now standing directly behind John, staring down at him. The move was not lost on him, and he was about to buckle but then to his surprise Bosa said, "Half of one percent of net profit, as and when the salvage is liquidated. Plus, I will gift you 100% of my interest in the dive operation now, in return for your absolute silence and unquestioning co-operation —provided that you bear all the costs of the salvage operation."

I thought that it was a little stingy for Bosa to throw that in. John had staff to pay at the shop and diesel to buy for the boat. I was very happy to pay the cost of our dives, but it was just like Bosa to penny pinch.

"It's a deal!" John said, as he held out his hand to Bosa.

"Very well, John. You are as tough a negotiator as I ever met! Mind you, you have Rose to thank for that! My own flesh and blood, negotiating against me! Sol will show you out."

John stood, and Sol escorted him to the gate. Just as they reached it, Sol placed a hand on his shoulder, leaned in, and whispered something in a local dialect—something that wiped the smile from John's face and put the fear of God into him.

Still, he was now the sole owner of his own dive operation he thought, and that night he would dream of how he was going to grow his business, unencumbered by any silent partner. The stories of sunken treasure in the Iron Bottom Sound, were legendary amongst islanders and he suspected that this was just one more. If they wanted to go off on a wild goose chase, then that was up to them. If they found anything, the half a percent he was going to get would be the cherry on the icing on the cake.

The threat that Sol had made to him was really unnecessary, he thought. He really doubted that there was any treasure in any case, but still, there was always the possibility. After all, why would Mr Bosa gift him the dive shop if there was nothing there? There had to have been hard evidence for him to go that far.

John didn't sleep all night, going over and over in his mind, fanciful dreams of just how much half a percent would be worth.

Chapter 26 The Pragmatist

Rose flung her arms around her father's neck and kissed him on his cheek.

"Dad, you are a softie! Half a percent!" She stepped back and looked at his reddened smiling face.

Bosa laughed. "My dear, you played your role to perfection. I am so proud of you but, had I not offered a tail to John Manu's commission, how long do you think he would have been able to hold his tongue and keep it secret?"

"Mmm, ever the pragmatist Dad, and I thought you'd just had a fit of generosity!"

Bosa feigned a hurt expression but wasn't fooling anyone.

Kate, Wiebbe and I were standing to leave. We had a busy day ahead tomorrow, prepping the gear for the salvage operation. Still, a quiet unease lingered in my mind about the whole operation.

Wiebbe and I were going to be at our most vulnerable when gassing off at our decompression stops. If anything went wrong on the boat once the gold was on board, we would not be able to surface until we had completed our stops.

Back in our hotel room, Kate gave voice to my concerns.

"What's to stop them taking off once the gold is on board and leaving you at your deco stop?"

"I know. I've been brooding on that, but I guess that there are two factors: You and Wiebbe and Rose's relationship. It's a risk, but blood is thicker than water as they say, and family ties are important. Add to that the way that Bosa and Rose played John, well, it has given me some comfort. Then of course, there is a third factor."

"What's that?"

"We'll be diving heavy," I said and smiled.

Chapter 27 The Salvage

That morning the talk around town was all about the small tremors that had shaken the ornaments off the shelves of the houses in Honiara.

An envelope had been slipped under the door of our hotel room containing a letter from the management to say that there was nothing to be concerned about and that small tremors were commonplace. We were assured that the hotel itself had been designed and built to the most exacting international standards in order to survive major quakes.

I doubted the veracity of the statement but having experienced many quakes in my time in the Pacific 'ring of fire', I was not overly concerned about the small tremors I had felt whilst lying in bed. A 2.3 on the Richter scale was barely worth reporting.

"Do you think the tremors will have moved the wreck, Dad?" Wiebbe said as we enjoyed a hearty breakfast in the hotel restaurant.

"No, hardly worth worrying about, although they may have stirred up some silt on the bottom."

"Could make things difficult, Dad."

I pondered Wiebbe's comment. "We could delay the dive for a few days and let things settle down but then again, I didn't notice much silt on the wreck when we dived it a year ago and there's been plenty of seismic activity over the last 60 years, far greater than the 2.3 we had last night."

"Are you sure it's safe?" Kate asked, looking across the table. "What happens if we get a biggie while you're in the water—or inside the wreck itself?"

I looked at the concerned expression on Kate's face and explained, "If we're in the water, we won't feel a thing. If we're in the wreck and the earth starts to move, we'll be so close to the exit that we'll just swim out. We'll lay down a guideline to follow if the viz gets bad, but remember, we'll only be down there on the bottom for 10 minutes in any case."

* * *

Rose greeted Wiebbe dockside with a huge hug. Bosa and Sol were already on their own boat and Sol had been given the job of skipper for the day. There really was little more to it than following John to the dive site and rafting up alongside.

Bosa grinned and looked upon his daughter with unabashed admiration.

"Ah, the way of the Islands, Mr Hawkins! It looks as though our family may be growing sooner rather than later!"

"Dad!" Rose shouted as she disentangled herself from Wiebbe's arms.

I couldn't help but share a smile with Kate as they busied themselves loading cylinders onto the dive boat.

The journey out to the site was uneventful and went quickly as we checked and re-checked all our gear. Once again, the weather gods had been kind to us and having successfully snared the wreck with our grapple, we were soon in the water, preparing for our descent.

Once in the water, Rose clipped the deco cylinders to our BCDs as she had done before, and we carried out our final in water checks. It was slack tide as we began our descent but this time, we rode the steel basket down to the bottom.

At 70 metres, it was clear that the tremors of the previous night had stirred up some fine silt, but we were still able to make out the shape of the ship's hull.

We wasted no time in making our way to the gaping hole in the hull and quickly found our treasure. It had taken exactly five minutes to reach the breach. Nevertheless, we had to move quickly.

Wiebbe and I removed our fins and clipped them to our BCDs. We immediately picked up ten gold bars and stacked them in the basket to stop it moving away should the boat drift or a current come up.

Shining our torches inside the hull, we laid down a line 10 metres inside and grabbed one box, which disintegrated. There were 50 bars inside. 50 kilograms of fine gold. $1.25m.

We methodically gathered them up and stacked them in the basket. Working quickly and silently, we counted another twenty boxes. There was no way that the davit would be able to lift them in one go; no way that we could salvage all that gold in one dive.

Wiebbe had determined that the safe working load of the davit was around 550 kilograms, so it would take at least two lifts to salvage the entire haul.

We had been on the bottom for 10 minutes and had loaded the basket with five hundred bars. Lifting at least ten at a time, it had still pushed us to our physical limit and despite the cooler water temperature at that depth, sweat was running down my forehead into my eyes—which I had to clear by flooding and clearing my mask repeatedly.

There were still as many, if not more bars left down there. There they would stay for another dive another day. They were no good to a dead man. Still, by my reckoning we had recovered nearly $12.5m worth of gold at today's prices. Not bad for a day's work. Even if we achieved 80% of that, John Manu's half a percent would be worth over $50,000—a fortune for an islander.

The last thing we did before leaving the bottom was to once again, exchange our lead weights for gold.

* * *

"They should be on their way up now, shouldn't they?" Bosa asked as he nervously checked his watch.

At that moment, three sharp tugs on the Dyneema rope signalled that John was to raise the basket.

Bosa was beside himself with excitement, which quickly spread to John, Kate, Rose and Sol.

"Bring it up, bring it up! Quickly," Bosa cried to John.

John was excited too, but not so excited as to lose his prize through undue haste. He knew that it would take at least 10 minutes for the basket to reach the surface at a retrieval rate of 10 metres a minute.

The davit rope became taut and the whole boat pitched alarmingly over to one side.

Rose saw the transom flex around the mounting bolts of the davit. At the same time, the metal let out a creak as the rope continued to take the strain. John quickly grabbed a thick mooring line and wrapped it around the top of the lower swing arm of the davit and tied it to the cleat on the opposite side of the boat.

"Move!" John shouted to Kate and Rose.

They quickly moved to the opposite side to balance the boat. Bosa, seeing a potential disaster, hurriedly instructed Sol to climb over and sit on the dive boat's port gunwale whilst at the same time, manoeuvring his own considerable bulk to do likewise.

The boat slowly returned to an even keel as the davit continued its relentless retrieve. Everyone sighed with relief—apart from John who was nervously watching the taut mooring line.

Rose looked over at her father and smiled. "Well Dad, I never thought I'd be grateful that you hadn't started that diet I recommended!"

"Cheeky little minx!"

The davit continued to bring up the treasure from the deep.

It was then that a cauldron of bubbles exploded on the surface of the sea. The boat rocked violently, and the davit let out a juddering screech which sucked the air from everyone's lungs and sent their hearts into overdrive.

"My God! What was that!?" Bosa gasped.

Sol looked up and pointed wide-eyed at the trees on the slope of the nearby island which appeared to be moving towards them.

"Earthquake, Boss! Land-slide!"

Chapter 28 Neptune's Bounty

Kate and Rose watched in horror as the beach—and the slope behind which Kate and I had picnicked on a year earlier—slid into the sea.

At the same time, the anchor rope went taut and then loose as the tines of the grapple holding onto the wreck straightened and let go of its purchase.

Wiebbe and I were 80 metres below the surface when the wreck below us started to shimmer. I still had the presence of mind to think that I might be hallucinating and automatically checked my dive computer and the mix that I was breathing.

Wiebbe grabbed my arm and pointed to the wreck, which was sliding backwards—faster and faster—off the ledge where it had rested, plunging over the edge into the abyss.

She rolled onto her starboard side as she went, hiding from our view the gaping hole which we had been in, only moments before. A huge blast of air which we had obviously expelled whilst in the hull, escaped from within the ship and raced towards the surface, expanding exponentially as it went.

Our ascent line was slack, but our grip was firm as we took in the sight of the great lady vanishing into the depths.

Wiebbe grabbed me and shook me, pointing toward the shore. What appeared to be a sandstorm rolling in towards us greeted my eyes. I realised that half the island must have slumped into the ocean and we were about to be engulfed in a total blackout.

I motioned to Wiebbe to continue our ascent. But with zero visibility we wouldn't be able to read our instruments—which meant we had no idea of our depth, our time, or when to switch mixes to complete our deco stops.

I looked at Wiebbe as we both realised that we couldn't stay where we were. We had to let go of our ascent line and make our way out to clear blue water, away from the dive boats.

The problem was, we had no way of communicating our intentions to the boats above us. I could only hope that Rose and Kate would follow standard operating procedure for lost divers, track our bubbles, and follow us.

* * *

On board, the gentle rocking of the boats returned as the ocean calmed. The davit continued its slow retrieve.

A sudden noise from the base of the davit drew John's attention as he stared at where it was bolted to the aluminium transom. The aluminium was bulging and starting to deform, the way it does just before it cracks. Another sudden movement might see their treasure disappear into the abyss.

"Shit! Are they OK?" Rose said, as Kate went to lean over the side.

"Oh, thank God. I can still see their bubbles."

But there was something strange about the bubbles coming to the surface. No longer white against a deepwater blue, they now shimmered with gold as the basket broke the surface.

John immediately swung the basket over the side to midships, at which point the aluminium transom finally gave and the davit crashed down on the basket, narrowly missing Sol's and Bosa's toes.

The shiny gold bars stacked inside—gleamed in the noon day sun—reflecting light across the faces of the passengers and crew.

Bosa leant forward and grabbed a bar, holding it up to the sky, and laughed out loud. Smiles and celebrations were the order of the day.

Bosa looked around and announced, "So, now we wait for Michael and Wiebbe to get back on board and then back to Honiara for a feast and a celebration, the likes of which you have never seen!"

Kate glanced back at the ocean to see a front of brown murky water advancing from the island towards them and quickly turned to Rose. "That's not good, is it?" she said.

"Shit, they won't be able to see their instruments. They won't be able to time their deco stops. I'm getting in the water. I can meet them at 20 metres and tell them to stay there until I return and then accompany them up to their next stop. Even though they'll be blind, they'll still know what gasses they have in which cylinders so they can make the swap at each stop."

"Rose, if they can't see their instruments, they won't be able to see you, and we haven't discussed this. How are you going to communicate your intention?"

"I'll figure something out," she said as she grabbed her BCD.

"Wait, look," Kate said as she observed our bubbles moving out into deeper, cleaner water.

"They're moving out to blue water. John, pull the ascent line and follow their bubbles. Everyone keep watch. We don't want to lose them if the wind gets up and stirs up the surface."

Kate pointed her arm at our bubbles as the rest of the crew untied the ropes, keeping the two boats together. As soon as they were separated, Rose joined Kate and kept her arm pointed at the bubbles as well. Standard operating procedure. Sol did likewise, although he wasn't quite sure why he was doing it.

* * *

In a little over an hour, we had drifted—well over a mile—from where the wreck had lain. We were able to make our deco stops mid-water and although we were getting close to our limits, we were never really in danger of running out of air.

After we had completed our staged decompression, Wiebbe indicated thumbs up. We could see the outline of John's boat, just a few metres above us. Wiebbe and I broke the surface next to the stern, to be greeted by Rose and Kate's beaming faces.

The relieved look on Kate's face reminded me of just how lucky I was, to have this woman in my life.

"Call that a dive," she said with forced nonchalance.

"Well, it's no lie when I say the earth really did move for me, honey!" I quipped.

We unclipped our stage cylinders and fins and handed them up before climbing aboard. Dumping our gear on the deck, we looked at the haul of gold bars as Bosa and Sol, pulled up alongside us.

Bosa insisted that the gold be brought to his house and that half of it be transferred to his boat immediately, in case ours sank.

The damage to the transom where the davit had been mounted didn't affect the seaworthiness of John's vessel, but Bosa wasn't taking any chances.

"There's just one thing," I said as I looked at Wiebbe.

We both pulled our dumpable weight pockets from our BCDs and let the gold bars fall onto the pile.

Bosa roared with laughter and waved his finger in our direction.

On the journey back to the harbour, I talked to Kate and Rose about our adventure.

"I realised as soon as I saw that cloud of shit moving towards us from the island that you wouldn't be able to complete any stops in a total blackout," Kate said. "Rose was all set to dive in and grab you at 20 metres. Fortunately, I saw that you had released the ascent line and your bubbles were moving out to the blue water, and I was able to stop her."

"Well, I'm glad you did."

"I guess it just goes to show that you can't plan for everything, but good basic training meant that we followed your bubbles, so you were never in any real danger."

"I love you, Kate… Did I ever mention that before?" I said.

* * *

Back at the harbour, we'd arranged to load the gold—now packed in sacks resembling those used for lead weights—into the back of John's truck to avoid attracting attention. From there, we'd head not to the dive shop, but straight to Bosa's house.

On arrival at Bosa's house, Wiebbe and I showered and joined everyone on the veranda which looked out over the tops of the trees to the Sound below.

The earth tremors we experienced last night were really a harbinger of things to come. The magnitude 6.5 that had followed that afternoon, had caused some structural damage to buildings in and around Honiara, but thankfully no reports of loss of life.

"The ship and its treasure that we had to leave behind are gone to the abyss," I said, as I described in detail how Wiebbe and I, had loaded what we could, into the basket and only escaped just in the nick of time before the ship had disappeared.

"How many bars did you leave behind?" Bosa asked.

"Forget it, Dad. We've more than enough and even if you could go down to 800 metres, the cost of the operation would be horrendous. Given what Wiebbe said about her rolling onto her side—as she slid out of view—it's entirely possible that the gold is buried beneath the wreck now, and the wreck itself is probably buried under half the island."

"I guess you're right, my sweet. But just imagine…"

Bosa turned to us. "The gold is secure in my strong room. You are more than welcome to view it, and I will make all the arrangements to liquidate it over the course of the next twelve to twenty-four months. I'll keep you all fully informed. I would like to gift one bar to Sol if that is alright with you?"

We agreed. It was difficult to say whether-or-not he was particularly happy, but it was a small price to pay for his protection and loyalty.

That night, Kate and I, went back to the hotel whilst Wiebbe elected to stay a little longer at the Bosa residence. Being too pumped up to sleep, we sat in our room drinking Johnnie Walker and champagne until the early hours, before eventually falling into a deep sleep.

It must have been 10 am when a frantic knocking at our door woke us and Wiebbe rushed in breathlessly saying, “It’s Rose, she’s been kidnapped!”

Chapter 29 Kidnapped

We arrived at the Bosa residence to find Joe Bosa pacing up-and-down in the lounge. Sol was standing stoically in the corner of the room with a large bloodied dressing on his head.

"What happened?" I said without preamble.

"Oh, my God! I called the hotel as soon as I heard," Bosa said. "Thank you so much for coming.

"Sol here was taking Rose to the shops this morning when no more than 100 metres from my own front gate, the car was rammed, and Rose was grabbed!"

Kate looked at me and turned to Bosa and said, "OK, we need to call the police."

"No. No, not yet."

"Why not?"

"Oh, Mrs Hawkins, it is the way of the Islands."

"Wait a minute! I'll show these bastards the way of Wiebbe Hawkins, when I catch up with them!" Wiebbe fisted the palm of his hand as he spoke.

Bosa went over to the drinks cabinet, and poured himself a large scotch.

"Mr Wiebbe, kidnappings in Honiara are not like they are in the movies or the Middle East. Often, it is small-time crooks who are looking for a few hundred dollars, and it's all resolved quietly and amicably. We can't involve the police just now; we have to wait for the call."

Wiebbe was so frustrated, he felt the need to break something. "How many kidnappers were there, Sol?" he said, "did you get a look at them?"

"No Boss Wiebbe. All Sol remembers is leaving house and waking up in car with blood on head," he said, raising his hand to his bandages.

"You should have that looked at properly at the hospital," Kate said.

"It's OK, Mrs Hawkins. Sol has hard head!" He smiled but grimaced a little at the same time.

"Nevertheless, I think you should get over to the hospital and get it checked out. Wiebbe will take you."

Wiebbe looked at his mum. He was clearly opposed to the idea and needed to be where the action was.

"You're right. What was I thinking?" Bosa said, as if noticing the bandages for the first time. "Sol, get a taxi over there now. Wiebbe, I want you here when the kidnappers call."

Bosa, who had been somewhat wary of Wiebbe up until this moment, seemed to want him by his side. Perhaps with his main muscle man out of the picture for a while, he felt safer with Wiebbe there.

The door of the lounge burst open, and Mrs Bosa stormed in, riding a wave of Chanel Number, 5 accompanied by a jangle of golden bangles. "Oh, my poor Joe!" she said. "Any word? Any demands?"

"No, nothing."

Ellie Bosa had made her dramatic entrance to good effect—as all eyes in the room landed upon her. Her brightly coloured Yves Saint Laurent kaftan trimmed with gold, billowed around her plump but shapely body, her finely manicured toes poked out of her open golden sandals which sparkled with brightly set rhinestones. Her naturally frizzy hair had been straightened and crafted into a bouffant style, no doubt at great expense to Mr Bosa.

It was difficult to guess Ellie's age, but I placed her in her late thirties or early forties.

I had found that it was often the case with the Islander women that they seem to age very quickly past the age of 25. Exposure to the sun took its toll. Ellie however, had obviously kept out of the sun and, with a judicious application of makeup, had kept her youthful looks.

Ellie looked around the room at Kate, me, and Wiebbe.

"You must be Wiebbe," she said as she approached and hugged him in a far too familiar embrace. She pressed her breasts hard against Wiebbe's chest, threatened to asphyxiate him with her overpowering perfume. Her dark brown eyes sparkled as she looked up into his.

"Rose has told me so much about you," she said as she took half a step backwards still holding onto his muscular arms, "but she never mentioned how handsome you were."

Reluctantly letting go of Wiebbe, she turned to Kate and I and shook our hands, carefully assessing Kate as only another woman can do. We completed the introductions just as the telephone rang.

Bosa picked up the receiver and put the call on speaker.

"No police. We have your daughter. We know you have the Nazi gold. Fair swap. If you want to see your daughter alive again, fifty bars."

"Wait! I want to speak to Rose."

The line went silent for a while, then Rose's voice came on. "Oh, Daddy, I'm so sorry."

Bosa's eyes filled with tears. "Rose, listen to me. Everything is going to be OK; I promise. Have they hurt you? Are you OK?"

Clearly, the phone had been snatched away from her as the kidnapper's voice returned. "Put the gold in a pickup and drive it to the Botanical Gardens. Leave the gold and the pickup in the car park with the keys in the ignition—away from the entrance—and walk away. We'll be watching, so don't get any smart ideas. Any suggestion of police and you'll never see your daughter again."

"If you do as you're told, we'll tell you where to pick your daughter up. Shortchange us and she dies. Any police, she dies. You have until 5pm."

The line went dead.

"We have to pay," Ellie said as she turned to face Sol, who had still not gone to the hospital. "Sol, get the pickup and bring it to the front. Wiebbe, Michael, Kate, come with me, we'll need all hands to load the gold into it."

Bosa sat with his head in his hands. Kate went over to him and squatted down on her haunches, taking his hands in hers.

He looked up with mournful eyes and said, "Ah, the way of the Islands. For a brief moment there, I was rich beyond my wildest dreams. I had everything within my grasp. Everything, but I can't let my baby suffer. I can't let my baby die."

"It's OK, Mr Bosa. We'll get Rose back—safe and sound. Don't you worry about the gold. It's only metal. Isn't that right, Michael?"

"I swear if they have so much as scratched Rose, I'll pull their fucking arms and legs off, and feed them to the fishes!" Wiebbe was already following Ellie to the strong room. For once, his mum didn't reprimand his language.

"I'll drive the truck," I said.

Chapter 30 The Botanic Gardens

I outlined the beginnings of a plan to Ellie and Bosa. Ellie was not impressed.

"Absolutely not!" Ellie said.

"I agree with Michael," Bosa said as we finished loading the gold into the back of the pickup.

"Come back inside and let's go over it."

"I'll drive the truck," Ellie said insistently.

"And exchange one hostage for two? I don't think so, my dear."

"Don't you 'my dear' me!"

"OK, look, it's not a good idea for Mrs Bosa, may I call you Ellie, to take the truck."

"I insist."

"No. That's not going to happen," I said.

Ellie's insistence was a little odd, but I let it pass. There really was no way that her husband would put her in harm's way.

The plan was hatched that I would drive the truck, with Sol, Bosa and Wiebbe following close behind, into the car park at the Botanic Gardens. I'd leave my phone under the driver's seat, then jump in the following car and drive away.

I turned to Ellie and said, "We have tracking on all our phones so it should be easy to follow the truck at a distance without being spotted."

“I don’t think that’s a good idea,” Ellie said. “What if they search the cab and find your phone or it starts ringing?”

“It’s OK Ellie, there is nothing on the phone to indicate it’s being tracked. They’ll probably just think it slipped from my pocket if it starts ringing.”

“Still, I don’t think you should do it. This is my daughter’s life you are talking about! Let’s just give them the gold and get her back.”

I looked over at Bosa who silently nodded at me, but then said, “OK, Ellie, you’re right. It’s a risk we don’t have to take.”

“And I’ll drive the truck?”

“No Ellie. Michael will drive the truck. You will wait here with Kate for when the kidnapper calls. Wiebbe, myself and Sol, will pick up Michael after he drops off the truck. He can call you on his mobile to let you know he’s made the drop.”

“But I want to drive the truck.”

“No, Ellie, and that’s an end to it.”

Ellie stormed out of the lounge to her bedroom. Kate got up to follow her, but Bosa held her back. “Let her be, Mrs Hawkins. She’ll be OK in a while. She’s still getting over her jet lag. It’s a wonder she’s functioning at all, given this terrible ordeal.”

“Here—take my phone,” said Kate, “You can leave it under the seat and track it on yours.”

“Way to go, Mum!” Wiebbe said.

“Now, we can assume that they’ll be watching. They won’t want to leave a pickup full of gold sitting there for very long, especially with the keys in the ignition, so we should be ready to move.”

* * *

The air was still and humid as I brought the pickup to a stop in the Botanic Gardens car park. Gravel crunched underfoot as I got out and looked around. The Park was closed now—an hour before sunset—and the air was heavy with the scent of the vegetation and some unpleasant odours emanating from the toilet block.

Sol drove up next to me and I got in the back seat.

I took out my phone as we drove away and called Ellie. Kate picked up the phone. "Stage one successfully completed. Put Ellie on, please.

"Ellie, it's Michael. We made the drop. I didn't see anyone. We're on our way home now. Should be back in an hour. Let us know on my mobile the minute the kidnappers call."

I truncated the call and Sol pulled into a small clearing about a mile down the road which was shielded from prying eyes.

"Now we wait," I said.

In no time at all, the pickup was on the move.

"Look it's moving. It's coming this way. Are you sure they can't see us?"

"We're fine, Dad, but I'm going to hide over there, so I can get a good look at this kidnapper." Wiebbe got out of the car and crept forward into the bushes as the car sped past.

A short time later he returned. "Looks like that kid who was hanging about the dock not so long ago," he said as he buckled up. "Where's he off to?"

"Looks like he's heading straight back to the docks."

"OK, let's assume he's just a messenger boy. I can't imagine he's the kidnapper. Let's keep a respectable distance behind and make our way down there. We'll hang back until we are sure that we have eyes on Rose or the real kidnapper."

We shuffled through the worst of the rush hour traffic as we made our way slowly to the docks.

At 6:20pm my mobile rang. "Where are you?" Ellie said.

"We're stuck in traffic, Mrs Bosa. Has the kidnapper called?"

"No, not yet."

The line went dead.

I wondered, had she had called to see if I still had my phone or, was she concerned about her husband's whereabouts?

"Stop, stop, stop," I called as I looked back at my tracking app and noticed that the pickup had stopped close by. Sol pulled into a space just before we ran onto the wharf.

We looked out over the jetty where a small boat, not dissimilar to Bosa's, was tied up alongside. The scene was shrouded in shadows and the faint glow of sodium lamps spread out along the jetty, creating pools of intermittent yellow light along its length.

The young man who had been driving the pickup wasted no time in passing the sacks containing the gold bars down onto the boat where eager hands received them.

"Come, let's go," said Bosa as he opened the car door.

"Wait, what are you doing?". Wiebbe said.

"I'm getting my boat!"

It was as plain to the eye that sees what was happening, and Bosa had been quick on the uptake. We all piled out and ran around to the other side of the jetty unseen, and got into Bosa's boat—just before the kidnappers' boat disappeared into the darkness and the pickup was driven away.

"Switch off the nav-lights," I said as we pulled away from the wharf.

Our kidnappers had not thought of taking this precaution and we were able to follow them unobserved. Eventually, they stopped alongside a yacht anchored some way off. Bosa brought up a pair of binoculars from the cuddy cabin and handed them to me.

"Do you see Rose?" he asked anxiously.

I brought the binoculars up to my eyes and brought the image into focus. One figure on the tender was passing the sacks containing the gold bars to another on the yacht. I could see a name on the yacht, a name that I hadn't seen for over twenty years: *Sea Dragon.* Lazarus's yacht.

Chapter 31 Better the Devil you Know

I gasped. "No way!"

"What? What is it? What do you see? Can you see Rose?"

Bosa took the binoculars from my grasp and tried unsuccessfully to focus on the image in the dim distance.

"I can't see anything," he said.

Wiebbe was quick to assess the situation. "Bosa, take the boat wide, upwind of the yacht. Dad and I are going to go for a little swim.

"Sol, you stay on board with Mr Bosa and let the boat drift back downwind after you've dropped us off. The current is running pretty fast, and you may need to help us get back in the boat if we miss the yacht. If we get on board and subdue the kidnappers, I'll call you by flashing a light."

Sol looked at me and, to my surprise, said, "Mr Hawkins, you are a lover, not a fighter. Please, take this." He reached behind him and pulled out a small snub-nosed revolver.

I was shocked.

"Sol, there is no way I'm going to take that. Besides, what's the chance of it working after it's been for a swim?"

"You take care, Mr Hawkins; you take care too Mr Wiebbe. Rose needs good man, and you are good man."

Taking a wide berth of the yacht, Wiebbe and I removed our shoes and slipped silently into the water. We were quickly grabbed by the current and propelled towards the yacht.

The tender which had delivered the gold cast off and motored into the night as we approached the anchor chain.

Wiebbe grabbed the anchor chain with one hand and my arm with the other, as I was in danger of being swept away. I managed to grab the chain and hold on, whilst Wiebbe climbed up onto the bowsprit. Once securely on board, he leaned over and grasped my wrist to help me up.

Slowly the current released its grip on my body as more and more of me emerged from the water. Getting our breath, we tiptoed silently on the teak deck, me on the starboard side and Wiebbe portside, until we arrived at the cockpit at the same time. There was no sound coming from the cabin and I motioned to Wiebbe to climb down with me.

Unfortunately, we had to go in single file and Wiebbe pushed me to the rear as he took a deep breath and recklessly burst into the cabin, ready for a violent confrontation with an unknown number of kidnappers.

Rose was alone, sitting in the cabin behind a table. Her eyes sprang wide as she saw her knight in shining armour come to her rescue and stood up, flinging her arms around him.

"Are you OK, Rose? Did they hurt you?"

"I'm OK, no, I'm fine."

A voice from behind caused me to spin around, immediately regretting I had not taken up Sol's offer of his gun.

"Michael. Wiebbe. So kind of you to join us. I wondered how long it would take you to figure it out."

"Lazarus!"

I saw the gun in his right hand, a revolver not dissimilar to Sol's. His left arm hung loosely by his side.

"It's good to see you both. It's been far too long. And Wiebbe! Just look at you! What a fine figure of a man you've become."

I could see Wiebbe calculating in his own mind whether he could get the drop on Lazarus, but a stray bullet in a target rich environment was too great a risk to take.

Lazarus seemed to be oblivious to the threat and continued, "I can't tell you how pleased I am that you two have hit it off. I'm really looking forward to the wedding."

I stood there open mouthed. The gall of this man was unbelievable.

At last, I found my voice. "Lazarus, you're supposed to be dead."

Lazarus smiled. "Ah! a little ruse to get you to come out to the Solomons. I'm afraid I didn't have anyone else that I felt I could trust. You see, despite our little misunderstandings, I know you will always do the right thing by me.

"Once I found the gold, I knew you'd come out and recover it for me. What a pity that half of it has disappeared into the abyss."

Lazarus looked at Rose, who downcast her eyes. "Rose has told me all about your adventures. I must say it was jolly exciting to hear about my old shipwreck, and I'm truly delighted that you both survived."

Wiebbe leaned forward menacingly and said, "The game's over, Lazarus. You can't kill us all. Bosa and Sol are astern and just waiting to board."

"I have no intention of killing anyone, young Wiebbe. But I do have a plan, and I think you're going to love it. Would you mind calling in Mr Bosa and that thug of his? This is likely to take some time, and I wouldn't want them to do anything foolish."

I looked at Lazarus and decided that he wasn't beyond using his revolver.

I turned to Wiebbe and said, "Call them over, Wiebbe. Let's hear what Lazarus has got to say."

* * *

Sol eased his muscled frame into the seat next to Bosa who appeared genuinely surprised to see that the mysterious Lazarus was indeed alive and well.

Wiebbe had hung the tender off the stern so that it didn't bang against the hull.

"Do I really need this?" Lazarus said as he waved the revolver around the cabin.

"You might want to keep it handy," Wiebbe said as he glared at him.

I glanced at Wiebbe and said "It's OK.

"Lazarus, put it away before someone gets hurt; no one's going to jump you, you have my word.

"Sol, you can put yours in the drawer with Lazarus's, please."

In the bright light of the cabin, Sol retrieved his revolver from the pocket of his pants and placed it on the table. It looked rusty, and I felt it was more likely to injure the shooter than stop an assailant.

Both guns were secured, and, despite my assurances, I could see that Wiebbe was still thinking about the chances of overpowering Lazarus before he continued.

"Very well. Now, firstly, I want to welcome you all aboard *Sea Dragon* and …"

"Get on with it, Lazarus," Wiebbe said. "I still haven't decided whether or not, to break your arms and legs."

"Patience, my boy,"

I looked at Wiebbe and motioned for him to back off. He sat back in his seat, but the tension was still visible across his shoulders.

"Secondly, I want to thank you all for recovering half my gold from my wreck." I placed my hand on Wiebbe's tightly muscled forearm. Lazarus continued, "Unfortunately, when I discovered the wreck, I paid a terrible price and she claimed the use of my left arm. I lacked the skills and knowledge to salvage the treasure that I had such a fleeting encounter with, two years ago.

"Now, however, you have a problem; how to realise the value of this bullion without raising suspicion. Of course you can use that bent jeweller, Mr Luke, but you can bet your bottom dollar he'll rip you off. Perhaps more concerningly, blab about it to anyone that cares to listen. Your secret will be all over Honiara in a matter of hours and your lives will be in great peril.

"Now, I have an alternative plan. I will take the gold back to Fremantle, and you will process it through your lease near Leonora. The same as you did with the bars you collected a year ago."

"Is there anything you don't know about us?" Wiebbe said with thinly veiled disgust.

"It pays to do your research, Wiebbe.

"To be honest, I am not sure I am fit enough to make the passage to Freo on my own and that is where you and Rose come in. You will be my crew. That has the added advantage of being able to keep your eye on the gold. Together, we will make the passage and rendezvous with your mum and dad in the Abrolhos. I'm fully provisioned for the voyage, and we can leave on the morning tide."

I stared at Lazarus in disbelief. "You are incorrigible, Lazarus! If Kate was here now, you'd be overboard!"

"Ah, if only," Lazarus sighed. "How is Kate? Beautiful as ever?"

Getting the gold out of the Solomon Islands was something we never thought to do and were quite prepared to accept a discounted price on it, but the transfer of funds from overseas was closely monitored these days and presented a huge problem for us.

Lazarus continued, "Now, having obtained the gold legitimately from your lease, you can sell it to Perth Mint and then invest in an overseas business in Honiara. I am sure that Mr Bosa has several businesses that are desperate for funds in order to pay his generous fees. You see, it will all be washed clean, and unlike the proceeds of crime, the full value of the bullion will be realised."

Rose piped up, "What he says makes sense, Dad. Isn't it better the devil you know than the devil you don't know?"

Bosa was struggling to accept the recent turn of events and, uncharacteristically, sat there in silence.

"Fuck!" Wiebbe chipped in. "I can't believe we are sitting here negotiating with a kidnapper. Why don't we just throw him overboard and sail down there ourselves?"

Lazarus smiled, "Appealing though that is, and in some way, I am looking forward to my own demise, you are not a murderer, Wiebbe, not if I am any judge of character."

At last, Bosa found his voice. "And what would your commission be on such a transaction, Mr Lazarus?"

"Mr Bosa, it may come as a surprise to you, but as I approach the twilight of my life, I have reached the conclusion that I have enough.

"I have all of my life's great and wonderful experiences to look back upon and this mere trifle is just that. An experience, a distraction, a plaything if you like, but you can't deny it has been a wonderful thing to play with.

"My commission? One dollar, Australian, of course!"

"One fucking dollar!? What's the catch?" said Wiebbe.

Chapter 32 Lazarus Has Risen

Kate stormed around the hotel room packing her suitcase. "I'm going to kill him. I am definitely going to kill him. That self-centred, narcissistic bastard. This was all a huge game for him, wasn't it? What for? A dollar! And now! Now, he has the gall to think that he can re-kindle a friendship that **he** destroyed over twenty years ago and use us into the bargain!"

I learned a long time ago that when Kate was in full flight, it was best to keep quiet and let her go-for-it until she ran out of steam. On this occasion however, she had been boiling over for the better part of an hour.

"And Wiebbe! What on earth was he thinking about? And Bosa! Letting his daughter sail down to the Abrolhos with that monster! I can't believe you agreed to this."

I was about to become the focus of Kate's rage and recognized the warning signs. However, Wiebbe was a grown man and more than capable of taking care of himself and Rose, and once his mind was made up, there was nothing I could do to stop him.

"Kate, you know Wiebbe. He has a stubborn streak about him."

"A stubborn streak? I wonder where he got that from?"

I said nothing but smiled, not attempting to answer her rhetorical question. Kate could not maintain her rage any longer and burst into a grin as she put her arms around me and held me close.

Eventually she broke our embrace and looked up at me and said, "Oh my. Are you sure they'll be OK?"

"Yes. I'm sure."

"Well, I still don't trust Lazarus. A leopard can't change its spots, and I just know he's up to something."

"I think that's a given, but what exactly he's up to, I have no idea."

* * *

"I am going to kill him," Ellie said to herself as she stormed around her bedroom, "that stupid philanderer, who does he think he is? We had a deal. I was meant to take the gold to him in the pickup and live happily ever after with him until he died, and die he would, sooner rather than later if I had my way. Then I'd be free of all this and live a life of luxury. Ha! If only he knew. Now, I still have to beg Joe for crumbs off the table—to buy clothes and trips to New York. I am going to kill him. I am going to find that bastard and make him suffer."

The irony was that Ellie had had no intention of delivering the pickup—and its gold cargo—to Lazarus. She had planned to lose the tailing car in the traffic and disappear into the night. She had been out-manoeuvred by her own step daughter and an interfering Aussie.

There was a gentle tap on her bedroom door, and she opened it to see her husband Joe standing there.

"Are you OK, Ellie? I thought I heard voices."

"Sweetheart. Of course, I was just thinking out loud. I wonder how Rose is getting on."

"Looking after our investment, I imagine."

"Oh, you are so clever, my darling sweetie-pie. I would never have thought of anything like that.

"We'll have to start planning the wedding soon!"

"Well, Wiebbe hasn't proposed yet, so don't you think that might be a little premature?"

"A woman's intuition, Joe. It's only a matter of time. I'll fly down to Perth to check out venues next week. Don't say you can't afford it!"

"You've only just got back from New York. Aren't you tired of travelling?"

"Oh, this is entirely different Joe, entirely different."

* * *

Kate and I arrived back in Fremantle and after a few days had arranged to charter a 52' Flybridge Cruiser called Strawberry Fields for a trip up to the Abrolhos. There, we'd meet up with the *Sea Dragon* in Turtle Bay, transfer the gold to our vessel and return to Fremantle 10 days later.

Sea Dragon would pull into the customs jetty, a few days after us, and go through the formalities with the Australian Border Force.

We'd decided on a stink boat rather than a sailboat for speed and comfort. It was also common for such boats to motor up from the Fremantle Sailing Club to the Abrolhos on fishing and diving expeditions. Kate had met up with several of the fisheries officers during her time on the Islands over the past twenty-five years. She was recognised as a frequent visitor, so to all intents and purposes, our trip would appear to be nothing out of the ordinary.

"You know, Michael, I'm really looking forward to visiting our old stomping ground together," Kate said as we packed our bags. "Don't you think it will be romantic?"

"Anywhere with you is romantic," I said as I held her close.

"Tease!"

After a short while and a quick check to make sure we had everything, I turned to Kate and said, "Well, I guess we are packed and ready to go.

"I'll take this down to the club and load it onto the boat, with our dive and fishing gear. We should look the part just in case fisheries board us."

I smiled and gave her a reassuring hug.

"The weather's looking great, so we'll leave at first light."

Kate hesitated. There was something troubling her I knew, but I chose to ignore her discomfort as I loaded the car.

Chapter 33 The Abrolhos

After a day's motoring, we pulled into Dongara and refuelled. We had decided to stay alongside that night, so that the sun would be behind us as we approached the Islands in the morning. This way the treacherous reefs would be highlighted, just as they had been over twenty years ago when I had sailed up there with the lecherous Lazarus on the *Sea Dragon*. Even with the latest in satellite navigation, it was good seamanship.

Kate had reluctantly packed a selection of fine wines, port and spirits on Lazarus's instructions to replenish his stocks upon arrival at the Abrolhos. We planned to stay there with *Sea Dragon* for a few days—to catch lobsters and fish, to complete the charade—before motoring back to FSC.

Arriving in Turtle Bay we found the place deserted and chose Lazarus's favourite mooring to tie up to.

The sun was high in the sky and warm on our faces. The turquoise water glistened around us as we made everything secure and ship shape.

I sat in the cockpit and was surprised and delighted to see Kate walk naked up the galley steps towards me, gently kiss me on the lips, then dive into the cool water.

"Who's going to see me?" she laughed. "Come on in, sailor-boy, the water's lovely!"

It was the following day that we saw the sail of *Sea Dragon* on the horizon. We had agreed to maintain radio silence so as not to raise suspicion but once in the bay, it would be natural to communicate and socialise with other vessels.

As the yacht came closer, I could see Rose on the bow waving enthusiastically, grinning from ear to ear. Phase one of our plan had been completed, it appeared, without a hitch.

As the day drew to a close, we gathered on the deck of *Strawberry Fields*, the gold already transferred to the engine room—buried beneath dive gear, ropes, and tarps. From a casual glance, it looked like nothing more than clutter. But we knew better. The charade was in motion.

"Michael, I cannot say how proud I am of these two youngsters. You really have done well. What a strong and competent sailor Wiebbe is. There is no way I could have got down here by myself given my disability, and Rose is both beautiful and smart to boot!"

Wiebbe's openly hostile attitude to Lazarus had ameliorated during his ocean voyage. He and Rose were becoming more of an item, finishing each other's sentences and sharing constant touches of affection.

Lazarus poured himself another large port and said, "We'll call Border Force when we leave the Abrolhos and let them know our ETA at FSC. That way, they can come on board and complete their formalities, and we can get ashore without delay."

"I can't wait to have a proper bath and sleep in a bed that doesn't move all the time," Rose said as she looked at Wiebbe.

"I think I can arrange that," he replied.

"What of yourself, Lazarus? What are your plans?" Kate asked as the sun sank over the island. She had been surprisingly accepting of his return from the grave and, rather than kill him as she had vowed, she cautiously accepted his embrace as he boarded our boat.

"I have a small cottage in Freo where I plan to spend the rest of my days, Kate. I have lived an interesting life, but—like Marley's

Ghost—I have forged many heavy links to my chain. It's time to make amends, although I seriously doubt, I'll be going to heaven!

"I have no one left now, Kate. You, Michael, Wiebbe and Rose are the closest thing to family I've ever had, apart from a number of blood sucking ex-wives, of course. You know, I see in you both and particularly in Wiebbe and Rose, everything I wish I could have been and everything I wish I could have had, but even with all the money in the world, it couldn't buy me happiness. It's a bit of a cliché, I know, but it's true."

That night, Kate and I lay in our bunk and talked softly to each other.

"Do you think that Lazarus is for real?" Kate said as she snuggled in close.

"I don't know. He seems genuine enough and well, let's face it, he's been good to his word so far and, don't forget, we do have all the gold."

"He's taken a bit of a shine to Wiebbe and Rose."

"Probably angling for an invitation to the wedding," I said.

"Ha! That'd be right! Do you think they'll get married?"

"They seem well suited, but I suggest we let nature take its course."

Kate paused, then said, "Wiebbe seems to like Lazarus well enough now."

"Yes, that's a bit of a turn-around, wouldn't you say? But then again this is Lazarus we're talking about. He'd 'sell ice to the Eskimos'. I did notice that you didn't assault him when he came on board Strawberry Fields."

"Oh, don't you worry about that," Kate said, "I was fit to punch him on his nose but when I saw him, he looked old and almost frail. His eyes were smiling at me. He was genuinely pleased to see me. He's still an attractive, loveable rogue, isn't he?"

"What is it that women see in that crusty old millionaire?" I said as I pulled her closer.

Kate's lips brushed mine and the romance of being on board a vessel moored in Turtle Bay overcame us and we made love softly with the movement of the boat before falling into a dreamless sleep.

* * *

In the morning, Wiebbe and I went diving and found the same bommie—still teeming with lobsters, just as it had been all those years ago, when I first arrived in Turtle Bay with Lazarus.

We caught twenty and froze sixteen in *Strawberry Fields'* freezer. The other four, Rose prepared with Lazarus in the cramped galley—fresh, fragrant, and destined for immediate consumption—alongside sand-whiting fillets that she'd hooked off the back of *Sea Dragon*. It was a feast born of stealth and saltwater, shared in whispers and laughter.

"You remembered the bommie, Michael?" Lazarus smiled as he split the cooked lobster tails along their backs.

"It's amazing that it's still full of lobsters all these years later," I said.

"Yes, but for how much longer, you may ask? You know, Michael, the world is changing. I'm a dinosaur. Can't be fussed with all this political correctness and stuff. I am a paradigm that has outlived its usefulness."

"Is there something you're not telling me, Lazarus?"

"I'm old, Michael, and I'm dying. I know it and there is nothing I can do about it. I've drawn up my will and left a sizable chunk of money to Rose's orphanage in the Solomons." He looked over at Rose who smiled and downcast her eyes, reaching out a soft hand onto his wrist.

"Thank you, Lazarus," she said.

"It's OK. I have discussed this with Rose. She'll set up a trust fund so that it's not squandered away. Hopefully, I'll leave a legacy of good in perpetuity. I've also left you a little something, but I doubt you'll be needing it. I'd like you to keep it for the wedding!"

"Lazarus!" Rose shouted and playfully hit him none too softly on his shoulder. "Enough of this foolish talk. Let's eat!"

The days went by and all too soon, it was time to say our goodbyes. We had a freezer full of fish and lobsters and a hold full of gold. Life was good. We hadn't been boarded by Fisheries and, although they may want to inspect our catch at FSC, it was unlikely.

Rose, Wiebbe and Lazarus would arrive a few days later and, once cleared by HM Customs, would join us at our house.

I was about to give Lazarus the address but then realised he already knew that, too.

Chapter 34 Marley's Ghost

Rose and Wiebbe crashed into the kitchen, dumping heavy bags of soiled clothes into the laundry on their way through.

"Where's Lazarus?" Kate asked, looking over Wiebbe's shoulder.

"It's getting late. He said he'd come over tomorrow, Mum. He wanted to go to his cottage first. I think he might want to have a bit of a rest as well."

"He's come home, hasn't he?"

Wiebbe looked at Kate and asked what she meant.

"I mean, he's come home to die."

"I guess so, Mum," he said as he shrugged his shoulders, "but don't write him off just yet. He's a tough old goat. You should have seen him on the yacht. Don't let the frail little old man act fool you!"

* * *

The cottage that Lazarus had bought some years ago was situated in the old town of Fremantle. It had been built in the early to mid-1800's and faced directly onto the road. Its single storey walls were made from thick local limestone blocks and the corners were of exposed brick in the colonial style with a tin roof which he recalled, heralded the first drops of rain in the autumn.

Behind the cottage was a beautiful walled garden which had been meticulously maintained during his extended absence by Jim's Gardening Services. Inside was neat, tidy, and clean. Lazarus had a contract with a local maid service that ensured the building was properly maintained even though it hadn't been occupied for many years.

He had thought of renting it out, of course, but he reasoned he needed a bolt hole. Somewhere that he could run to if things got hairy, and the thought of renters trashing the place had sent shivers up his spine.

Opening the lead-light windowed front door, he was greeted by the spartan surroundings and rather dated décor. He'd have to do something about that, he thought.

He'd called the agency and asked for the fridge and pantry to be stocked at the same time as he had made the call to the Australian Border Force, and also asked them to place fresh flowers on the kitchen table. Nothing like a few fresh flowers to make a place feel like home.

He placed his keys on the hall table, picked up some letters from the floor and moved down the hallway to the kitchen where he put the kettle on, unaware of the person watching him through the back window.

Scraping its legs noisily along the flagstone floor, Lazarus pulled out a chair from beneath the kitchen table and sat down heavily, cupping a steaming mug of tea in both hands. A single Australian dollar coin lay on the table.

They'd forgotten the flowers. He made a mental note to delete those from their bill.

The letters and flyers were normally dealt with by the managing agent—so these must have come today. Looking at them, he quickly tossed them aside as junk mail. Rubbish, he thought.

It was then that a gentle waft of air stirred the top page of the Harvey Norman catalogue.

Shit, I must have left the front door open, he thought and stood up, slowly making his way to the hallway. It was dark and a shadowy figure called out his name. "Lazarus, you bastard!"

A shot rang out, and his world turned monochrome—the muzzle flash briefly illuminating everything in front of the shooter. He staggered into the kitchen and fell hard, cracking his head on the flagstone floor.

The pain in his left arm surged to a crescendo as he glimpsed the figure looming above him, revolver raised, eyes unreadable. Then, everything went black.

Chapter 35 Salting

Kate and I had originally decided to smelt the gold bars in our garage, making small one-ounce ingots which could be easily transported and sold. We'd get about 32 Troy ounces to the kilogram and could add a little bit of copper or silver, to match the chemistry of the small nuggets we'd found on our lease. Say 32 troy ounces to the kilogram, 500 kilograms 16,500 Troy ounces. Our little furnace would need to work overtime.

"Perhaps we'd be better off creating 1kg bars. We really just need to get rid of the swastika and add a bit of copper and silver," Kate said.

It was a nice problem to have but we'd have to use a few different gold buyers in addition to Perth mint to make sure we didn't raise too much suspicion. Fortunately, there were plenty around in Western Australia and they didn't appear to talk to each other or keep a central database. We'd be OK.

"OK, one kilogram of salted gold. 500 kilograms, that's 500 bars. A bit more manageable," I replied.

"Morning, Mum, Dad," Wiebbe said as we were rearranging our garage.

"Afternoon, son," I said, making a show of looking at my wristwatch.

"Mmm, that time already? Is Lazarus here yet?"

"No, haven't heard from him," I said. "I expect he'll be here soon enough. He wouldn't want to miss this. Is Rose up yet?"

"Yeah, she's in the bathroom. I'm on breakfast duties."

"You'd better call it brunch!"

It was late afternoon, and Lazarus still hadn't turned up.

"Do you think he's OK?" Kate asked, a slight concern in her voice. "Do you have his number?"

"I'll call him," Wiebbe said, taking out his mobile.

"Hmm, that's odd, no reply."

"Probably off womanising," I said.

"At his age? Dad, that's gross."

"Hey, don't knock it. You'll be old soon enough. I still have lead in me pencil, my son!"

"Oh, please!" Kate groaned. "Wiebbe go around to his place and see if he's OK."

"OK, Mum. I'll take Rose. Do we need anything at the shops?"

"No, oh yes actually, can you get a couple of litres of skinny milk? I only have full cream."

"No worries."

Wiebbe and Rose strolled off hand-in-hand towards Lazarus's cottage which was just a short walk across town. On arrival Wiebbe rapped on the front door and, having received no reply, was about to walk away when Rose bent down and looked through the lead light window.

"Wiebbe, I think I can see something," she said, as she tried to peer through the textured glass. "Here, have a look."

"Fuck, he's collapsed."

"Can you open the door?"

Wiebbe tried pushing it hard but to no avail. "Let's try around the back."

Rose and Wiebbe raced along the side passage to the back lane and climbed over the locked gate into the garden. Approaching the back door he saw Lazarus through the glass window—sprawled out—his body half in the hallway and half in the kitchen, his head resting in a pool of blood.

He tried the handle and then, finding it locked, rammed the full weight of his shoulder against it, smashing the frame around the deadlock and sending wooden splinters and glass, across the floor.

Kneeling by his head, Wiebbe felt for a pulse. He lowered his face to an inch above his nose. "He's still breathing, Rose. Call an ambulance."

* * *

"Shot? What do you mean, shot?" I quickly switched my mobile phone to speaker mode so Kate could hear the conversation.

"Shot, as in with a gun, Dad. The police are here and the ambulance has taken him to Fremantle Hospital. It's a mess. The whole place has been ransacked. Who'd want to kill Lazarus, Dad?"

I thought it might be easier to draw up a list of who wouldn't want to kill him but said instead, "OK, I'll meet you at the hospital. The police will want a formal statement from you. Just tell the truth and you won't go wrong. You might want to leave the bit about the gold out of the story. They don't need to know about that. We're old family friends that met up in Honiara and you offered to help him sail *Sea Dragon* back, with Rose."

* * *

"Are you the next of kin?" the ward clerk asked as Kate and I, fronted at the nurses' station in the hospital.

"He doesn't have any next of kin. We're the only family he has," Kate said.

"I'll call up and see if someone can talk to you."

A young doctor came through the doors and spoke briefly to the clerk who nodded in our direction.

"He's lost a lot of blood and, to be honest, he's still very poorly. He's in recovery now and we'll be moving him up to the ward shortly. We'll have a better idea of the prognosis tomorrow.

"However, the good news is that the wound isn't serious. I suspect that he fell backwards with the impact of the bullet and knocked himself out. He has a haematoma on the back of his skull but no fractures. The bullet passed through his left arm which appears to be quite atrophied, possibly due to an accident some time ago. We sometimes see that on motorcycle accident victims where the brachial plexus nerve is damaged or, in severe cases, severed. Was he a biker by any chance?"

"No, I think that he may have acquired that injury from a diving accident," I said.

"Ah, that could account for it. Just 15cm to his right and the bullet would have passed straight through his heart. It was really the blood loss that we were concerned about. However, we gave him four units in theatre, and he's now stabilised. He's a tough old boy, I'll give him that."

Wiebbe and Rose turned up just as the young doctor was explaining.

"You may as well go home and come back tomorrow," he said. "He's not going to be up to seeing any visitors for a while. Go home and call tomorrow. The ward clerk will let you know if it's worth your while coming in."

I thanked the young doctor as he turned to go back to a noisy ED where some drunk or druggie, was throwing things around.

Wiebbe, myself, Rose and Kate walked out into the car park. "They want us to go to the police station tomorrow and make a full statement," Wiebbe said. "They seemed pretty happy that we'd discovered him and called the police and ambulance. I told them that it was me that had broken down the back door after I saw him lying in a pool of blood, but I hadn't noticed any sign of forced entry.

"The officer said I'd done the right thing, although forensics would need to take our fingerprints to eliminate us from their enquiry, when we go to the station tomorrow." Wiebbe paused, "Who could have done this, Dad? The place was a tip—every drawer, every cupboard open, the contents thrown around the room."

“Lazarus was the kind of guy who found it easy to make enemies,” I said.

“The officer reckoned it was a burglary gone wrong but was concerned about the gunshot wound. He said that most burglars in Freo wouldn’t know one end of a gun from another. You could see it was a real worry for him, to think that burglars were now arming themselves with guns and were not afraid to use them.”

“Come on, let’s get home. I need a drink,” I said.

“How’s the smelting going?” Wiebbe asked, keen to change the subject.

“It’s good, Wiebbe, although your mum and I, have decided to recast the bars into 500 new one kilogram bars to get rid of the swastikas, rather than thousands of one-ounce ingots.”

“Sounds good to me,” Wiebbe said as we completed the rest of our walk in silence.

Chapter 36 A Surprise Visitor

Ellie sat in her room in the Parmelia Hilton, just off St. George's Terrace in Perth. Her hands were still shaking as she swallowed the contents of the last of the miniatures from the minibar. She stood up, went to the bathroom and glanced at her reflection in the mirror. She looked as though she had aged ten years in the last twenty-four hours. She promptly threw up.

An hour later the phone in her room rang just as she emerged from her en-suite, dressed in the fluffy white gown provided by the hotel, her hair wrapped in a towelling turban.

"Ellie, sweetheart! Have you met up with Rose yet? How is everyone? Any news on the wedding?"

"Oh Joe, I've been that busy. You wouldn't believe the number of beautiful venues here. I'm going down to Freo to check out the Esplanade Hotel tomorrow. I'm planning to pay a surprise visit to the Hawkins then. You haven't told Rose I'm here in Perth, have you?"

"Of course not! It's going to be a wonderful surprise. Our little secret," he chuckled, "and while you're at it, make sure the gold is being held securely."

"Of course, dear."

* * *

Ellie had spent all afternoon listening to the local radio for any news on the murder. She had fully intended to blow that bastard's brains out but hadn't the heart to do it. When she shot him, a fine mist of blood had filled the air as he was propelled backwards onto the kitchen floor. He had stared wide eyed up into her masked face before losing consciousness.

For her part, she had looked into those seductive eyes, which even in death held that boyish mischief about them, and simply failed to deliver the *coup de grâce*.

Whilst not quite sure where the bullet had hit him, she was pretty sure he was dead, and had then spent the better part of an hour, ransacking the house, but to no avail.

The house was as sterile as her hotel room. Practically no personal possessions and certainly nothing worth stealing. The Hawkins had clearly retained all of the gold. Rose was her only guarantee that they wouldn't double-cross her or her corpulent husband. Even so, she held a niggling doubt about her own stepdaughter. Trust no one, she thought.

Ellie had been surprised at just how calm she had been as she left the house. She made sure that she dropped the latch on the old Yale lock as she closed the front door. She was wearing her face mask and a baseball cap pulled low over her eyes. Her baggy coat might even have served to conceal her gender from prying eyes and CCTV cameras, she thought.

She had carried her Coles shopping bag down the street and blended in with other shoppers before ducking into the restroom of a local pub. There, she ditched her attire for a more flattering dress.

The revolver she had naively but successfully smuggled into the country was disposed of in the river.

It was the following day that the news broke about an armed robbery and a shooting in Fremantle.

The radio blurted out: *"882 6PR News. In breaking news, WA police report that a seventy-one-year-old man has been shot and seriously wounded in a home invasion in Fremantle. Police are yet to issue a description of the assailants but Detective Sergeant Grant said that they were concerned about the escalation of violent crime in Fremantle, and particularly the use of firearms.*

While the Premier was unavailable for comment, Shadow Police Minister Ms Ledger, said "I have repeatedly called upon the Premier to strengthen the police force. He has consistently failed, and failed miserably to do his job, and this is the result."

In other news, Perth Zoo is to get a facelift..."

The words on the radio drifted into background noise as the news of Lazarus's survival spun Ellie into a panic. Lazarus was still alive. Had he recognised her? Had he spoken to the police?

She needed to keep it together. She could do this, she told herself.

* * *

Arriving at the Hawkins' house, she knocked on the front door and was greeted by her radiant looking stepdaughter.

"Surprise!"

"Mum! What on earth are you doing here? Is Dad with you?" Rose said as she glanced over her mum's shoulder.

"No, he's back in Honiara counting all his money and moaning about my credit card bills as usual. Hi Wiebbe," she called out as Wiebbe appeared behind Rose.

"Mrs Bosa, well, this is a surprise. Come to check up on us I see!"

"Oh, don't be silly, Wiebbe. I would trust you both with my life. Are your mum and dad in?"

"No, they've popped over to the sailing club to move Lazarus's yacht, to one of the vacant pens. I think Mum was intending giving it a bit of a tidy-up before the cleaners got on board. But don't just stand there, come inside!"

Rose glanced at Wiebbe as he stood aside, enabling Ellie access to the house. He turned around to see Rose tilt her head and offer her best 'WTF' expression. Wiebbe just raised his eyebrows silently, his half-smile unseen by Ellie and followed her inside.

Sitting in the lounge, Rose offered to make some tea and left Wiebbe and Ellie to their own devices. Alone together, Ellie turned to Wiebbe and said, “So, Wiebbe, when are you going to make an honest woman of my daughter?”

The forthright question shook Wiebbe, who was lost for words.

“Neither of you are getting any younger. I was married to Mr Bosa when I was 21. Now, I don’t want to interfere, but you should both really think about having children while you are both still young enough to enjoy them.

“Children do so much better with younger parents. And have you thought about where you are going to live? You’ll have your choices of places here in Australia and the Solomons, and you’ll need a large guest room or granny flat for when granny and grandad come to visit.

“Of course, the wedding is going to be spectacular. I’ve already identified lots of lovely venues and Mr Bosa will pay for everything, although he’ll whinge about it. I don’t want my daughter to feel as though she has to scrimp and scrape. It will be the society wedding of the decade!”

Rose walked in on the tail end of her mum’s speech.

“Mum! Back off. Wiebbe and I are very happy together the way things are and, if and when we develop any plans for anything else, we’ll be sure to let you know.”

There was a sharp knock at the front door.

“That’ll be the police,” Rose said as she got up to answer it.

Part III

Murder

Chapter 37 To Catch a Murderer

Ellie stiffened in her chair.

"Police? What's going on?"

"Oh, Mrs Bosa, you wouldn't have heard but there's been a shooting," Wiebbe said. "Mr Lazarus was attacked in his own home and shot! Rose and I discovered him barely alive. We called the police and the ambulance. He's in hospital recovering."

Ellie's mind was racing, and she quickly began asking questions as the detective walked into the lounge with Rose.

"Oh, my goodness, did they catch the gunman?"

"This is my mum, Ellie. She's visiting from the Solomon Islands," Rose said as Detective Sergeant Grant appeared in the lounge.

Grant glanced around the room, removing his hat as he did so and turned off his walkie-talkie.

"Would you like a cup of tea, detective?" Rose asked as he took a seat opposite the settee on which Ellie was sitting.

"That would be lovely. Thank you, Rose."

Rose left the lounge to make tea, leaving me, Wiebbe, Kate and Ellie with Grant.

Grant was a career policeman on a fast track within the force. His keen eye and intellect had been noticed by his superiors. Over his time with the force, he had been given several opportunities to prove himself, all of which he had successfully exploited. His relaxed style not only overshadowed a ruthless ambition to succeed but also a genuine interest in making the community a safer place—particularly for Aboriginal youth in rural and remote WA. You had to do time in the 'bush' to really succeed in WAPOL, he reasoned, and whilst many saw this as a dead end or something to be endured, Grant had worked hard to connect with disaffected youth in the State's far north and—to everyone's surprise—had succeeded where others had failed or simply given up.

Ellie couldn't help but notice the gun holstered on his hip.

Grant appeared relaxed and did his best to set everyone at ease with his easy smile and open body language.

"Hello, Mrs Bosa, I'm Detective Sergeant Grant. I must apologise for barging in like this. I'm sure this is not the welcome you were expecting upon visiting Freo."

Ellie did her best to smile as she continued to fidget with her wedding ring on her left hand. If Grant had noticed, he didn't let it show as he removed his pencil and notebook and said, "Did you know Mr Lazarus as well?"

Ellie glanced around the room quickly, half expecting someone to answer for her. How much had he already been told about her relationship with Lazarus? she wondered. There had been no time to ask Rose and Wiebbe what they had said to Grant, and she was concerned about getting her story straight. Eventually her eyes settled back on the benign officer's face.

"Oh, I think I only met him the once, just before he sailed down here with Wiebbe and my daughter Rose. He was a client of my husband's. My husband's a lawyer in Honiara, you know," she said as she regained some of her composure.

"I see."

Ellie wanted to pump the officer for as much information as she could, but forced herself to react as she thought any innocent party might.

"Have you caught the gunman? Did Mr Lazarus get a good look at him? And to think this happened in Fremantle, of all places. Honiara I might expect, but Fremantle!"

"Unfortunately, not yet. Mr Lazarus was knocked unconscious in the attack and has no memory of the incident. The last thing he remembers is arriving home and opening his front door. After that, waking up in hospital."

Ellie seemed relieved at the explanation and her shoulders involuntarily relaxed as the officer made a brief note in his notebook before continuing. "The doctor said that memory loss was quite common in trauma like this, but that over time, it may come back, so we'll keep in touch with him and see if he remembers anything. In the meantime, it looks as though he'll make a full recovery."

"Oh well, that's good news, isn't it? I mean, what a terrible thing to happen."

"You OK, Mum?" Rose said as she entered the room with a tray full of mugs of tea. Rarely had she seen her stepmother looking so out of sorts.

"Yes, of course, dear. It's just all come as a bit of a shock."

Turning to Wiebbe and Rose, Grant said, "The doctor said that you two can visit him tomorrow if you like. He's a tough old bloke, that's for sure."

"Thanks, detective, I was going to call the hospital today," Wiebbe said. "Thank you for coming around in person."

"That's OK, I was in the area in any case, helping to organise the door-to-door enquiries."

"Door-to-door enquiries. Do you have a suspect or description?" Ellie said.

"Fremantle is a small-town, Mrs Bosa. The street where Mr Lazarus lived is full of busy bodies and we have quite a few leads to follow up. Everyone is keen to help. It's only a matter of time until we apprehend the person or persons responsible."

"Person or persons?" Ellie asked.

"There was one report of a person seen leaving the property wearing a baseball cap and a mask. Bloody frustrating these masks. The crims love 'em.

"In the meantime, can you think of anyone that would like to do harm to Mr Lazarus? People that he owed money to maybe, or people in Honiara?"

"I thought it was a burglary or a home invasion gone wrong."

"What makes you say that?"

"Oh, just something I heard on the radio this morning. I just put two and two together you know and, as I said, I hardly knew the man, so no, no idea."

"We're following up all lines of enquiry at this stage, Mrs Bosa. The thing is that no other homes were targeted in the street, which suggests this might be personal. We haven't had this MO on our patch before, so it's doubly concerning. Leave no stone unturned and all that. Can you tell me the name of your husband's practice in Honiara and how I can get in touch with him?"

"Oh, I wouldn't waste your time, detective. Really, I don't think that Mr Bosa had very much to do with him, either. He never mentioned him to me before we agreed that Rose and Wiebbe would help him sail his yacht down to Fremantle."

"Nevertheless."

Ellie rummaged in her handbag and took out a business card of her husband's and handed it to Grant. She was perspiring despite the room being air-conditioned.

"Thank you, Mrs Bosa. How long are you staying for?"

"Oh, I have an open return ticket. I was planning to stay for maybe a week or two but I think maybe I should get back."

"I see. I don't suppose either of you two have remembered anything else that may be of help?" he said, turning to Wiebbe and Rose.

"No, we just went around to see if he was OK, as he wasn't returning our calls. Has the property been made secure? I'm afraid I made a right mess of the back door."

"Yeah, don't worry about that. Forensics are finished and the door has been boarded up.

"I was thinking that it might be nice if you could tidy the place up a bit for when he gets out of hospital. I dropped the keys off at the hospital today so you could ask him for them when you visit."

"Definitely, absolutely," said Rose. "Wiebbe and I will go over and get things sorted tomorrow after we've seen him. I wonder if he'll have remembered anything by then?"

"If he has, call me straight away. Here's my card. Also, here's the name of a local builder who'll be able to fix up the door frame. They're good lads who won't rip you off. Especially if you tell them that Detective Sergeant Grant sent you. Don't be put off by their jail tats. It's just a few of my lost sheep—trying to make it on the straight and narrow. Knowing I referred you will make sure that they'll do a first-class job.

"And Wiebbe, you did good. Both of you did good. Lazarus wouldn't be alive today if you hadn't shown up.

"Nice to meet you, Mrs Bosa, I'm sorry that your first visit to Freo has been so traumatic. It really is a very safe place normally. I hope you'll enjoy the rest of your stay."

"I hope you catch him, detective."

"Well, we're not sure it is a 'him' just yet."

Detective Sergeant Grant left the house and Rose and Wiebbe returned to the lounge to see Ellie looking quite perturbed.

"Mum, are you OK?"

"Yes, of course, I just felt like I was being cross-examined like a common criminal by that detective. Who does he think he is?"

"He's just doing his job, Mum."

"Well, I don't like the way he kept writing things in his notebook."

"I think you need a drink, Mum!"

"Yes dear. Oh, what a day! What ward did you say Mr Lazarus is on?"

Chapter 38 Investigation

Detective Sergeant Grant called a team meeting back at Fremantle Police Station and reviewed the case in a small, cramped room.

"So, what have we got?" Grant asked rhetorically, "71-year-old male attacked in his own home by a person or persons unknown. No signs of forced entry. One gunshot wound to the left arm caused by a .38 special—possibly fired from a revolver at close range—with powder burns on his clothing. Home rifled. We can't say for sure if anything is missing just yet, not until the victim returns to the scene. But he has informed us that there was nothing of value in the cottage, not even a TV, as he'd been overseas for several years and was only maintaining the property through an agency for future use. He'd intended fully kitting it out upon his return—this week as it happens.

"One suspect was seen leaving the house carrying a red bag, possibly a grocery store bag, at or around the presumed time of the assault. Approximately 5'4" to 5'8", identity unknown, possibly female.

"No similar *modus operandi* on our patch, and no other houses targeted in the area."

"Looks personal," PC Simon Ward said out loud.

"Simon, can you check with the agency and see when they did their delivery—date, and time? I understand that Lazarus had organised the upkeep of his property with a Jim's franchise and asked that his fridge be stocked by the housekeeping agency prior to his arrival. Get a log of their visits. Let's exclude the bag lady if we can.

"Jill, can you draw up a list of the usual suspects and see what they were up to. Put some pressure on your informers, find out what the word on the street is. Anyone shouting off his mouth or waving a gun around?"

"Sure thing, Boss. Has Lazarus remembered anything yet?"

"No, and he may not."

"What about the couple that found him?"

"Thirty years of policing says they're not involved, but Rose's mother Ellie Bosa was acting very strangely. I think she may know more than she's letting on but then again, she's just got to Australia and been confronted with a violent crime so, no, in the absence of motive, opportunity and means, we may well be looking at a home invasion gone wrong as our friends in the 6PR newsroom, have already decided for us.

"But let's not let them cloud our judgement. We'll solve this by good solid police work. We won't cut corners and let the media do our jobs for us. As Sherlock Holmes once said, 'When you have eliminated all which is impossible, whatever remains, however improbable, must be the truth', so let's get to it. I'll talk to Mr Lazarus about Ellie Bosa and see if I get a reaction."

The door of the briefing room opened, and Inspector Evans poked his head around the corner. "Detective Sergeant Grant, there's something I'd like you to look at in organised crime when you have a minute.

Don't want to stretch you too thin but I suspect that you are just the man for the job."

Grant nodded that he'd be there in a moment—unsure of just how far the Lazarus case would run.

* * *

Rose and Wiebbe were surprised at just how perky Lazarus was, when they visited him as he sat up in his hospital bed. It appeared that he had lost none of his charm and the nurses were enjoying his flirtations and mischievous teasing.

"I really don't know how he does it," Wiebbe said to Rose as they were leaving the ward. "He is an absolute rogue!"

"Yes, but apparently a loveable one and a very wealthy one. He's been showering the nurses with chocolates and little gifts."

"He looked pretty good for a man who only a few days ago was playing the part of a frail old sea dog on his final voyage," Wiebbe said.

"That's Lazarus for you." Rose, too, had apparently fallen under his spell.

They practically collided with Detective Sergeant Grant as they left the ward.

"Hello you two, how's Mr Lazarus doing?"

Wiebbe was first to respond, "Remarkably well it appears. He's got the nurses running around for him and is in good spirits."

"Did he say if he remembered anything?"

"No. The whole episode is a blank. One moment he was at his front door, the next he was waking up in crisp white sheets in a hospital bed."

"And how's your mum, Rose? She seemed quite shaken up when I met her at your house."

"Yes, she was, wasn't she? But then again, it must have come as a huge shock to her. She's OK now, calmed down. I wouldn't worry about her. She'll be fine."

"Did Mr Lazarus give you the key to his house?"

"Yes, we're going to go over there now to tidy things up."

"You're good friends to have," Grant said as they turned to leave and walked off down the corridor.

* * *

"Ah, Detective Sergeant Grant."

"How are you feeling, Mr Lazarus?"

"I'm feeling remarkably good, considering I've been shot!" Lazarus said as he propped himself up against the pile of pillows that had been puffed up behind him by the attentive nurses.

Grant smiled, pulled up a chair and sat down, taking out his notebook and pencil. "How's the memory? Anything come to mind? Anything at all?"

"I'm afraid not, Detective. As I said to Rose and Wiebbe a moment ago, one minute I'm at my front door and the next I am waking up in a hospital bed."

"Don't worry too much but anything would help, and one memory can often trigger others. So something that might seem innocuous, a shadow, a perfume, a noise, anything at all really, would help."

Grant had deliberately used the word perfume rather than smell and watched Lazarus's eyes for the slightest reaction, but there was none.

"Do you know Mrs Ellie Bosa?"

Lazarus's face twitched almost imperceptibly before answering. "Mr Bosa's wife. He's my lawyer in Honiara. I think I've only met her a few times. Why do you ask?"

"She's here in Perth, staying at the Parmelia Hilton."

"With Joe Bosa?"

"No. He's back in Honiara.

"I asked her if she knew of anyone that might want to do you harm. But she said she'd only met you once, and that was before you set sail for Fremantle with Rose and Wiebbe."

"Ah yes, it probably was just the once, come to think of it. Please excuse me, I'm not thinking all that clearly at the moment. Must be the drugs." He managed a weak smile.

Lazarus was lying, of that much Grant was sure. His rapid transformation from a sprightly patient into a frail old sea dog—was almost comical.

"Surely I'm not famous enough for someone to take out a contract on me, Detective? I'm just an old man with some small business interests, providing a comfortable living in retirement. No, I think you're barking up the wrong tree there. I've probably ruffled a few feathers in my business dealings over the years but, then again, who hasn't? Certainly nothing so egregious as to invite a 'hit', as they say in the movies.

"You could give Mr Bosa a call. I have his contact details in my phone, but I'm sure he'll tell you the same thing."

"I will. Mrs Bosa kindly supplied those contact details already but thank you, in any case."

Lazarus closed his eyes and let out a sigh.

"I think I may have over-exerted myself, Detective, or perhaps it's the painkillers. Would you excuse me? We can continue this conversation at a later date. I'm afraid I'm quite exhausted. Maybe when my mind is a little less foggy, I'll remember something of value."

"Thank you, Mr Lazarus. I think you're right. It's easy to get confused with those drugs in your system."

Lazarus laid back as Grant stood up to leave.

All Lazarus could think of was his own safety. "Detective Sergeant Grant, do you think that there might be a real threat to my life? Because if you do, I'd like some police protection outside my room."

"In the absence of any information to suggest that, I can't afford the manpower unless of course, there's something you'd like to tell me?"

Lazarus hesitated. "No Detective, nothing at all. I guess I'm just being paranoid, having been shot and all."

"Get some rest, Mr Lazarus," Grant said, and turned and left.

This was going nowhere fast, he thought. The Inspector had pushed a major organised crime investigation his way, involving WA Bikie gangs. Unless there were significant developments arising from their door-to-door enquiries, this would have to be put on the back burner.

* * *

Stupid, stupid, stupid, Lazarus said to himself as he lay in his hospital bed. Memories flooded back into his mind from that night. So, Ellie was here in Fremantle and armed with a gun. He thought he had recognised the voice—and her perfume—as she had called out to him. He had always planned to double-cross her, so maybe he had got what he deserved. But she was a loose cannon for sure. He just never imagined that she'd take it so personally. After all, her husband was getting his fair share of the gold, and she'd have trouble spending it all in her lifetime. No—this was personal. She was a woman scorned. But more worryingly, she was a woman scorned with a gun.

Chapter 39 Fremantle Hospital

Lazarus woke early the following morning and called the ward nurse over. "How long before I can leave?" he said.

"You're doing really well, Mr Lazarus. The doctor thinks you may be well enough to be discharged tomorrow, providing there's someone at home to look after you. If not, I can ask the social worker to arrange some home help. Lucky for you, there are no broken bones, and the flesh will heal pretty quickly. You'll be coming back to get your dressing changed, of course, and you'll have to keep up your physio to make a full recovery. But, as I said, it's all looking good."

"I feel fine. I'd like to go home today."

"Oh, I'm not sure about that. Of course, I can't stop you, but I really think you should talk to the doctor first, before making any rash decisions."

Seeing the doctor in the corridor, Lazarus motioned to him and asked the nurse, "Would you ask him to come over and talk with me now, please?"

Following Lazarus's gaze, she appeared slightly flustered. "Of course," she said, as she turned around to intercept the young doctor and explain the situation.

"Now young fella me lad, what's all this nonsense about discharging yourself?" the doctor said as he sat on the edge of Lazarus's bed.

“I feel fine, Doc, really. I hate being in hospital and would feel so much more comfortable in my own little cottage. Rose and Wiebbe can take care of me. Not that the staff here are awful. I mean, they have been wonderful, but I really want to go home.”

“One more night. And if you feel the same in the morning, we can let you go then. What do you say?”

“I don’t believe you can keep me here against my will, can you?”

“Well, no, of course not, but if you were to go home today, it would be against medical advice, and you’d have to sign a waiver of liability. So just to be on the safe side, one more night isn’t going to kill you now, is it?”

“Get the waiver. I’ll get dressed.”

The young registrar was resigned to Lazarus’s stubborn insistence. He realised that there was no persuading him otherwise.

“Alright, Mr Lazarus. Look, I’ll give you some painkillers to take home and a script to get some more.”

A short while later, he returned to find Lazarus sitting impatiently in the chair next to his bed.

“There’s some paracetamol and tapentadol. Take the paracetamol four times a day to keep any pain or discomfort, at bay. If it gets bad, then use the strong stuff. It’s best, however, not to wait. Keep on top of it. There are no medals for suffering in silence.

“Of course, no driving or operating machinery whilst on the strong stuff,” the young doctor smiled.

The nurse provided a discharge form which consisted of a number of check boxes, designed as much to absolve the hospital of any liability as to provide guidance to the patient for post-operative care.

Lazarus thought that it was highly unlikely he’d be driving anytime soon, given that he only had one good arm.

He ordered a taxi to take him back to his cottage. Soon enough, he was wheeled down to the pick-up point, where a slightly distraught discharge nurse explained that she was supposed to hand him over to a responsible person. She needed to get them to sign the form to say that they accepted responsibility for his care.

"Don't worry about me, lass," he said, "No one's going to come back and sue you—I can promise you that."

Lazarus eased himself out of the wheelchair and into the back seat of the taxi.

"Change of plans," he said to the driver as he pulled away. "Take me to the Parmelia Hilton."

Chapter 40 Mrs Bosa

Arriving at the Parmelia Hilton, Lazarus realised his mistake. The taxi company might have a record of his new destination, and whatever plans he had for Ellie Bosa would have to be changed.

The best he could hope for, was a peace treaty with his would-be assassin. Given his current state of health, he was in no position to engage in a physical confrontation. No, this would require all of his charm and guile.

As she opened the hotel suite door, he saw it—the look on her face was a picture. Fear, love, anger, guilt and sympathy all fighting for dominance, all flickering across her features in a single, breathless moment.

"Ellie, my love," Lazarus beamed, with what he hoped was his most innocent schoolboy smile. Dropping his head, he looked up at her with his practiced puppy dog eyes.

Ellie was lost for words as her jaw literally dropped.

"May I come in?"

Ellie stepped back from the door and Lazarus silently entered her suite, making his way to the large bay window which overlooked the Swan River.

"Oh, Lazarus, I'm so sorry," she said as she started to move toward him.

"I forgive you, my sweet. How could I have been so foolish? The love of my life. I was in a bad place, and I made some bad decisions…"

"I shot you! I could have killed you!" Ellie was wringing her hands.

"Yes, my dear… but you didn't. And I think—perhaps—I may have deserved it anyway. Being shot that is, not being killed." He made an attempt at a guilty smile. "You don't still have a gun, do you?" he glanced a little nervously around the suite.

"Oh, Lazarus." Ellie moved toward him and he braced for the pain as she stretched out her arms in preparation for a bear hug.

Lazarus managed to lift his injured arm above hers, not without a little discomfort, as she squeezed him. Her ample breasts pressing hard against his chest, her face pressed against his. Tears were flooding down her cheeks.

"Ellie, would you take this old sea dog back if he asked you?"

"Lazarus! I tried to kill you!" she said, as she disengaged from her hug and looked at him incredulously.

"I know, but you missed and, well, we make a good team, don't you think?"

Ellie was stunned but her mind was still racing. What was this loveable rogue up to now? she thought.

She decided to play along. After all, Lazarus still had money and, with a little judicious play on her part, she was even more keen to relieve him of it than ever before.

"You are a rogue, a pirate, a philanderer, a thief, a …a… a…"

"So, the answer is, yes?"

"No! Of course it's not yes. How could you even begin to imagine…"

Lazarus moved towards her and slipped his good right arm behind her, moving his hand up her spine to her hair, and gripping it firmly as he planted his lips against hers.

Ellie struggled—just enough, she hoped—to convince Lazarus she was genuine in her attempt to escape the embrace, before finally succumbing… and surrendering to his kiss.

There was a raw lust in her as she pushed hard against him and, despite the pain from his left arm, Lazarus felt it too.

There was an almost comical disrobing as Lazarus groaned and winced, as Ellie helped him get naked and then joined him in bed. She was surprised at just how lustful she felt as she mounted him and rode him.

Lying next to him that afternoon, she played gently with the hairs on his chest and wondered how on earth this was all going to play out.

Chapter 41 Lazarus is Missing

I felt as though I was interrupting something very important when I asked the ward clerk "What do you mean, he checked himself out?"

"Mr Lazarus was quite insistent, Mr Hawkins."

"Well, did he say where he was going?"

"Yes, I think he said he was going home. Back to his cottage in Fremantle. The discharge nurse heard him talking to the taxi driver before he got into the car."

I sighed with frustration. This was, however, just like Lazarus to disrupt the system.

"Thank you," I said and turned to Kate. "I think we'd better go down to Freo and pay our loveable rogue a visit."

"Why can't he, for once, just once, behave like a normal human being?" Kate asked rhetorically as we got into our car.

Arriving at his cottage, we were surprised to see it locked up and Lazarus was nowhere to be seen. Kate's mobile rang. It was Wiebbe.

"He discharged himself?" I heard her say.

"No, we're there now. He's not here, and it doesn't look as though he's been here either."

* * *

"I am sorry, sweetie, I just can't stay here a moment longer," Ellie said to Rose as she fussed about packing her bags in her room at the Parmelia Hilton. "Your father needs me back in Honiara and well, to be honest, things haven't been right between us for some time now, and I need to go back and sort things out."

Ellie's comments came as no surprise to Rose—who had often wondered how the marriage had survived as long as it had.

To her credit, Ellie had tried valiantly to replace Rose's mother after her death but there was always an unspoken void between them. Rose had been just five years of age when her mum had succumbed to breast cancer. The doctors in Honiara had caught it too late and there was little they could do to prevent a rapid decline. It was less than a year between diagnosis and her death. When her father had re-married, Ellie had moved into the family home.

Joe, her father, had insisted that Rose call Ellie, Mum. Rose's stubborn refusal to do so waned after a heart to heart with her dad, who had explained to her that they were trying to make a new life together and whilst no one could ever replace her real mum, she now had a new mum who loved her very much.

Her father had had tears in his eyes as they spoke and, as they ran silently down his cheeks, her resolve melted and she reluctantly forced herself to call Ellie Mum. It wasn't for her, but for her dad.

"Did you know Mr Lazarus has gone missing after he was shot?" Rose said, keen to change the subject.

"Really? No, I didn't know that, but I can't say I'm surprised. He always seemed to be a bit shifty to me, and I suspect there is more than one person who would like a piece of him!"

"So, you don't think it was a robbery that went wrong?"

"Rose, sweetie, I really don't know what to think any more. I just know that I need to get home."

Ellie was hiding something, of that, Rose was sure. Her reluctance to talk about the shooting seemed odd, since everyone in Fremantle appeared to have an opinion on it.

"Now, don't you worry about me. And don't worry about the wedding. It will all sort itself out."

"Mum, Wiebbe and I haven't even talked about getting married. We're happy with things the way they are for now."

Ellie appeared not to hear what Rose was saying.

"It's important for your future, Rose, that you get things formalised. You don't want to find yourself cast out on the street barefoot, penniless and homeless if things don't work out. Trust me, it can happen and while it's all a bed of roses now, things can change in an instant."

Rose leant on the lid of the last of Ellie's cases, snapping the locks closed, contemplating her last comment.

"Mum, it's not like that in Australia," she said.

"Oh Rose, you are so beautifully naïve." She placed her hands on the side of Rose's cheeks and pulled her towards her, kissing her gently on her forehead. "How I long for the innocence of youth!"

"Will you at least say goodbye to the Hawkins before you go?"

"Oh, my dear, I'd really rather not. This whole episode has been too traumatic for me, and I just need to get away."

The phone rang in her suite.

"Yes, please send him up now," Ellie said before replacing the receiver.

"Well, sweetie, my ride is here. Don't worry, I'll be back soon enough. It's really just a little bump in the road."

"It'll be OK, Mum. Wiebbe and I love each other, and you know that love conquers all."

Ellie reached out and hugged her in a stilted embrace. A gentle tap on the door announced the arrival of the porter, thankfully interrupting the awkwardness of the moment.

Rose followed Ellie to the reception area and watched her slip into the back seat of the taxi. She didn't look back. It was the last time Rose would see her stepmother.

* * *

Back in Honiara, it soon became apparent that Joe Bosa had used all of his legal training to protect his family's fortune and leave Ellie with, according to her, nothing.

"I don't give a fuck about a piece of paper!" Ellie screamed at Joe. "You owe me, Joe Bosa! I'll get what's mine and you'll get what's coming to you!"

"It's over, Ellie."

"Over! Over! I'll tell you when it's over! You'll see! Now get out of my house!"

"This is my house, Ellie. If anyone is leaving, it's you, and right now!"

Ellie looked at Joe incredulously. If she had had the pistol that she shot Lazarus with in her hand, she would have emptied its chambers into the smiling, self-serving, fat face of her corpulent husband, there and then.

"Sol, get the car! I'll be staying at the hotel," turning to Joe she said pointedly, "at Mr Bosa's expense!"

Joe sat down heavily in the armchair as the front door slammed so hard it cracked the plaster around the frame. He poured himself a large scotch and picked up the phone to dial reception at the hotel.

"Mrs Bosa will be staying with you for a few days," he said. "Please ensure that her room charges are debited to my account for one week, after which she will be responsible for her own charges." He replaced the receiver and took a large swig from his glass.

The week of grace would give Ellie time to sort herself out. Get a rental somewhere and arrange for her clothes and personal possessions to be sent over. It was the least he could do.

He knew of her philandering and her secret personal bank account but had chosen to turn a blind eye to them. It was, after all, the way of the Islands, but as they had grown increasingly apart, the animosity between them had grown ever stronger.

Bosa was comfortable that the pre-nuptial agreement—and the various legal structures he had established for his business interests—protected him and his family's fortune. Ellie had brought a small dowry with her into the marriage, but he had insisted that this was hers and, as far as he knew, she hadn't touched it. She would be wealthy by the standards of the islanders and really want for nothing, but of course, that was a far cry from the lifestyle he had afforded her.

Ellie was quick to engage her own lawyer but shocked to find that her claims barely covered their fees. Bosa had been meticulous in his work.

Ellie's mind now turned to her own survival, and that meant finding Lazarus—fast. Securing her future wasn't just important now… it was critical. Every second counted, and the stakes couldn't be higher.

Lazarus had seduced her in her own hotel room. The fact that she had shot him seemed to do little to dampen their ardour. Could this be love? A volatile love that was for sure, but why did love always have to smell of roses and not cordite, she thought with a smile.

That bastard had disappeared again.

Lazarus had a bolthole in Fremantle and was known around Honiara, well, at least up until the time he had faked his own death. He hadn't returned to his cottage in Freo after their tryst and, whilst there had been plenty of places he could have sailed to in his yacht, that was still sitting seemingly abandoned in a pen at FSC. The truth of the matter was, it was in desperate need of a re-fit before it could be considered seaworthy again.

A few calls and exchange of monies to Immigration in Honiara indicated that he hadn't returned to the Solomons, so that led Ellie to recall pillow talk about his upbringing in England. She realised that the bastard had dual nationality. Two passports. Shit.

Another call to Immigration and another bribe found out that he had used his British passport to leave Australia on a flight to Dubai.

The net was widening. Theoretically, he could have flown from Dubai to any one of nearly 30 countries in Europe, but something told her he was more likely to be in England. Now where the fuck in England would he be? Where the fuck was his hometown?

Ellie wanted to get as far away from Joe Bosa as possible, but more importantly, she wanted to find Lazarus. The thing was, did Lazarus want to find Ellie and if he did, what was likely to happen?

Ellie was under no illusions. She had doubted his intentions when he had turned up at her suite at the Parmelia, but lust and a need to feel forgiven had overcome her fear. The only reason he hadn't killed her there and then, she reasoned retrospectively, was because he just couldn't get away with it. Did he have a contract out on her now? Was seeking him out now such a good idea? Would he find a way of getting to her before she got to him?

Lazarus had to die, that much was clear. This time, she would get it right and make sure the bastard was dead. But before he died, she had to somehow steal his fortune in gold.

Ellie decided to hide her trail as much as possible, flying to Europe via Turkey and weaving her way between countries within the EU with few border controls.

Once in the UK, she would appoint a private detective to find him. It couldn't be that hard. Of course, she'd need protection and a weapon. It wasn't that easy to get a pistol in England, but there were plenty of opportunities in her first port of call in Eastern Europe.

Ellie disappeared from the Solomons.

* * *

In Fremantle, Grant's team had been forced to shelve the Lazarus investigation following the disappearance of their only witness to the crime, Lazarus himself. There was a record of him leaving Australia a few days after he'd checked himself out of the hospital, but with other pressing priorities, Grant had been forced to consign the investigation to the archives.

Chapter 42 Sea Dragon

We never did see Lazarus again after he checked himself out of the hospital. I liked to imagine that he travelled away to some tropical island to spend his days in the arms of an island girl, or two, knowing him. Living off his gold or perhaps sitting in a bar somewhere, telling tales of pirates, treasure and love lost. He was a rogue for sure but as Rose said, a loveable rogue.

I was informed by Detective Sergeant Grant that he'd left Australia and may have gone to the UK but hadn't left a forwarding address, so the case had been shelved. Something inside me wondered if the UK was just a stepping stone to somewhere more exotic, a red herring maybe.

His cottage had been maintained by a team of gardeners and housekeepers but after a few months, their visits became less frequent and eventually, a year down the track, the property was sold. I discovered, after a bit of digging, that the proceeds from the sale had been paid to Rose's orphanage in the Solomons. Typical of Lazarus, in a way. Always full of surprises.

That year saw the final recasting—and sale—of the Nazi gold. As agreed, we purchased some disastrous investments in Honiara which, of course, benefited Mr Bosa enormously—to the tune of several million dollars. Thus, our end of the deal had been completed. And we settled down to what we imagined would be a quiet, comfortable life.

Lazarus's yacht had been seized by FSC as a lien against unpaid pen fees. After some protracted negotiations, we bought it from the club and spent a small fortune refitting it for an ocean voyage. No expense was spared. It was completely gutted: new mast, rigging, sails, engine, genset, electronics, paint and antifoul. The interior fit-out alone was over $200,000. In total, we must have spent well over half a million on her.

It would have been cheaper to buy a new one by the time we'd finished but there was something about the *Sea Dragon* that held a special place in our hearts. We spent a long time discussing whether we should re-name her. Wiebbe was insistent that, if we did so, we would need to find a virgin to piss in the bilges—in order to appease the wrath of Neptune. We joked that finding a virgin in Fremantle was problematic, so we agreed to stay with the name *Sea Dragon.*

When at last she was lifted back in the water she was the envy of just about every member of the club, including the stink boat section.

Kate cracked a bottle of Veuve Clicquot over the bowsprit, much to the consternation of the shipwrights who had polished her to a mirror finish. We were unaware of a figure watching from the shadows.

I looked at Wiebbe and Rose and passed them the keys. "Happy anniversary," I said.

"Whoa! Dad! You're joking!"

"Take her, Wiebbe. You and Rose can do that trip of a lifetime before you start your family. You know, once kids come along, your priorities change. Go now, while you have the chance."

Rose flung her arms around me, then hugged the breath out of Kate.

"Thanks Dad. Are you sure about this?"

"Of course, Wiebbe. I have absolutely loved refitting her, but she's a young man's boat and needs a young couple to sail her. I just have one request. Could you drop Mum and me off in the Abrolhos when you decide to leave?"

* * *

Unbeknown to us, Lazarus had quietly returned to Australia on a fleeting visit. He had snuck into the yard of FSC the day-before she was lifted back into the water, as the shipwrights and labourers had knocked off. He had climbed aboard the *Sea Dragon* whilst she was still on her hard-stand and had meticulously examined every inch of her, inside and out. Somewhat begrudgingly—he admitted to himself—they had done a pretty good job. Actually, she was better than new.

After a thorough examination he sat himself down at the helm and grasped the wheel in both hands, looking up at the naked mast and rigging, with the eye of an experienced skipper. He let his imagination run freely as, once again, his spirit soared, and he imagined himself on the ocean with a following breeze.

If she'd been in the water, there would have been little to stop him casting off and stealing her. Not so much stealing as repossessing. *Sea Dragon* was still his after all, he reasoned.

A noise from the adjacent hard-stand shattered his reverie as one of the power section owners working on his own vessel exhorted a flood of profanities—as he attempted and failed—to reach some inaccessible bolt head, on his flybridge.

Lazarus didn't recognize him, and the man paid little attention to Lazarus, which suited him just fine, but also made him realise that he had spent more time on *Sea Dragon* than he had planned.

There was, however, one last thing to do before he left her. A parting gift for Wiebbe and Rose, or perhaps a final atonement for himself.

Out of his pocket he retrieved a soiled piece of waxed sailcloth, and carefully unfolded it to reveal a jewel-encrusted, golden brooch. It was the brooch that Michael and Kate had found on East Wallabi Island—the brooch that he had stolen from them so many years ago. He had never had the heart to sell it, always believing that it held its own destiny—like Tolkien's one ring to bind them, maybe. He was but a caretaker for it. Today the circle was complete, and he felt it was time to pass it on to its new custodians.

Moving down into the cabin, he remembered stories of young sailors taking their girlfriends down into the bowels of their ships to 'see the golden rivet', a mythical rivet of pure gold hammered into the keel of the ship, during the keel laying ceremony. Of course, it was little more than an excuse to find some privacy for some hanky-panky. The thought made him smile as he lifted the floor hatch to reveal the keel bolts which attached the lead-filled keel to the hull. It may not be discovered for a while, he thought, but then again, as the keel had only recently been re-fitted it would be incumbent upon the owners to check the torque on the bolts after a couple of trips. He carefully placed it snugly between the bolt heads and wished that he could be there to see their faces when they discovered it.

His hand shook as his fingers left the package in place, reluctant to let it go. He felt like Baggins in the *Lord of the Rings*, letting go of his 'precious'. A reluctant release. A weight lifted. And yet, something hollow in the space it left behind.

A sudden noise from the stink boat next door and an outpouring of yet more expletives, indicated it was time to go. His fingers tightened into a fist as he strengthened his resolve and replaced the hatch. As he turned to leave the cabin, it was all that he could do not to look back. Had he done so, he was unsure whether his resolve to leave the brooch behind, would have held.

Chapter 43 Lazarus's Legacy

Sea trials for the *Sea Dragon* had revealed the usual bugs which needed fixing up, but overall, these were minor. The shipwrights had done a great job and she handled beautifully off the Western Australian coast, cutting through the waves as water slipped around her highly polished hull.

Wiebbe and Rose had felt like they were once again at home as they sailed out past Rottnest Island into the deep blue waters over the Perth Canyon. A spinnaker made the most of a strong easterly in the morning before it veered around to bring them back to shore in the afternoon.

Kate and I were dockside when they returned, eager to see how she had performed.

"Better than new, Dad!" Wiebbe said excitedly as I threw the pen lines to Rose on the bow.

"So, when are we off then?"

"Well, the weather's looking great, so we were thinking next week."

I looked at Kate and smiled. "Up for an adventure?"

"Oh, Mr Hawkins, I thought you'd never ask!"

"We'd better check the torque on the rigging bolts, and don't forget the keel bolts. I take it that you gave her a flogging over the canyon?" I said, as Rose was making everything secure.

"Yes, Dad, that'd be great. I have the settings somewhere on board. Those guys at Fremantle Shipwrights did a great job."

"So they bloody well should have, the amount they charged!" Kate said, only half tongue in cheek.

"The torque wrench is in the garage at home. I'll come down in the morning and make an early start," I said as I helped Rose off the boat.

"Yeah, no worries, Dad, that'd be great, but don't go thinking you can climb up the mast. I'll do the high bolts. I'll see you here at, say, eight, before it gets too hot."

The sad reality was that many sailors failed to check their keel bolts for tension and corrosion as often as they should. On at least one such occasion, to my knowledge, a keel had fallen off, resulting in a fatal accident.

It was 7am the following morning when I found myself dockside. I should not have been surprised to see Wiebbe and Rose already hard at it. Wiebbe was high in the rigging, sitting on a bosun's chair, checking not only the stays but every nut and bolt on the mast.

"I thought as much!" I shouted up to Wiebbe.

"Afternoon, Dad!" he said, mimicking the way I would theatrically look at my watch when he had turned up later than expected.

It was just like Wiebbe to get an early start on the day. Part of me realised that he was also wanting to ensure that I didn't do any high rope work.

Rose took one wrap off the winch and let him down smoothly to level of the radar just above the spreaders. "Last thing to check," he said, as the torque wrench clicked on the nuts holding the dome secure against the mast.

Wiebbe stood up as soon as his feet touched the deck. "Thank you, sweetheart," he said as he kissed Rose on the cheek.

"Cup of coffee, Mr Hawkins?"

We sat in the lounge sipping coffee and going over the work that needed to be done, and plans for our departure the following week.

Wiebbe said, "I managed to borrow another torque wrench from the guy who was on the hard stand next to ours."

"What, the stink boat owner? I did wonder," I said.

"Come on Dad, he's a rough diamond but not all stink boat owners hate yachties."

I smiled. The banter between power boat owners and yachties was the same the world over, but at the end of the day, we were all sailors and would always help each other out if we could.

"OK," I said, draining the last of my coffee, "I'll start below on the engine, genset, keel bolts and desalinator mounts."

"Great. There's a checklist here with torque settings for each bolt, so just mark them off as you do them, so none get left behind. The back bolts on the genset are a pig to get to, so call me or Rose if you need a hand. Rose can squeeze into incredibly small spaces."

He looked at Rose, who returned his smile and said, "Well, at least I'm useful for something!"

It was with a sense of annoyance that I lifted the floor-hatch over the keel bolts to see a dirty piece of sail cloth wedged between them. How could anyone have been so lazy? I thought to myself. Such materials could trap water and lead to accelerated corrosion.

It was only when I reached down to retrieve it that I felt the weight within. A shiver ran up my spine as I unwrapped the parcel and saw the brooch. I had last seen it on the Abrolhos Islands, moments before Lazarus had stolen it from Kate and myself.

"You bastard," I uttered under my breath as I stood up and made my way to the cockpit. I glanced around the yard, half expecting to see Lazarus looking down on us, but there was no one there.

"What have you got there, Mr Hawkins?" Rose said as she was joined by Wiebbe. "Oh, my! That's beautiful," she said as she plucked the brooch from my hand and held it up to the sky.

Sunlight sparkled through the emeralds, rubies, and diamonds.

Wiebbe and Rose both looked at me expectantly.

"Fucking Lazarus," I said.

* * *

That evening we all sat down around the kitchen table as Kate and I took turns to reverently examine the brooch.

"It's a part of the story we haven't told you before, Wiebbe," Kate said, looking at me as though seeking permission to reveal that dark moment in our past. I nodded for her to continue.

"I believe that the brooch is part of the fabled treasure of the *Aagtekerke*. Your dad and I uncovered it in the Abrolhos Islands where we first met. Lazarus was with us as you know, but what you don't know is that he basically cracked our skulls, left us for dead, and made off with it."

Wiebbe and Rose were stunned to silence. By the time Kate had finished, Wiebbe and Rose were ready to find Lazarus and send him quick sharp to Davy Jones' locker.

"Calm down, you two," I said. "That's water under the bridge now, and if we'd wanted to hold Lazarus to account, we'd have done so a long time ago."

"So, what now?" Wiebbe said.

"Well, the brooch is obviously yours now. How he managed to get it there, I don't know. You could ask the shipwrights if they'd left it there on his instruction, but I'd put money on it that Lazarus himself has been on board. You know, I just had a feeling as soon as I found it that he was watching us. It was really spooky. I mean, I physically felt his presence."

"We don't even know if he's in Australia," Kate said.

I looked at Kate who suddenly checked her anger. "You're right. That bastard," she said.

"Do you think that it's good luck to keep it? I mean, maybe it is a talisman. Lazarus obviously never sold it. I wonder why not?"

"Maybe he didn't have the heart, or maybe it was just too risky," Kate said. "You see, the intrinsic value of the brooch would be far greater than its bullion or gem value if it was broken down. If you could link its provenance to the *Aagtekerke*, it would be priceless."

"I think we should donate it to the Maritime Museum," Rose said. "I really don't feel comfortable keeping it, and even less so knowing that Lazarus violated our boat with his presence."

"It's not that easy, Rose. Firstly, donating it anonymously would raise all sorts of questions about its origins and authenticity. Its real value comes from knowing it's from the *Aagtekerke* and establishing that provenance from an anonymous donation would be speculative at best."

"Then all we need is a marine archaeologist to discover it in situ," Wiebbe said, looking at his mum.

"I'm not sure I could maintain the deception for very long," Kate said. Perhaps it would be better for you to find it. I can give you the supposed location of the *Aagtekerke*, well, the site where they found the ivory tusks in any case, and maybe you could 'find' your brooch there?"

"Sounds like a plan, Mum. I suspect that it will result in another extensive maritime archaeological excavation on the site, but hey, you have always said that more excavation work needed to be done!"

"Isn't that illegal?" Rose said.

"Only if you get caught!" we replied in unison.

Part IV

Lazarus's Story

Chapter 44 Tring

Sitting in my little cottage on the outskirts of Tring in Hertfordshire, I can see through the window across the field. The leaves on the trees are starting to turn to hues of brown and crimson, as autumn approaches.

And so it is with my own life, as I enter my autumnal years. All too soon, winter will be upon us, and my life will be over.

It's strange, even now in my 90s, I feel that dying is something that happens to other people and could never happen to me.

Of course, I have been blessed with good health and despite the abuse I have subjected my body to over the years, I can say that I am a medical marvel. My doctors say I have the constitution of a 65-year-old, and they're not wrong.

Now the air is filled with the scent of mushrooms and cow dung—as the farmer spreads muck across the pasture at the end of my garden— bringing hope and new life from death and decay.

You get to thinking about such things as you get older. How you will be remembered and what you have done with your life, and so without feeling too melancholy about it, I have decided to document my life and— if time permits—secure my own place in the history books. The worst that could possibly happen is that I leave the world without making a difference.

So, how to begin this memoir? To call it a book would be far too pretentious even for me, so a memoir it will be. It's likely to take a while, as my left arm and hand are so weak these days that

I am restricted to typing almost exclusively with one hand. A secretary that I could dictate to might help but in some ways, I want to spend time reading and re-reading the written word to ensure it is the unabashed truth.

Truth, now, that has been a strange concept to me over my life…

"Dad, what are you up to?"

"David, don't you knock before entering my study anymore?"

"Sorry, Dad. There's a Detective Chief Inspector Barratt at the front door, asking for you."

'Dad' now there's a surprise. Yes, I have a son, a prodigal son as it happens; the product of a fling in the Solomon Islands nearly half a century ago. He sought me out after I returned to England and in many ways, he has become my closest friend. His dark blue eyes and shock of black hair, now greying at the temples, had been a sure-fire seduction for any female foolish enough to cross his path. He's mine. No doubt about that. Like father, like son.

I straightened my back and aching knees as I stood and made my way from my study, down the hallway to the front door.

"Inspector Barratt? I'm Lazarus. I understand you're looking for me?"

Barratt looked to be a man in his late fifties or early 60s, his hair greying, his face lined with the scars of a life in the force. His Marks and Spencer suit was clearly past its best-before date, but it was apparently going to have to last until his retirement which I guessed was not that far off.

"Yes, sir. I'm following up on a cold case review concerning the disappearance of a Mrs Ellie Bosa. May I come in?"

"Please do," I said. "Would you like a cup of tea?"

"That would be lovely, thank you."

"David, why don't you put the kettle on while the Inspector and I sit in the lounge?"

"Yes, Dad. You want biscuits as well?"

I nodded to David as he retreated into the kitchen.

My lounge room was quite small but comfortably attired, with soft furnishings sitting on a deep pile Axminster carpet. The walls were adorned with memories of my life, a photo of me at the helm of *Sea Dragon*. I forget who took it now. A beautiful painting of Fremantle Round House and a seascape by a local artist who captured the wind and waves perfectly, as they billowed the sails of a clipper from the late nineteenth century. My old sextant sat next to some photos in their silver frames on top of the bookcase which lined one wall. It contained an eclectic range of books, ranging from astronomy to archaeology, business, and a fair smattering of fiction. I do like Wilbur Smith.

"Now, how can I help you, Inspector?" I said.

"We've had a request from the Solomon Island Police to interview you in relation to the disappearance of Mrs Ellie Bosa some twenty years ago. It's a cold case review which they are conducting."

I drew a deep breath. Time was not on my side, but if I was determined to tell the truth, then now would appear to be the right time, although I was not quite ready to tell the whole truth to this gentleman. I needed to talk with him a little while longer to get the measure of the man, but something told me that this stranger was a person sent to me for my confession.

We sat in our comfortable lounge, me in my favourite chair under my standard lamp and Barratt on the settee.

I began, "I first met Ellie when I was in the Solomon Islands. She was married to Joe Bosa, my lawyer, as it happens."

"Yes, sir," Barratt said whilst fumbling in his pocket to retrieve his notebook and a recording device. "But before we begin, in a case of this nature, it's standard operating procedure these days, for me to read you the Police Caution. I also want to tell you that, should you decide to talk with me, it will be regarded as a voluntary interview. You don't have to answer any of my questions and if you prefer, you can also have a lawyer or a support person present. I can come back at another time, or we can arrange a time for you to come down to the station with your lawyer or a support person."

"Inspector Barratt, I am well aware of my rights and presumption of innocence, and I am more than happy to co-operate with your investigation."

"Thank you, Mr Lazarus.

"May I have your full name?"

Lazarus smiled. It was a question he had been asked many times before but for as long as he could remember, he had always been; just Lazarus. In fact, all his documentation stated that single name.

"Just Lazarus," I said, "I know, it's a little unusual. You should try filling out forms without a first name or a surname! Sometimes I use Smith when I must but no, just Lazarus will do. Use it as you will."

Barratt took the small recording device and pressed the record button, entering the date and time of the interview, my name, and other details for the record. He also stated that the voluntary interview was being recorded. This seemed odd since the recording device sat between us, but I guessed it was part of Barratt's SOP.

"Am I under arrest, Inspector?" I said.

"No, sir."

"Will I get a copy of the tape?"

"It's a digital recording, Mr Lazarus, and depending on how we go, I'll be happy to provide you with a copy and a paper transcript if necessary."

My luck seemed to be holding. Here I was about to get a free secretarial service from the Hertfordshire County Police. I had better make this good. I smiled at the thought.

"As I said, Joe Bosa was my lawyer back in Honiara over a quarter of a century ago."

"Yes, sir, we're aware of that. That's one of the reasons we wanted to talk to you. You see, we have reason to believe that you and Mrs Bosa were having an affair, prior to her divorce and subsequent disappearance." Barratt stopped and sat silently, waiting for my response. I gave nothing away.

"Inspector Barratt, the Solomon Island community runs on gossip, rumour and hearsay. You won't have to look very hard to find as many stories as you like of infidelity, sunken treasure, and even murder. So, what are your reasons for believing that I had an affair with Mrs Bosa?"

Barratt had nothing, of that much I was sure, and I wasn't going to give him anything. Well, not just yet, in any case.

"Apparently, Mrs Bosa had a reputation as a bit of a party girl, which eventually led to an acrimonious divorce from her husband, Joe Bosa."

The term 'party girl' made me wince a little but Barratt appeared not to notice.

"Ah well, Inspector, there you have it. A jealous husband and a scornful wife. I'd look no further if I were you. I'm sorry I couldn't help you."

The door of the lounge room opened to a clinking of cups and saucers as David entered, carrying a tray.

"Tea?"

"Thank you, David."

"Perhaps you're right, Mr Lazarus. But Mr Bosa came up clean, and it appears that Mrs Bosa made her way to Europe and possibly on to the UK. The Solomon Island Police seem to think that she was looking for you."

"Oh my, that was so long ago. I'm afraid I really can't recall now. But maybe I could refer back to my journals and something will spring to mind? Perhaps I could do some digging and call you in a week or so?"

I wanted time to think, and if need be, time to arrange my affairs. I also wanted to set myself a deadline. A target if you like, to get my story straight, warts and all.

Barratt settled back in the settee and realised that this was going nowhere fast.

"That would be most useful if you could," he said as he removed a business card from his pocket. "Please call me if you remember anything that may be of help.

"Interview terminated at 11.05 am."

It was obvious that Barratt's heart just wasn't in it. The cold case desk was frequently seen as God's waiting room. A place where ageing officers worked before retirement. Of course, there were the young guns who specialised in forensics and loved to find DNA on a victim's clothing to nail a perpetrator, sometimes decades on from a crime they had committed. In this instance, however, it was a missing persons case from a place both physically and culturally about as far apart as you can get from the UK, with no body and no forensics.

Barratt drained his tea and stood to leave. I shook his hand firmly and looked him in the eye. Yes, I felt that this was a man I could trust.

* * *

I decided to do some background-checking into DCI Barratt. It was easy given his length of service with the Force and the internet's insatiable appetite for trivia.

It turns out that he was a career police officer from the time he left school, rising through the ranks through a mixture of good fortune, attention to detail and some good, old-fashioned policing that may well be frowned upon today. I knew I'd like him.

Not afraid to clip a young lad around the ear to set him back on the straight and narrow or take him home to mum for a good thrashing. His style was increasingly at odds with the values of today's Force, which was becoming more an extension to social services than an enforcer of the law.

At the height of his career, Barratt had solved a particularly intriguing and, at the time, scandalous murder in Berkhamsted, just down the road from me. He had brought together an eclectic team of young professionals to solve the case. It was in many ways his last hurrah, but it demonstrated to me his capacity to move with the times and embrace emerging technologies to get his man.

His relaxed paternalistic style was disarming, and I was sure that it had pulled in many a confession. Whilst he had now been shifted sideways in the twilight of his career, this highly decorated officer was still a force to be reckoned with.

I had to be careful not to underestimate him.

A week after our initial chat, I invited DCI Barratt to my home once more.

This occasion was a little more relaxed as we exchanged niceties.

David had placed a set of mahogany occasional tables strategically to accommodate tea and cakes for myself and the Inspector.

“You might be interested to hear what I have to say, Inspector, but I’m afraid it will take some time.”

“Ironically, I have all the time in the world, Mr Lazarus, so please don’t rush. Please also remember that last week I read you the police caution, so anything you do say may be admissible in a court of law.”

“I understand, Inspector, or may I call you Ignatius?”

Barratt looked decidedly uncomfortable and not a little surprised at the revelation that I had done my homework so thoroughly.

“Inspector, is fine,” he said.

Chapter 45 The Orphanage

So here we are. I have a self-imposed deadline for my confessional. Just what I needed.

I realise now that I am a survivor. Yes, against all odds, I have always found a way to survive. More than that, not only survive but to flourish and prosper, often at the expense of other's misfortune or—more often than not—through my artful manipulation of them.

I am an orphan. Not just in real terms, but in so many other ways.

I have rehearsed my confession carefully over the past few days and I admit I found it difficult to tell the truth even to myself. But this is my last chance to set the record straight, so I didn't want to muck it up.

* * *

I looked over at DCI Barratt sitting on the settee. "Inspector, what I am about to tell you may very well incriminate me. For my part, however, I have resolved within myself to tell the truth, the truth that is as far as I can recall. I'll tell you my story and leave the rest up to you. You'll have to decide for yourself how much of it is the reliable memory of a 92-year-old man, and just how much veracity you can attribute to some of my more 'colourful' memories.

"Many of those who would testify against me or corroborate my story are long gone, but here we are, and time is running out so, to coin a phrase, 'If you're sitting comfortably, then I'll begin.'"

I placed my steepled fingers against my lips and momentarily closed my eyes. Yes, the time was right. Opening my eyes, I stared at Barratt and took a deep breath.

Barratt clicked record on his digital recorder and settled back on the settee. He was experienced enough to know not to rush things.

"I was born in England in 1932, to an alcoholic mother and an abusive father. I'm not making excuses, you understand. Just laying down the foundations.

"My father thankfully abandoned both of us when I was just five years of age. I learned later in life that he was killed in World War II. It was matter-of-fact news to me and although I felt as though I should cry, I never did. He had beaten me with his leather belt on more than one occasion, usually when he returned home from the pub, drunk and penniless. I felt nothing for him. I had nothing left to give him, dead or alive.

"My mother had a nervous breakdown after my father left, and at the ripe old age of five years and two months, I was taken away by social services and placed in an orphanage in Royal Tunbridge Wells in Kent. I never saw her again."

Barratt sat in silence, knowing better than to interrupt a subject when the words were flowing freely.

This was a missing persons cold-case review. Many less experienced coppers might rush to the finish line. Barratt knew that listening to Lazarus's life story could not only flesh out the circumstances behind Ellie Bosa's disappearance but may also lead to new lines of enquiry, if the finish line was not yet in sight.

I took a moment to remember the good things about my mum. Her smiling face and rosy cheeks as she would tuck me into bed at night with my teddy bear. Those memories were becoming increasingly vague as I got older, and I realised that one day soon, they may fade altogether.

I continued, "The orphanage was annexed to the local boy's school. Words cannot begin to describe the brutality of those institutions. The orphanage building itself was designed by some Victorian architect called Wichcord, in the early 19th century. Apparently, he also designed the Kent Lunatic Asylum, later renamed Oakwood Psychiatric Hospital, and the Maidstone County Jail, all of which may give you a bit of an insight into his architectural style.

"Grey skies and a perpetual drizzle coated the orphanage's granite façade and instilled in me a terrifying foreboding of what was to come.

"I remember vividly being unceremoniously dumped at the front door, clutching my small brown leather-look suitcase. It contained all my worldly possessions, a spare set of clothes and my striped pyjamas. I held my threadbare and patched teddy bear 'Poo', under my arm.

"The towering buxom matron was dressed in a dark blue uniform with a starched white collar. She had big, flared nostrils. It's funny the things you remember from your childhood. Anyway she took me by my hand and, with as far as I recall, little more than a nod to the social worker, dragged me inside.

"I vividly recall the social worker leaving in her black Austin, the gravel crunching under its tyres. I desperately wished that I was going with her. She had seemed nice, and reluctant to hand me over."

"You don't recall paperwork and the like being handed over?"

"No. I was five years old, Inspector. I could barely write my own name." I paused.

"Well, it didn't take long for me to learn the ropes at the Royal Tunbridge Wells Orphanage Asylum."

Barratt raised his eyebrows. "Asylum?" he said.

"Yes, they really did call it an asylum. There was a clear pecking order, underpinned by a violence and brutality that was handed down from the teachers in the annexed school to the older boys and so on to the bottom of the food chain."

"I can imagine."

"No, Inspector, with respect I don't think that you can.

"The first casualty was Poo, who was ceremoniously burned at the stake by the older boys as I was forced to watch. I recall them hooting, laughing and shouting into my face 'cry-baby cry!' I refused to give them the satisfaction, even though inside, my heart had broken.

"As one of the youngest, and certainly the newest orphan, I was at the bottom of the pecking order. There was little that I could do to completely avoid the ire of the older boys and the staff, many of whom were sadists and paedophiles."

"Jesus."

"Yes, Jesus indeed.

"In those days, it was easy for these criminals to hide in such institutions. No one outside of the system seemed to care about our well-being and turned a blind-eye to what was going on behind closed doors, as long as the perpetrators were discrete.

"Yes, Inspector, that includes your lot as well, as it happens."

I took a sip of my tea as I forced myself to reflect on the horror of those days.

"How did you survive?" Barratt said, to fill the growing void of silence that threatened to derail my confession.

I refocussed my attention and continued, "I was street smart, and I was fleet of foot. That's the two things I had going for me and, although I received my fair share of beatings and abuse from the older boys and some of the staff, I was able to joke my way out of conflict and on occasion, out-run the orphanage bullies.

"I also discovered that I could find sanctuary on the school's farm. There was a very kind biology teacher, Mr Giles. Farmer Giles the kids would call him. Ex-military, like many of the teachers were at the time. Whilst he had little or no formal teacher training to speak of, he showed a special interest in me as I was always keen to learn, and loved to care for the animals we kept on the school farm.

"The good thing about those animals is that they never showed malice, and whilst I tried desperately not to become attached to them, as I knew they served another purpose entirely, sometimes I just couldn't help myself.

"I had to be careful to hide any such feelings, of course, as sure enough, they'd be exploited by the older boys. They would take delight in torturing to death a favourite rabbit if they knew I was fond of it but, because of those experiences, I imagined that one day I might become a farmer myself.

"The sow we had bred gave birth to a litter of nine piglets; five girls and four boys, as far as I recall.

"About 5 months later, as they reached adolescence, Mr Giles asked me if I would like to see how the boys were castrated. He explained that farmers removed the testicles of the boy piglets in order to avoid boar taint. Apparently, the testicles, if left in place, give the pork an unpleasant odour when being cooked, although it didn't appear to affect the taste."

"I can't see that happening today," Barratt said.

"Well, it was different in those days, Inspector. I was keen and not at all squeamish.

"I trotted down to the farm with Mr Giles, past the greenhouses to the paddock outside of the pigsty and watched as he lifted one of the piglets up, pushed its head backwards between his legs and tucked its rear legs underneath his wide leather belt, exposing its nether regions.

"Taking a small scalpel blade, he made a two-inch-long incision and popped out the testicles, like shelling peas from a pod. "The blade must have been so sharp that it appeared to cause little discomfort to the piglet, which surprisingly didn't appear to notice.

"He pointed out two veins attached to each testicle that had to be cut in a certain sequence, following which the testicles fell to the ground. As soon as they hit the dirt, the sow who had been watching close by snuffled them up.

"Mr Giles asked me if I'd like to have a go and although nervous, I was keen to try."

I smiled as I recounted the story to Barratt. "Unfortunately for the piglet, my first cut was too tentative, not cutting decisively or deeply enough. The piglet escaped my grasp and set off at breakneck speed, squealing and running around the paddock in circles before I re-captured it and finished the job."

Barratt laughed. Clearly, he was envisaging the scene.

"As I grew older," I continued, "I grew tall and powerful for my age. I was already over six feet tall and broad across my shoulders as I approached my 15th birthday. I also developed those street smarts I mentioned. I used those and my physical presence to build a following amongst some of the boys. That gave me an insight into how to manipulate people into doing my bidding, a skill I would continue to hone for the rest of my life.

"One thing I couldn't control however, was the unpleasant attention of the school's Deputy Head, Mr Stent, or Stench, as the boys would call him. A nasty piece of work." I gritted my teeth even now as I recalled his behaviour.

Barratt placed his hand over his mouth and chin in what appeared to be concentration, but I figured it was to stop himself from interrupting me.

"Of course, Stench was a corruption of his real name. It took little imagination to come up with that, especially given the fact that his personal hygiene left a lot to be desired.

"Stench was the worst of a bad lot; A sadist and a paedophile. He preyed on the young and not so young boys in the orphanage. Short, well, shorter than me, slightly built with a large aquiline nose, dyed black hair plastered down with Brylcreem, his piercing blue eyes would seek out the most vulnerable. His evening tutorials were a euphemism for his extracurricular sexual perversions; something to be avoided at all costs.

"Matron would change the bloodied sheets of the boys that had been to the tutorials the following morning, silently complicit in his nefarious activities."

"Good God!" I glanced at Barrett; his eyes wide. "Was Stent ever brought to justice?"

"In a way, but perhaps not how you would imagine. Please let me continue."

"Of course."

"It was eight or nine years after I had arrived at the orphanage and I had risen almost to the top of the pecking order, when a particularly frail looking young lad of around nine years of age arrived. It must have been sometime in 1947. His name was Peter Meister. Yes, a German in our midst. You can imagine given that the war had only just ended, he instantly became the target of just about everyone, even though from memory he was second or third generation English. Why his parents hadn't changed their name to 'Masters' or something similar, as so many Meisters had done before, I'll never know.

"He was also, unfortunately for him, small for his age, skinny and clearly malnourished. Skin and bones really. His dark eyes were sunken into his sallow complexion beneath a mop of wayward black hair, and his clothes hung off him, three sizes too big, his sleeves completely covering his hands.

"I have to admit, even I laughed, when I saw him. He didn't even make it to the dorm before being set upon by the other boys, calling him a fucking Nazi and, somewhat paradoxically, a fucking Jew boy! Antisemitism was alive and well in those days, Inspector.

"I was seated on a small mahogany hall table in the oak panelled corridor and watched the abuse for a while, enjoying the banter and the teasing. Then it got physical. I laughed as he got smacked in the face and went down like a sack of spuds. There was nothing particularly odd about that, but then a few boys started laying into him with their boots.

"Now these days, it appears that it's acceptable to kick a man when he's down but, back in my day, there was the unwritten rule: Once a man went down, you waited for him to get up, or you accepted his submission if he stayed down. These boys weren't about to do that."

"What happened?"

"Well, oddly enough, something snapped inside of me. I'd been enjoying the spectacle of the beating but then I felt an uncharacteristic desire to intervene. I called out, 'Enough! Leave be! He's had enough!' Two of his assailants looked over to me and backed off immediately, laughing as they did so, one even saying, 'Welcome to the asylum!', much to the amusement of myself and the gathered onlookers.

"Two older lads however continued to lay into him as he cowered in a foetal position on the floor, trying his best to protect his head and guts.

"I leisurely slid off the hall table I had been sitting on and stepped over to them. That was enough for one of them to back off as I looked him in the eye. The other, Smithy, just glanced at me and said, 'Fuck off, Lazarus, this cunt is getting what's coming to him.'"

I saw Barratt grimace at the vulgarity of the language emanating from my mouth.

"Yes, Inspector, like you I still find the C word incredibly offensive."

Barratt smiled a tight-lipped smile, supressing the urge to interrupt me as many less experienced coppers would have, preferring instead to let me put meat on the bones and perhaps even incriminate myself further.

"Smithy's violent verbal outpouring and blatant disrespect for me had hit a nerve. He had humiliated me in front of the crowd, and I needed to re-establish my authority, and quickly. Such was the psychology of boys at the orphanage."

"I understand," said Barratt, obviously recalling his own experiences of playground politics.

"You see, Smithy had been a long-term rival of mine. He'd come to the orphanage shortly after me. His violent home upbringing had made it easy for him to fit in, whilst the timing of our arrivals made for a natural, albeit uneasy. alliance.

"His arrival took the heat off me as the new boy for which I was immensely grateful but, having said that, he never seemed to shoulder as much of that heat himself as I had.

"Smithy seemed to treat me as someone he could relate to, although we were never to be friends. He very quickly gathered his own following and became one of the orphanage's bullies.

"As we grew we appeared to be evenly matched physically, so much so that a sort of détente had existed between us and, up until then, we had avoided a face off."

"What happened next?"

"Well, as Smithy wound up his leg for another boot to Peter's guts, I swept his standing leg from under him, and sent him crashing backwards where his head met the corner of the table I'd been sitting on, knocking him senseless.

"I saw the opportunity for what it was, and quickly straddled him, sitting down heavily on his chest, knocking the wind out of him. I raised my fists and pummelled his face until my arms were heavy and tired, and his lips, nose and eyes were a pulpy mess."

Barratt winced at the picture that I had thrust into his mind's eye.

"I realise now that my actions were not so much in defence of Peter, as to vent my anger at the humiliation I had just experienced, assert my authority over Smithy and move one rung higher up the pecking order. The funny thing is that although Smithy was a terrible bully, he never sought revenge for the beating I had given him, preferring instead to try to befriend me, but I was never interested and kept him at arm's length.

"I recall gasps and hushed whispers around the corridor as I stood up, leaving Smithy in a bloody heap groaning on the flagstone floor. I grabbed Peter by the scruff of the neck, lifted him up and half threw him toward the dorm, making light of his injuries as he winced in pain.

"In the months that followed, I'd sometimes overhear softly spoken words about being a Jew boy lover. It mattered not. My position was cemented in place. I had achieved legend status amongst the boys, and no one fucked with Lazarus after that.'

I paused to take a sip of tea.

"Please continue, Mr Lazarus," Barratt said seemingly engrossed.

I placed my empty cup back on the saucer and locked my gaze on Barratt's eyes. I was right about this one, I thought. Smart enough to entrap a suspect. Give them enough rope and they're sure to hang themselves.

Well, I was 92 and had resolved to rid myself of as many links of the chains I had forged in life—like Marley's Ghost—and if that meant spending what little time I had left as a guest of His Majesty's then so be it.

In truth I was enjoying my confession. Talk about cleansing the soul!

I continued, "You know, in the year that followed Inspector, rarely did I need to resort to physical violence, and I enjoyed the ability to intimidate other boys with a glance or a stare. I believe it was Lord Acton that said, 'Power tends to corrupt and absolute power corrupts absolutely' or words to that effect. I fell in love with the power and relished the fact that I could delegate boys to administer a beating to a rival, but strong as this love was, it never usurped my love of gold, Inspector. But more of that later."

"And Peter?"

"I discovered that Peter's parents were interned for the duration. After the war had ended they had abandoned not only each other, but him as well."

"Poor bastard. I guess there were a lot of stories like his, after the war."

"Yes, I saw in Peter a vulnerability, I myself, had felt when I first arrived at the orphanage, and I made it my business to ensure that he didn't suffer the way I had. He was under my protection and my growing physical presence and frying-pan-sized fists—as they became known—were at his ready disposal should he need some moral or physical support."

"What happened to him?" Barratt said.

Vivid images came flooding back into my mind and although I had rehearsed my confession over and over, those images now threatened to derail it. I forced myself back on track.

"Well, Inspector, I couldn't be everywhere at once and he got a fair amount of attention from some of the other boys, but it wasn't them I was terribly concerned about. A bloody nose is just part of growing up, isn't it? No, it was Stench that was the real worry."

Barratt smiled, obviously recalling his own scraps and bloody noses but then refocussed at the mention of Stench's name.

"Stench had had his eye on Peter from the moment he arrived at the orphanage. Fortunately, his current tutorial group had kept him preoccupied and away from Peter for the first year.

"Then one day, after some of the boys in his tutorial group had left the orphanage, to find their own way in the world, Stench turned his attention to Peter.

"To this day, I regret not somehow preventing his participation in the tutorial group, but as I said, I couldn't be everywhere at once."

I sat in the lounge, contemplating my failure to protect Peter. I remembered his face which he would contort into a seemingly endless range of hilarious expressions and his quirky sense of humour. He was quick-witted, and often had me in hysterics—mimicking one of the teachers, or casting me a glance over some remark I'd made, in which he'd spotted a double entendre.

"So, what happened?" Barratt said, interrupting my silent reflection.

"Well, Inspector," I continued, "that very night, I found Peter softly whimpering in his bed with the sheets pulled up around his eyes. I knew immediately what had happened and my blood rose so violently within me, that I was all set to pay Stench a visit that very evening and give him what-for.

"I recall gently pulling back the sheet from Peter's bony little fingers. He had a split lip to complement his black eyes and rapidly swelling head. He was barely recognisable. His breathing was ragged and shallow. He whispered to me, 'Forget it. Please Lazarus, don't do or say anything'.

"I was just a kid. I should have raise the alarm, but I didn't. I let him drift off into sleep. I tucked him in as best I could. I was unaware of just how serious his injuries were. How could I? I made my way back to my bed in the adjacent dorm. As I lay there awake, I wondered just how Peter and I were going to escape the madness. I resolved that we'd talk about it in the morning. I also promised myself that Peter would never attend one of Stench's tutorials ever again."

Chapter 46 Runaway

Barratt and I were sitting in my lounge as I continued my confession. "What became of Peter?" he said.

"Well, in the morning, I sauntered into Peter's dorm to see how he was recovering; Peter was gone, his bed had been stripped. I looked out of the window and saw Matron walking across the quad, towards the laundry. She had bloodied sheets under her arm. I guessed that they were Peter's."

"Gone? Gone where?"

"Just gone. I was told he'd been adopted by a couple that had lost their son in the Blitz. I didn't believe a word of it then, and I still don't now, nearly 80 years on.

"There's a housing estate built on the site of the orphanage these days, but I bet that if you dug down deep enough, you'd find human remains of the boys who had mysteriously vanished. Peter is there for sure."

"Seriously?"

"Mark my word, Inspector, you have no idea."

Even though Inspector Barratt was recording the interview, he had his notebook out. I saw him scribble a note orphanage, bodies, schoolboy gossip? He'd follow that up at a later date for sure.

"What of Mr Stent?"

“Stench, you mean,” I spat the word out. “I had managed to avoid Stench’s attention myself for the better part of 10 years when after one morning assembly, I was called to his office.

“I remember that office vividly. Dark oak panelling lined the walls on which hung smoke-stained copies of landscapes from nineteenth century English artists. His large mahogany desktop was inlaid with green leather, embossed around the edge with gold leaf. To the left of his blotter was a wooden in-tray filled with papers held down by a heavy glass paperweight from the Isle of Wight. It encased a red-and-white lighthouse against a white cliff. Funny the things you remember.”

Barratt’s eyes narrowed as he was obviously trying to envisage the scene.

“Next to his in-tray was an ashtray overflowing with cigarette butts, their aroma competing with the smell of lavender furniture polish. To my right, a black Bakelite telephone sat under a green-shaded desk lamp, proudly announcing his importance and status to any casual visitor. Not many people had ‘phones in those days, Inspector.”

“Yes, it’s difficult to imagine. These days I don’t know how we’d cope without our mobiles and instant access to everything.”

Barratt took a sip of tea from his cup, gently returning it to its saucer as though the sound of china clinking might derail me.

“You know, I recall that the partially drawn blackout curtains were still in place over the tall windows. Windows so high that you couldn’t see out of them. They let in a sliver of morning light which illuminated the dust mites and heavy tobacco smoke that hung motionless in the air.

“As was required, I stood to attention on the soiled rug in front of his desk as Stench leaned back casually in his leather chair. He took his time to draw down on his cigarette as he stared at me. ‘Lazarus, I have some tragic news for you,’ he said, ‘your mother is dead.’ Just like that.”

Barratt let out a sigh and nodded. Whether it was in sympathy or acknowledgement of the way that things were done in those days, wasn’t clear.

"Although I had long given up any thought of ever seeing my mother again, my knees went weak as I entered a silent state of shock and disbelief at the abruptness with which the news had been delivered.

"Stench was watching me through a haze of smoke. Those piercing blue eyes, looking for any kind of weakness, any opportunity to break through my resolve and take advantage of me.

"He leaned forward and continued, 'Apparently, she drank herself into a stupor and slashed her wrists in the bathtub.' Still, I recall him looking for weakness. It was painfully clear to me that the bastard was enjoying the pitiful suffering he was able to inflict upon me.

"He stood up from his leather chair and slowly moved around to sit on the edge of his desk in front of me. Looking up into my eyes he raised his hand gently to my cheek, then slid it down across my back to my buttock. 'At times like these…' he began, but he never got to finish his sentence.

"I clenched my right fist and with all my might and anger, I hit him fairly and squarely on his fucking beaky nose. It felt so good. He fell backwards onto his desk, holding his face with bright red blood and yellow snot pouring out between his fingers."

It mattered not that Barratt was there. I realised that, even after all those years, I was still clenching my fists as I recounted that defining moment of my life. I forced myself to relax.

"It was his turn to be in shock," I said. "Stench stared back at me in wide-eyed disbelief. Before he could retaliate however, I grabbed the heavy glass paperweight in my left hand and, again with all my pent-up anger, I brought it down into his face, smashing several of his teeth, alternating blows with my right fist.

"My violent assault continued as his arms flailed about in an ineffective defence against my onslaught. It was as though every blow I landed was taking back the months and years that had been stolen from me. Every blow was in retaliation for what he had done to Peter and countless other young men over the years.

“Eventually his arms stopped moving and he lay there motionless, sprawled across his desk.

“I was just shy of my 16th birthday and as far as I was concerned, I had just done the world a favour, ridding it of this spiteful, evil excuse of a man.”

Barratt sat in stony silence as I continued my story. He must have been doing the maths. Stench would be well over a hundred years old now if he had survived and, in any case, he would have been unlikely to press charges against me, particularly if he had had anything to do with Peter’s disappearance or abuse of young men.

“I rifled his desk and retrieved two five-pound notes, six one-pound notes, a shilling, a sixpenny piece, and a few pennies. Just over sixteen quid total. Enough to get away. There was also an almost-full packet of Player’s Navy Cut unfiltered cigarettes, a cigarette lighter, a penknife and a whistle which I stuffed into my pocket. The keys to every door in the school were clipped to his belt like a gaoler.

“I unclipped the keys and then, I don’t know why but remembering how Mr Giles had taught me to castrate the pigs on the farm, I unbuttoned his fly and extracted his balls. I took the penknife from my pocket and castrated that bastard there and then.”

Barratt was clearly shocked but did his best to hide it. There were many atrocities committed in WWII and not just by the Axis powers. We did our fair share, to be sure. Stories like mine were commonplace as soldiers gave in to their blood-lust in the heat of battle. I reckoned that this was pretty much the same sort of thing.

“My only regret was, and still is, that the bastard hadn’t been conscious to appreciate it.”

“Did he survive?” Barratt asked, his eyes wide as he leant forward in his seat.

“I was convinced that I’d killed him. I’d never seen a dead body before and I didn’t know how to check for signs of life, but I do recall being surprisingly rational. I knew I had to get away. My plan was simple; I would run away to sea.

"What of Mr Stent…Stench?" Barratt said, correcting himself.

I smiled as I recalled, "I did learn some years later that the bastard had survived my attack, but it was not without a little satisfaction, I confess, that I imagined the miserable, impotent life that he faced, without his balls."

Barratt suppressed the beginnings of a smile. "What happened then?" he said, as he slipped back into the comfort of the settee.

"Well, having completed my impromptu surgery, I glanced around the office and retrieved his ex-army greatcoat and flat cap from the cane coat stand in the corner. This disguise served me well as I briskly exited his office, locking the door behind me and walked the mile or so to Tunbridge Wells Railway Station. There, I bought a second-class ticket to Charing Cross.

"I got off the train at Charing Cross and walked down Villiers Street to the Embankment to catch the tube to Victoria Station, where I bought another second-class ticket to Gillingham. It was about an hour's ride from there, stopping at all stations, and then just over a half an hour's walk down Brompton Road to the dockyard through the bombed-out streets.

"During my train journey to Gillingham, I pondered the enormity of my crime. Had I killed Stench? Had he bled out? My hands started to shake, and I was convinced that every eye in the carriage was looking at me.

"I pulled down my recently acquired flat cap, turned up the collar on my greatcoat and feigned sleep, resting my head against the steamed-up carriage window. I was good at pretending.

"The guard came around calling for 'tickets please' and I fumbled for my ticket, convinced that at any moment he would recognise me from a hastily printed wanted poster that had, in my mind, already been circulated to all railway stations, ports and airports.

"My ticket was clipped, and the guard went on. Rivulets of sweat ran down my back, even though it was cold.

"Chatham Docks was hidden behind a high brick wall, which was the highest wall I had ever seen in my life, topped with broken glass and barbed wire. Its security gates and attendant guard meant that no one was getting in or out, without a pass. I watched the east gate for a while until the sun started to set and the few remaining streetlights that hadn't been trashed by the Luftwaffe started to come on.

"Innocently, I wandered up to the gate and asked the guard if I might secure a position on a merchant vessel as a deckhand."

"He looked at me and said, without any preamble, 'How old are you, son?' Clearly, I wasn't the first young lad he had come across that had plans of running away to sea.

"I'm eighteen," I lied, taking out one of Stench's Player's Navy Cut cigarettes and offering a smoke to him. "Just looking for work, don't you know?"

"He eyed me suspiciously as he took the smoke. I hurriedly took another from the packet and tapped the unfiltered cigarette on the back of the pack, the way I had seen Stench do in the classroom so many times before. I took the lighter and held it up before the guard and he inhaled the coarse tobacco smoke into his lungs. I followed his example and realised too late my mistake, as the acrid smoke burnt the back of my throat and seared my lungs. I bent over double, coughing, retching and eventually puked by his feet.

"I remember the guard sniggering at me. 'Went down the wrong way, did it, son?' he'd said.

"I stubbed the cigarette out with my boot.

"I recall the guard's expression softening a little as he said to me, 'Look son, I don't know what sort of trouble you're in, but you're going about it all wrong. Go down to the Sail and Anchor. It's a pub just around the corner there.' He nodded in the general direction. 'It's popular with the merchant crews. Ask about, you might just get lucky. Watch yourself though. Some of those lads can be a little, how shall I say, affectionate!'

"I remember telling him, 'I can take care of myself,' as I bid my farewell, my mouth still full of the taste of the revolting tobacco and vomit."

Chapter 47 The Antipodean Queen

Barratt seemed comfortable enough sitting on the settee in my lounge as I entered into the next chapter of my life story.

I felt my shoulders relax as I recalled far happier times.

I began, “Even though the war had been over for two years, Inspector, the scars of the Blitz were everywhere to be seen.

“The docks had taken a pounding from the Luftwaffe but miraculously—like St. Paul’s Cathedral—the Sail and Anchor pub, had survived amongst a sea of devastation, albeit with some boards still over shattered windows. Glass was hard to come by. Other windows still had a criss-cross pattern of brown parcel tape over them. The thick green paint on the door was deeply scarred from shrapnel, showing just how close it had come to obliteration.

“I found the pub easily enough. Opening the door, I was wrapped in the glow of amber light and a gust of warm humid air laced with the strong smell of stale beer and tobacco. Do you remember those spit and sawdust days? It seems as though they are long gone now.”

“Yes indeed, how things have changed, eh?” Barratt said as he took a sip from his tea.

"Yeah, you could say that.

"Well, my entrance to the pub was met with a few curious stares from the locals, but it was clear that most of the patrons were itinerant sailors passing through, getting their last drinks in before setting sail.

"I recall the rather rotund barman lifting his head as I approached the counter, flicking a tea towel over his shoulder. He asked me 'What'll it be, son?'

"I put on my deepest voice and said a pint of best bitter, please rather politely, which appeared to amuse him. I watched him as he took a 'jug' and pulled down on the porcelain pump handle with a practiced arm, half-filling it with a cloudy amber liquid and frothy head. The second pull filled it to the brim so that the level of the liquid finished expertly at the top window and just a little froth slid into the slops tray below. I took out a shilling and placed it on the counter.

"I asked him if he knew who might be looking for crew. I was concentrating hard not to let my voice waver. It had broken a few months before but I was still prone to the occasional falsetto.

"The barman looked up, placed both hands on the countertop before him and nodded over in the direction of the bay window. 'Billy over there, might have something,' he said. The barman had indicated a stocky but clean shaven, dark-haired man with heavy set features in his late 40s, sitting on the window seat. He was cradling an empty glass in his hands. I recall he wore a heavy donkey jacket with scuffed leather stitched across its shoulders. His grubby moleskin trousers were short over his heavy, ex-army boots. The red neckerchief tucked into his grey flannel shirt also appeared to have seen better days.

"I wandered over, carrying my—as yet—untouched pint of bitter in my hand. He watched me and set his dark brown eyes on my beer. I was pretty quick on the uptake in those days, Inspector, and placed it in front of him. "I hear you might be looking for crew," I said.

"'Maybe,' he'd replied in a thick Slavic accent. His eyes scanned me as though he was assessing my potential there and then. I felt almost naked before his stare.

"I told him I was looking to join a vessel as soon as possible. 'I've plenty of experience and I'm fit, I'm strong, I'm willing to learn and work hard.'

"He asked me, 'Who've you sailed with, lad?'

"That was it, my subterfuge had been blown all inside of 30 seconds. "I'll work for my passage," I said, rather too desperately, as he continued to interrogate me with his stare.

"I recall him saying, 'In a spot of bother, are we?' to which I replied, 'Who isn't these days? Fucking commies, eh? I thought they were meant to be our allies?"

"He asked me if I was a Bolshevik? "I wasn't sure what a Bolshevik was, but I was pretty sure he didn't care for them and that meant that I didn't either, 'No! no way!' I said.

"The tension seemed to ease, and his stern expression softened as he said 'So, how old are you really?'

"I lied again and told him I was 17, adding, 'but I pass for eighteen, don't I? I mean, I couldn't have bought you a pint if I didn't, could I?'

"Billy cracked half a smile and said, 'Which eye did George look at you with? His right or his left? His real one or his glass one?' I hadn't noticed, but I was pretty sure it was the colour of my money rather than the lack of stubble on my chin that had secured the sale.

"He asked me 'What's your name, son?'

"Lazarus, I said, to which he replied, 'Just Lazarus? No first name or surname?'

"I hadn't used a surname since I was five and a half years old and wasn't about to start now. Just Lazarus. Use it as you will,' I said, regaining a little of my bravado.

"It was then that Billy leant forward, his large hand making the pint jug I had placed in front of him look tiny as he threaded a finger through its handle. He took a big gulp of the bitter, draining half the contents. He looked at the empty space in front of me and said, 'Not much of a drinker yourself, then?'

"I told him that I'd never developed a taste for it.

"It appeared that Billy had reached a decision. Staring me in the eye he said 'So, you got any papers?' I said that I'd lost them some time ago and hadn't got around to getting a replacement. Somewhat abruptly he asked, 'How much money you got?'

"Now Inspector, I wasn't so naïve as to disclose my entire wealth to a stranger. I told him, 'I have a five-pound note to my name and a few coins.'

'Give it to me,' was all he said.

"I was a little taken aback and asked him 'what for?'"

"He said, 'I'll need to get you through the gate in the morning and for that, I'll need to get you some paperwork.' It was as simple as that.

"I was pretty shocked, not to say suspicious, but what could I do? 'Five pounds is a bit steep, mate! It's all I have,' I complained.

"He told me, 'OK, forget it. Find yourself another ship.' I recall he leaned back into his seat, drained his pint, wiped the back of his hand across his mouth and looked at me expectantly.

"I walked over to the bar and slapped my five-pound note on the table and ordered another pint of bitter, receiving four pounds and nineteen shillings change from George the barman. Grasping the change in one hand and the pint in the other, I returned to Bill and slapped both down in front of him.

"I was cocky alright. 'Four pounds nineteen shillings and a pint. I'll see you in the morning,' I said.

"Billy had smiled at me and said, 'Alright, Lazarus, if that's your real name, be at the east gate tomorrow at 5 am.'

"I was a little taken aback but managed to say, 'Great,' and 'thank you.'

"He told me to save my thanks, adding, 'We're bound for the colonies and, mark my word, you're going to wish you never met me before too long. I'll promise you that.'

"'I doubt that very much', I said, although I wasn't quite sure why I should regret meeting him."

"So, what happened next?"

"Well of course, I had nowhere to sleep that night and I was reluctant to spend what little I had left on board and lodgings, so I made my way through the bomb sites to a local park and sat on a damp, slatted bench, willing away the hours until dawn.

"I could see an illuminated clock-tower in the distance which seemed to be frozen in time. I shivered as I pulled the collar of my greatcoat up around my ears and dozed fitfully until around 4 am when I woke with a start as my fists sank into Stench's skull. I gave up trying to sleep and wandered around until the streets slowly started to come to life.

"I bought a pint of milk from the milkman's horse-and-cart and drank it down greedily. Another five pence from my dwindling supplies. I nicked another bottle from a doorstep and drank that, too. I felt as though the taste of tobacco and vomit in my mouth was proving hard to get rid of, even though it must have been long gone." I paused as I remembered those days so long ago, yet still so fresh in my mind.

I wasn't sure how much of my flashback I had relayed to Barratt in my confession and how much was in my mind's eye. I looked up at Barratt. "Not going to arrest me for petty larceny, I hope, Inspector?"

Barratt smiled. "I think you are way past the statute of limitations on that count, Mr Lazarus. Please, continue."

"Well, approaching the east gate, I noticed that the guard on duty was different to the man I'd encountered the previous afternoon. I stood back on the opposite street corner until I spied Billy and company, walking towards him. Their breath clouded the freezing early morning air as they strode along the pavement. Billy caught my eye and with the slightest nod indicated I should join them. I rushed across the road, hands deep in the pockets of my greatcoat, which was heavy and wet from the morning dew.

“Billy pressed his palm into the gate keeper’s hand and with a casual wink of his eye, a surreptitious exchange of notes took place between them.

“I was in. I was dockside.” I paused as I remembered the sense of freedom passing those gates: the feeling that I had got away with Stench’s murder.

“We walked in silence for a while up towards a large steamer whose deck was stacked high with barrels and crates. No shipping containers in those days, Inspector. Emblazoned across her stern and bow were the words *Antipodean Queen*. She looked to be in great shape, obviously built recently as part of the war effort.

“I was on my way to Australia.”

* * *

“Billy, whose real name was Zvonimir, turned out to be the captain of the *Antipodean Queen* and a veteran of several North Atlantic convoys during the war bringing much-needed food, arms, and ammunition from the USA before and after their somewhat late entry. He was what you might call a rough diamond. Hard working and no stranger to using his fists to settle an argument. He proved to be a good leader and mentor and was widely respected by his crew, many of whom had sailed with him in the convoys. He introduced me to the crew as a general deckhand rather than a cabin boy, which I was quite pleased about. He made it clear to everyone on board that I was under his personal protection.

“Dinner in the mess was a chance to hear stories of those Atlantic crossings and the German U-Boats that hunted the convoys in Wolfpacks. I must say, it all sounded very exciting and I was really quite disappointed that I had missed out on the conflict, on account of my age. Part of me desperately wanted to be part of this band of men, a brother-in-arms. It was a feeling of being an outsider that I couldn’t shake until I, too, found a way to serve my adopted country sometime later.

"The first couple of days after we cast off from Chatham docks were plain sailing as we made our way down the Thames Estuary into the Straits of Dover and the Channel. When I was not assisting cook or being shouted at in the hot and noisy engine room, I kept myself busy either exploring every nook and cranny of the ship or on deck checking cargo lashings, revelling in the feeling of the salty wind in my face. Captain Bill, who had taken me under his wing, showed me the bridge and went through all the controls and gauges.

"His stories of U Boats and their torpedoes, destroyers, and their depth charges which shook the hulls of the convoy vessels so violently that they thought they'd pop the rivets, and the shrapnel flying, had my undivided attention. He seemed pleased to have such an attentive audience.

"Crossing the Bay of Biscay, I encountered my first ever experience of seasickness. Ever been seasick Inspector?"

"Can't say I have, Mr. Lazarus. Bit of a land lubber me. Closest I get to the ocean is the Grand Union Canal." He smiled.

"I envy you. Words cannot adequately describe the feeling. I understood immediately Captain Bill's prediction that I would wish that I had never met him as, for three days, I vomited until I had nothing left to bring up. I felt as though my ribs had all cracked, my stomach muscles were torn to shreds, and all my strength had deserted me.

"On the third day, it was a Sunday as I recall, Captain Bill came to my quarters and asked if I wanted to be put ashore in France.

"'I'm here for the duration, Captain,' I'd said weakly, struggling even to raise my head.

"He slapped me on the shoulder, none too gently, initiating another bout of dry retching which he thankfully ignored. 'Good lad!' he roared. 'Now listen up Lazarus,' he said, 'Cook has, on my orders, prepared Sunday lunch for you, and a pint of sweet tea. You will get up, freshen up and eat up every scrap of lunch and, drink all of your tea. You'll then go to the heads and throw it all up. Clean up any shit and return to the mess where Cook will serve you another Sunday lunch and another pint of sweet tea. You'll eat up and drink up and when you're finished, you'll resume galley duties and wash all the dishes, pots and pans. If you do this **exactly** as I say, you will never be seasick again. Do we have a deal?'

"My God, did we ever, I thought. I was so desperate to get over that terrible malaise that I would have eaten a dead cat if he'd told me to.

"So far, the captain had been good to his word and whether it was mind over matter or some miracle cure, I really had no idea and quite frankly I didn't care, but to my delight and astonishment it worked. I've never been seasick since."

Barratt smiled.

"The crew got on well together and whether it was because of my guardian angel or my 'can-do' attitude, they all seemed to warm to me to various degrees. There was none of the sadistic bullying I had experienced in the orphanage, and I felt as though I had found a new family. They'd all donated some hand-me-down clothes to me as I had joined the ship with just the clothes I was wearing. I suspect it was as much in their own interests as it was in mine as I was certainly a little high on the nose after a couple of days.

"Our first port of call was Lagos in Nigeria. As the youngest member of the crew, much of my time in port was spent keeping watch on board, however, I was able to watch the goings-on around the port from the deck.

"You can imagine the assault on my senses coming from a British orphanage and a bombed-out London. I don't think I had ever seen a Negro before and here were millions of them, all running around barefoot, smiling, and happy. Lagos, and more to the point, Nigeria wasn't like it is now. In those days, it was a friendly, bustling port of activity, trading gold, timber and ivory. The oil industry was still in its infancy. We did, however, top up the bunker oil, off load and take on some cargo. We also took on fresh food supplies prior to setting off for the Cape and Australia. I remember tasting my first banana. It was like nothing I had ever tasted before.

"The journey down to the Cape of Good Hope was smooth and trouble free. Captain Bill took time to introduce me to the science of celestial navigation, using marine charts, the ship's chronometer, a sextant and an almanac, lifelong skills which I would treasure in the years to come.

"The toughest nut to crack was the fiery Scottish Chief Engineer, Angus McBride. But after a couple of weeks of verbal abuse in the engine room learning the names of the tools, even he seemed to tolerate me to the point that when I was to leave the ship, he seemed genuinely reluctant to let me go. I recall him saying to the captain, "Waste of my fucking time training up **my** new apprentice to such a high standard only to see him run away." Clearly Angus had taken possession of me in his own mind. Praise indeed!"

* * *

"By the time we stopped in Cape Town to again off-load some cargo, refuel and pick up supplies, I considered myself to be a veteran.

"Danny, the ship's purser who had mysteriously disappeared in Lagos only to reappear looking slightly worse for wear, asked me if I'd like to go ashore with him to trade with the natives. I explained that I had nothing to trade but for Stench's whistle. I was keen to keep the cigarette lighter, but I'd go along with him in any case.

"Danny showed me his sea chest full of trinkets, costume jewellery and nylons bought for a few pennies or traded with the American GIs for smokes back in England. He then lifted out an internal shelf to reveal a compartment containing a number of German Luger pistols and ammunition. He told me, 'These are the real beauties, Lazarus,' and handed me what looked to be a brand-new pistol. 'Liberated by our boys in Germany. Worth their weight in gold, they are,' he said.

"He could no doubt see the look of concern on my face. I had never held a firearm before and, although keen to try it out, I was also worried about arming the natives in what I understood to be a volatile country. I asked him if what we were doing was illegal, to which he replied, 'Only if you get caught.'

"Oddly enough, Inspector, that's a phrase that has dogged me for most of my life.

"Danny said, 'Don't worry about arming the natives, Lazarus,' as he saw the look of concern spread across my face. 'If they want to try before they buy, they'll fire up perfectly but in truth, they'll be pretty useless once they get a bit of dirt in them.' He explained that the German engineers had made the Lugers to such exacting tolerances that the slightest bit of shit in the mechanisms would jam them up. Of course, that didn't stop them becoming a favourite souvenir of our boys though. There were plenty of squaddies returning to England, down on their luck, who would happily trade-in their spoils of war, for a few quid. Danny explained that the earlier models were a different calibre, but the blacks didn't care. It was all about kudos for them.

"I remember feeling the weight and shape of the pistol in my hand. It fitted really well. I asked Danny how much he thought he'd get for them.

"He replied with something of a wry grin, 'As I said, son, they're worth their weight in gold, literally. These black bastards go out for days into the bosch, or bush as we call it, with little more than a stick and a loincloth. They pick up nuggets all over the fucking place. No point in us going looking for 'em ourselves. That's a fool's errand,' he said. He told me that they had their secret places. 'All I do is put the Luger on the scales and wait until it's balanced out with gold and that's it. Job done and trade made.' He told me to make sure that the pistol had a full magazine, though. You see, empty it weighs nearly two pounds; with a full magazine you can add another three Troy ounces. 'That totals 34 ounces for a fully loaded pistol,' he said.

"I think that the price of gold then was around US $34 an ounce, a princely sum of $1,156 apiece. Not bad when you consider that they cost about $100 a pop to manufacture."

I looked at Barratt and saw his empty cup. “More tea, Inspector?”

Barratt leant forward as I poured another cup from the pot, careful not to drip on the freshly laundered tea cosy.

“I’ve thought a lot about that moment over the years. I reckon it was the start of my love affair with gold. You see, gold became my talisman. It never corroded or tarnished and would always be tradeable. Gold was both a safe financial harbour and a psychological fortress all wrapped up into one. Of course, I had no idea how it would also increase in value in recent years. Up until the early 70s the price didn’t really change, but then it more than doubled to US $97 an ounce in 1972 and increased again the following year to over $150 an ounce. What’s it now? Over $2000? It had been an incredibly stable commodity up until then. Now, I could see a whole new world of opportunities opening up before me.

“I’m afraid I don’t really keep up with the gold price, Mr Lazarus, but please continue.”

“As luck would have it, Danny got a severe case of gut-rot on the day we came alongside in Cape Town. Unable to leave the ship he entrusted me to go ashore with his trinkets and the all-important Lugers and ammunition. We agreed that I would receive a small commission on any sales.

“Even though Danny had given me strict instructions and directions to meet with the potential buyers, I made sure that the Lugers were empty but parcelled up the ammunition in lots of 25 rounds wrapped in waxed cotton, which I made sure were added to the scales.

“The conflicting sights, sounds and smells of Cape Town were like nothing I had ever encountered before. With my sack of goodies slung over my shoulder, I walked through narrow dirty streets overflowing with raw sewage and— in stark contrast— past pristine edifices of government offices glaringly white against the cloudless blue skies, all overshadowed by the most remarkable flat-topped mountain I had ever seen.

"Eventually I reached the address that Danny had given me and I made my way inside a dimly lit, smoke-filled room. As my eyes adjusted to the low light, I observed several men who appeared more Arabic than Negro, sitting around on cushions on the floor. They looked up as I entered and mumbled to each other in a language that I could make no sense of.

"I was beckoned forward and asked to join them. It was then that I wished that I'd had the foresight to have a loaded Luger in my back pocket.

"They wanted to know where Danny was, and I explained that he'd fallen ill after we had stopped off in Lagos. That seemed to be a source of amusement to them as they speculated on exactly the nature of Danny's illness.

"We soon got down to business, however. I was a tough negotiator, and I explained to the buyers that the price had doubled since Danny's last visit. They were none too happy about that but, such was their desire for a genuine article, that they mostly met my price, sometimes making up the difference with small soapy feeling rocks that they assured me were uncut diamonds from the kimberlite pipes, whatever they were. I was immediately suspicious but as I was making a great deal on the gold itself, I decided to take a risk. As it turned out, some of those little rocks were worth far more than the bullion that they were supposed to substitute.

"My pièce de résistance, however, was when I 'reluctantly' retrieved Stench's whistle from my pocket and strung along a story in whispered tones of how it had been found by Howard Carter in the tomb of Tutankhamun in 1922."

Barratt's eyes narrowed, full of scepticism.

"You see, Inspector, I told them that it was so precious that knowledge of its existence was known to only a few. I explained that my father had won it from Carter in a card game. It was fabled as the whistle of virility. Legend had it that if you blew it hard as you came, your wife or concubine would conceive a healthy, powerful son who would rise to greatness. Of course, if you were weak and didn't blow it hard enough, you would be cursed with a weak and lazy daughter who would eat all your food and spend all your money."

I could see the beginnings of a smile cross Barratt's face.

"I got rather more for the whistle than a Luger," I said. "Danny and the crew laughed for days at the thought of the whistle announcing to the world another ejaculation. For days afterwards, lights-out on board the *Antipodean Queen* would be heralded by a number of shrill whistles, much to the amusement of the crew.

"I gave Danny his fair share of bullion and pocketed the rest. Don't get me wrong, I told Danny I'd made a bit on the side, which he was very happy about as it meant that he didn't need to pay me a commission. Just how much I'd made, however, was never discussed. I am not sure how he was treated on his next visit to the Cape when he discovered just how much I had made, or whether he ever received any feedback on the efficacy of Tutankhamun's whistle. I figured that I had well and truly burnt my bridges in that transaction.

"We left Cape Town after a week, with fresh fruit, more bananas, and ivory amongst other things and headed east towards Australia.

"Our arrival at Fremantle saw me leave the *Antipodean Queen*, much to Captain Bill and Purser Danny's apparent dismay. My offer to work my passage was conveniently forgotten and Danny handed me an envelope containing over a month's wages. Try as they might to persuade me to stay on for the Adelaide leg, I was determined to leave the ship and try my luck in the lucky country. We parted friends with the promise of a 'wet bed in the bilges' if ever I wanted to return.

"And so it was that I left the *Antipodean Queen* and, shortly thereafter, managed to secure my Australian citizenship on the eve of the Korean War."

Chapter 48 The Korean War

I felt that things were going well with my confession to Inspector Barratt. At least he hadn't fallen asleep.

"Cashed up and bold as brass, I acquired two hundred acres of land south of Fremantle in Western Australia and tried for a couple of years to make a go of it. My only experience at farming was rearing the cows, pigs, sheep and rabbits on the school farm. After clearing the land of thorny scrub, trying and failing to extract any goodness from the shitty soil, I realised that I just wasn't cut out to be a farmer. Two hundred acres in England was a good-sized farm in those days. Here in this barren desert, stocking levels were a fraction of what I had foolishly anticipated and soon the farm was in trouble. I decided to cut my losses and look for something else.

"It was early in 1950 and tensions on the Korean Peninsula made enlistment in the Australian Army a relatively easy and attractive proposition. It would also give me the war experience I had longed for as I had sat around the mess table on the *Antipodean Queen*, listening to the stories of the crew. I was just eighteen years old. I think it was late June that North Korea finally made its move on the south and by Christmas, I was in the thick of it.

"You know, Inspector, the Korean war has often been referred to as the forgotten war, coming so close on the heels of the Japanese surrender at the end of WWII. I was constantly surprised in later years at just how many kids I spoke to didn't even know that it happened. It was, from many perspectives, an ideological war between capitalism in the West and communism in the East—a battle ground for the United States and the forces of China and Russia to play out their ideologies against each other. Why the fuck Australia had to get involved I have no idea, but get involved we did. Robert Menzies was Prime Minister at the time and, apparently, he was committed to send Australian troops to the peninsula in support of the UN—which basically meant the Yanks."

I paused, remembering those days. Barratt took a sip of tea.

"It was a fucking disaster overall," I continued, "maybe three million casualties, military and civilian. And for what? A piece of paper declaring an armistice which no one signed, and a demilitarised zone separating two ideologies which is still there to this day. Fucking pathetic, if you ask me. I soon changed my opinion about going away to war. It's definitely not all it's cracked up to be.

"But Inspector, war was also an opportunity. Despite the bitterly cold winters and scorching hot summers, there was always a buck to be made. South Korea had seen a massive influx of refugees from the North, and their need for clothing and food was great. The money they had was worthless, but many had brought gold with them. Working in logistics, I was able to provide refugees with both food and clothing in exchange for a few gold coins.

"Those without gold would offer me their bodies but I mostly refused, although there may well be a few little Lazarus's wandering around Seoul," I smiled. "I'd give most of those who had nothing to trade but their own flesh, a couple of ration packs and tell them to fuck off. I'd make them swear to secrecy—on the lives of their families—not to tell anyone of my largesse. The last thing I wanted was a line of refugees asking for charity. They were by-and-large illiterate and superstitious, so that played nicely into my hands.

"I rationalised that trading army surplus for gold was in fact, an act of humanitarianism. After all, without my careful and conscientious diverting of army surplus, many refugees, both women and children, would have perished."

Barratt looked at me accusingly.

"Oh, Inspector, let me be clear. None of our troops went hungry or naked because of my activities.

"The Australian Army-issued greatcoats were pretty useless. I swear that some of them were left over from the First World War. However, that in itself was an opportunity. You see, the US Army had vastly superior gear—their winter coats were filled with eiderdown—and I was able to secure a number of these from my counterparts in the US army. I gave these to select Australian personnel to—how shall I say—lubricate the distribution channels of surplus stores my way. Quid pro quo and all that," I smiled.

"I take it you didn't get caught. Did you see any action in Korea?"

"I was fortunate but also frustrated that I didn't see direct action but I demobbed with a very healthy balance in both cash and gold which, together with the proceeds from the sale of the farm, allowed me to invest wisely in the property market on my return to Perth at the end of 1953.

"I was 21 and had seven houses by the time I turned 22. After a few physical altercations with tenants, I moved into industrial property and shopping centres, partnering up with other entrepreneurs in Perth. It was a crazy time where just about anything went.

"Life was good. It was about then that I re-discovered my love of the ocean, and I bought my first yacht, a little 26-foot Folkboat. I became a member of the then vestigial Fremantle Sailing Club, and I learned how to sail.

"My properties gave me a good income and whilst I was constantly pressured to join the so-called 'high society' in Perth, I resisted the temptation to strut around like a peacock, preferring instead to feel the salt spray in my face.

"My first big solo voyage was on a much larger custom-built carvel planked yacht called *Sea Mist*. She was big, heavy and slow but oh, what a beautiful girl she turned out to be. I had acquired her second-hand and kitted her out to sail to Indonesia via the Abrolhos, and then over to the Solomon Islands.

"My yacht and apparent wealth made me a target for every gold-digging woman in Southeast Asia. Of course, I tried hard not to flaunt my wealth in such places. I found adopting the persona of a penniless sea gypsy worked occasionally but I soon found myself seduced by pleasures of the flesh.

"A boy needs to sow a few wild oats, wouldn't you agree, Inspector? It wasn't my first encounter with the fairer sex, but in Southeast Asia I was like a lamb to the slaughter. I think I may have escaped five marriage proposals in as many weeks."

"Is that where your love affair with the Solomons began?"

"I hadn't really thought about it, Inspector, but I guess you could say that.

"I returned to Fremantle almost a year later to find that my business partners had completely fucked things up. I had to work hard to recover and rebuild my portfolio, but at least I wasn't starting from a zero base.

"I reluctantly concluded that if you wanted a job doing properly, you had to do it yourself. There were a few harsh words spoken with my business partners and at least one fisticuffs that I recall, effectively dissolving any partnership that could have existed. Still, I was young and well capitalised, and I was able to dust myself off and start all over again.

"What became of *Sea Mist*?"

"Unfortunately, she'd suffered greatly from poor maintenance whilst in Southeast Asia and marine worms had eaten well into her hull and keel, making refurbishment and restoration a fool's errand. Despite a few attempts at bringing her back to her former glory, she was eventually scuppered off the west end of Rotto." I paused as I remembered fondly my days aboard. Funny thing is, that you always see the past through rose-tinted spectacles and gloss over the hours spent cramped up in the engine room trying to get the bastard running—or the broken fingernails from furling the sails.

"By the time I was entering my 40s, things were pretty good. I commissioned a new 50-foot cruiser, and my businesses were largely running themselves, thanks in no small part to some loyal and competent staff and more than a modicum of luck. And from time to time, a little intimidation on my part!

"My gold reserves had risen in value to nearly $200 an ounce, which meant that my property portfolio had basically cost me nothing.

"It was time to spread my wings again and set off into the wild blue yonder. It was then that I met Michael."

Chapter 49 Michael

Time was racing on and it wouldn't be long before the sun set, but DCI Barratt had shown no indication that he was bored or restless as I continued my confessional.

"I liked Michael as soon as I saw him. In many ways he reminded me of what I'd quite like to have become. Or rather, what I might like to have been in an earlier life. But in reality, my mould was already cast. I had perfected the look and the persona of a crusty old seadog, which was scary enough to keep most people at bay. Just the way I liked it.

"Michael. It was always Michael for some reason. Even though Australians were renowned for abbreviating every word they could, Mike or Mickey or other such derivatives never stuck, and so Michael it was."

Barratt frowned. "So, who's Michael, and where does he fit in?"

"Ah, Inspector, all will become clear shortly. Please bear with me."

Barratt seemed to reprimand himself silently for the interruption. I was on a roll, and he must have felt that he'd risked the possibility of derailing me with his interruption.

"Michael was working at a law firm in the city as I recall. Clerk or some such position. I don't think he was training to be a lawyer, more of an accounting, admin type. One thing I knew for sure was that his heart wasn't really in it. He was born for the ocean. Why he hadn't followed his dreams was a mystery to me. But later I learned that his parents had been extremely risk averse. They had worked hard, although unsuccessfully, to extinguish any sense of adventure in him. Job security and a pension for life seemed to be their mantra. I guess his parents' and grandparents' attitudes had been shaped by living through depressions and recessions.

"Michael was a regular at the sailing club, always helping out with the bosuns and crewing whenever he got the chance. I therefore had very little hesitation in asking him to join me on the *Sea Dragon's* maiden voyage to the Abrolhos when he brought some papers over to my yacht to sign.

"The *Sea Dragon*, that's what I called my new cruiser.

"Michael's youthful enthusiasm was refreshing after having dealt with some of the old money in Perth. He must have been nineteen or twenty when we made what was to be a fateful journey up to the Abrolhos and where he met Kate, his future wife.

"I recall Michael had this far-fetched cock-and-bull story of buried treasure: a secret map which his dad had left him. I didn't believe a word of it. Actually, that's not quite right. As the mystery developed I became convinced that there was an element of truth in it, and let's be honest, who doesn't like a good treasure hunt?

"Of course, I did my best to hide my growing curiosity from him. But if there was treasure to be found, then the gold dragon within me needed to be fed—and if that meant relieving Michael of his haul, then so be it. After all, he wouldn't have been there at all but for me, would he?"

I glanced at Barratt, looking for a sign of approval but received none.

"The lovely Kate, however, was a complication that I hadn't foreseen. She was, and still is, a very beautiful woman and, not lacking in self-confidence, I half imagined conquering her myself. How wrong was I? Nope, she only had eyes for Michael."

Chapter 50 A Family Affair

The evening was drawing in and I asked Inspector Barratt if he would like to stay for tea or perhaps continue our discussions the following day.

"Let's keep going, Mr Lazarus," he said.

"Well, in that case I think we should invite you to stay for dinner."

"Thank you but no. May I remind you that this is still a voluntary interview, and I really don't want to cloud it with a social interaction. You are still under caution, Mr Lazarus."

There it was—a reminder that Barratt was an inspector in the Hertfordshire constabulary, not a friend or a priest, but a copper. I took a deep breath. Was I to stop now 'halfway through my confession' or was I to keep going? No—the time was right, I had gone too far now to back off. I looked at Barratt and sighed before continuing.

"Well, now I was in my early 40s—well OK, my mid 40s—and Kate must have been in her late teens or early 20s when we met in the Abrolhos. Notwithstanding the difference in our ages, she definitely had the potential to be a 'new ex-wife'. Michael on the other hand, had other ideas and, as it transpired, I got the gold, and he got the girl.

"I often wondered who got the better deal, but if I am being perfectly honest, I reckon we both did alright. They're still together now, you know.

"Kate gave birth to a strapping son, Wiebbe, and acquired a wonderful daughter-in-law Rose who has now presented them with a grandson and granddaughter!"

I could see Barratt trying to make sense of my lyrical storytelling as he must have felt that I was wandering off track.

"Rose is Ellie Bosa's stepdaughter," I said by way of explanation.

Barratt leant forward, grasping his hands together between his knees. I sensed that he was gathering more pieces of the puzzle and they were starting to fit together. I had deliberately said 'is', rather than 'was', to see Barratt's reaction, but if he had noticed, he didn't show any sign that he had.

"Inspector, I may have been slightly economical with the truth when we spoke last week but when you hear the rest of my story, I am sure you will understand why I felt the need to be, how shall I put it, 'circumspect.'"

I continued, "After I had left Michael and Kate in the Abrolhos, I made myself disappear for nearly two decades as I sailed around Southeast Asia. I tried to make sure that I was never in one place long enough to be regarded as anything other than a sailor passing through.

"Actually, when I say 'left', I mean, I robbed them of the treasure we found and left them in a shocking state on West Wallabi Island. It's something that I have since regretted, but at the time, I saw no other way. I can't tell you how relieved I was to find out that they had both survived. And I did console myself with the fact that I'd left them with a few gold coins which, I understand, paid for the deposit on their first house."

"So, what do you mean, a shocking state?" Barratt enquired.

"I cudgelled them both, smacked them on the noggin with my spade, took the gold and left them to die."

Barratt sat looking at me, clearly not sure whether to believe me or not.

"That's right, Inspector. I wasn't always a frail 90-year-old man."

"92 actually," Barratt said.

"Touché, Inspector. 92 it is." I smiled.

"After years of sailing around the South China Sea, I felt a need to put down roots, but I felt that returning to Australia was just not right. I had kept a small cottage in Fremantle, and more of that later, but really, I had no desire to live there.

"I ended up in Honiara and became a frequent visitor to the bars and clubs. Working my way through a bottle of rum and a girl or two a night seemed to be my destiny. It was then that fate dealt me a hand—and I met Hans."

Chapter 51 Hans Müller

Barratt leaned forward in his chair and asked "Who is Hans?"

"One evening I wandered into a tiny bar that I hadn't visited before and befriended a German by the name of Hans Müller. Hans was in his early 60s, weary of life and well on his way to drinking himself into an early grave. He was, however, an entertaining conversationalist—until that is, he had polished off the second half of a bottle of whisky. After that, he became belligerent and would eventually find himself being thrown out of the premises or, more often than not, left to sleep it off in a corner.

"Hans looked a lot older than he was. Although he still sported a full head of blonde hair, his weather-beaten, pockmarked face bore testament to the hard life of a German expatriate living in the tropics.

"Hans was down on his luck. He never seemed to have any money, so he was happy to sit and talk with me about the good old days—as long as I kept him supplied with alcohol. My rat instincts told me that there was more to Hans Müller than met the eye.

"For Hans, the good old days were the Third Reich. Hans was a proud Nazi and believed that had Germany won the war, the world would be a better place. He had an unwavering belief in his own racial superiority and regarded Churchill and Eisenhower as war criminals.

"One evening, half way through a bottle of Johnnie Walker, Hans admitted to me that he had been an *Undteroffizier* or Sergeant in the Wehrmacht, the German armed forces, during the war, and that he had arrived in the Solomons towards the end of the war on a secret mission to accompany several high-ranking officers of the Waffen-SS. I tried my best to look suitably impressed, which obviously worked since he leant across the table between us and, glancing furtively from side to side, whispered in my ear, 'I know vhere ze gold iz.'

"Now my ears pricked up. I said to him, 'What are you talking about, Hans?

"He replied, 'Not here. Too many, how do you say? Nosey farters.' I remember laughing and correcting him, "nosey parkers you stupid Kraut. 'Right, nosey parkers,' he'd replied.

"It was a few weeks later that I managed to get Hans to revisit the conversation that he had begun—and subsequently forgotten. When I caught up with him again, Hans was not well. His tremors had worsened, and his rakish cough brought blood into the palm of his hand.

"I had arranged a modest lodging for him, above the bar where we had met. It wasn't an act of charity but purely self-interest. If Hans had some inside information on the location of Nazi gold, then I wanted to be the first to know about it. Mind you, if he really did know anything, then it begged the question, why was he living in such a state of abject poverty?"

I recalled the conversation to Barrett using my best impersonation of Hans's thick German accent.

"Hans said to me, 'Vhen I vaz *Undteroffizier*, I vas part of ze most secret mission. I vaz to guard a huge haul off gold zat ve liberated from ze Jews, und take it to Japan wiz ze officers from ze Waffen-SS. Ze route zat ve took vas—how do you say?—Very dizzy?'

"'Circular,' I corrected him—although to be fair, his English was much better than my German.

'Ya, das is right, circular,' he'd said.

"I remember laughing as he explained 'Ve ended up in ze fucking Solomons just as ze whole fucking US Navy arrived in Savo Sound und blew za crap out off us. My Officers ver killed, und I alone survived. Ze gold went down wiz ze ship.'

"Fanciful stories about fabulous sunken treasure in the sound were commonplace, Inspector, but there was something about Hans's story that rang true. Have you heard of the Iron Bottom Sound?"

Barratt shook his head.

"Well, it's a stretch of water between the Guadalcanal and Savo and Florida Islands in the Solomons. It used to be called Savo Sound but, after literally hundreds of ships and planes were sunk there during WWII, the US Navy re-named it the Iron Bottom Sound.

"That evening, I pressed Hans on the location of his treasure ship but still, he was reluctant to tell me and entered into another coughing fit before passing out in his chair.

"The following morning, I visited the bar and was told he was still asleep in his room upstairs. There was nothing particularly odd about that. He was probably sleeping it off.

"After an hour or so, there was still no sign of Hans, so I left the company of the proprietor at the bar and made my way up the narrow wooden staircase towards his room. The treads were bare and the green and cream paint on the walls was flaking off. Holes in the walls bore testament to pictures that had been hung there in the past but repeatedly knocked off as people and furniture had negotiated the narrow confines.

"Hans's door was on my left and slightly ajar. I pushed it open with the toe of my white canvas plimsoll and saw him lying on his bed, still wearing the clothes from the night before.

"The shutters on the single window were closed, making the room dark. My eyes took a moment to adjust to the low light.

"Hans had his back to me. I put my hand on his shoulder and rolled him towards me. Instantly I knew Hans was dead. He was cold and stiff, and his lips were blue. Dried vomit stained the bed beside him and clogged his airways.

"My initial reaction was to rush downstairs, inform the proprietor, and call the police. However, something inside me made me hesitate. If Hans had been telling the truth about a cargo of gold, then maybe he had kept a record of where the ship was lying. That might explain why he was living in abject poverty if he could not retrieve it himself. So close and yet so far.

"I looked around the room and then started to search it methodically. Not that there was much there in terms of personal possessions. There was, however, a large sea chest, not unlike the one that Danny had had on the *Antipodean Queen*.

"I opened it easily to reveal a collection of neatly folded clean clothes. I lifted up the internal sliding shelf to reveal a copy of Mein Kampf and some newspaper-cuttings written in German that I couldn't read.

"As I set the copy of Adolf Hitler's autobiography to one side, an old black-and-white photograph fell out from between its pages. It was of Hans with the Fuhrer himself. But Hans was not wearing the uniform of a *Unteroffizier* from the Wehrmacht but the uniform of an *SS-Obersturmbannfuhrer* or Lieutenant Colonel as we would have called him. The striking lightning *SSs* were clearly visible on his right collar.

"'So, Hans, my little lying Nazi,' I thought, 'What else have you been hiding?'

"I pocketed the book and the photo and rolled him gently off the bed to search under the mattress. Hans's body landed with a thump on the wooden floor and for a moment I was fearful that the noise would bring the proprietor up the stairs, but the continued clinking of bottles from the bar below afforded me some comfort.

"Under the mattress I discovered a large leather folder, tied together with a leather thong.

"It was then that I heard a heavy footfall on the stairs outside and I quickly stuffed the folder beneath my shirt and down the front of my trousers, leaning over Hans just as the owner entered the room.

"I looked back over my shoulder at him and said, 'Poor old Hans. Looks like he's died in his sleep.'

"The proprietor looked at me suspiciously and then glanced at Hans's body. 'There's rent karamapim tok wanpela kago bihain long to be paid,' he'd said in Pidgin.

"I said I'd make good any of Hans's bills and asked him if he could please call the police and the undertaker for me, while I tried my best to make him look decent. He wasn't keen to stay in the room with a dead body and made his way back down the stairs.

"I did my best to lay Hans back on the bed, and arranged his arms and legs with some dignity. I had no idea of what atrocities Hans may have been responsible for in WWII but to me, he was a human being. I felt a strange duty to treat his body with respect. That respect, however, didn't prevent me conducting a thorough search of his room.

"That search revealed no more than a few items of personal clothing, some coins and notes in his bedside table—which I left in place, and a Knight's Cross of the Iron Cross, with its red, white and black ribbon, which I pocketed.

"I learned later that it was a prerequisite of this award that you had to have already received the first and second-class Iron Cross. Hans was apparently a brave soldier and a war hero in his time.

"The police arrived and quickly determined that the elderly Hans had died in his sleep. Which, I thought, was nicer than saying he'd drowned in his own vomit. No one seemed to know of any living relatives, so I suggested that his belongings and the small amount of cash I had found, be given to the proprietor of the bar to help cover any outstanding debts. The proprietor wasn't too happy about it until I told him that I would make up any shortfall."

Chapter 52 Consequences

Barratt asked "What was in the folder?"

"That evening, I retreated to the *Sea Dragon.* I placed the folder on my galley table. Untying the leather thong, a sheaf of papers slipped out, consisting of a marine chart and some notes typed in German. The chart and the notes were annotated with scribbled handwriting and would you believe it, an X marks the spot on the chart.

"I grabbed my English-German dictionary and started painstakingly to translate those pages and the handwriting.

"It looked like the freighter Hans had been on, was the victim of an airborne torpedo attack. There was some question as to whether it was friendly fire or an American Douglas TBD Devastator. My dictionary didn't include swear words, but I got the drift when I read the scrawled text next to the X on the chart: 'Zu verdammt tief! Ficken!!!'"

Barratt raised an eyebrow.

"Too damn deep! Fuck!!!

"My heart raced. If this ship did indeed have Nazi gold on board, then the chances were that it was still there. I had discovered the location of the freighter—but it was far beyond recreational SCUBA diving limits.

"I should have known, but rarely had I fallen foul of the law and I imagined foolishly, that the laws of physics didn't apply to me either.

"The next morning, I got two SCUBA tanks filled at the local fire station and sailed *Sea Dragon* over to the site of the wrecked freighter. It took the better part of a day to get there, despite a swift following breeze. On arrival, I let down a grapple and was excited when it snagged with a reassuring metallic clunk on the wreck over 100 metres below.

"My two tanks were never really going to be enough, but I reasoned that this would be a simple bounce dive.

"I was, however, shocked at the rate that I emptied the first tank. Soon my breathing became laboured, and I reached behind me to find the pushrod that would give me access to its reserve. We don't have those sorts of tanks these days, Inspector. At the time there was no such thing as a reliable submersible pressure gauge, so the tanks were designed to increase breathing resistance as they emptied, until the reserve was met. At that point, you reached behind your back and pulled the pushrod to give you access to your reserve.

"The wreck of the freighter was magical. I'll never forget the way that she appeared out of the gloom as I descended. I was quite mesmerised. I found the hole in the hull as I sucked in the last of the air from my first tank and finned quickly towards it, holding my breath as I did so.

"Then I saw them. Gold bars everywhere, spilling out of the hold where the torpedo had violently ruptured the hull. My excitement was beyond words. It was all that I could do to remember to breathe. I was narked off my head as I stretched out my arm and grabbed just one of those bars before I realised that I was in big trouble.

"Something told me I didn't have enough air to make a safe ascent. Grabbing more than one bar and I wouldn't have been able to surface at all. But then again laws didn't apply to Lazarus I thought, and I quickly stuffed the bar down the front of my swimming costume. No wet suit or BCD in those days either, Inspector.

"Now, these days we have sophisticated computer algorithms to assist SCUBA divers in making safe ascents, including deco stops and safety stops. In those days, all we had was the US Navy's human experimental data to guide us.

"My mind was so foggy with the nitrogen narcosis that I thought I might just get away with it. Coming to the surface, I felt fine."

"Fine?"

"Fucked-up, Insecure, Neurotic and Emotional," I laughed.

Barratt smiled. "What happened next?"

"Well, if you know anything about decompression diving, it's really the last little bit that gets you. You see, the change in pressure from 100 to 50 metres is 50%. The change, however, from 10 metres to the surface is 100%. It's that, which causes nitrogen bubbles to form in your tissues and blood as the gas comes out of solution. Like taking the top off a bottle of fizzy drink. Do it too quickly and you get a mess."

"You got the bends?"

"I waited as long as I could at 5 metres but very quickly, I had to pull the pushrod on my tank to access my reserve. I tried to breathe slowly and deeply, not that it would have helped, but after what seemed to be but a few breaths my tank ran dry.

"I could see the surface and the hull of *Sea Dragon* tantalisingly close above me and had no option but to swim for it. I didn't have any more tanks on board or a means to fill them, so even a risky in-water decompression was out of the question. Had I had a spare tank on board, I could have dropped back down to 5 metres to attempt an in-water deco stop. It's risky, but given no alternative, it would have to have been better than nothing.

"As it was, I recall lying on the deck gulping air at one atmosphere as the pain started to wrack my body. I don't know how long I was there, but I do remember being woken by the bright light of the morning sun on my eyes and a burning sensation down my left side. I tried unsuccessfully to move my left arm and noticed the skin crackled as I rolled onto my side, trapping my arm against the teak decking. Nitrogen in my skin was still trying to escape. I managed to get to the cabin and drank pint after pint of water.

"I stayed there anchored up to the wreck for another two days. It was longer than I wanted, as I was keen to avoid attention, but I was in no fit state to skipper. After a couple more days, I was just about capable and set off back to Honiara to seek medical attention. Although I had recovered some use of my left arm, it was, however, too late to make a full recovery. My diving days were over."

I lifted my left arm with my right and said, "I've got my arrogance to thank for this, Inspector."

"What of the gold, Mr Lazarus? Did you manage to keep it?"

"I retrieved one bar of gold—but oh! The agony of leaving the others behind was almost too much to bear. Whilst I was forced to accept that my diving days were over, I had no one in the Solomons that I felt I could trust to recover the remaining bars.

"That's when I remembered Michael and Kate. As you know, I felt guilty about leaving them for dead on the Abrolhos, and I surmised that they would be none too pleased to hear from me, so calling them up and asking them for their help was never going to work. I had to devise a plan.

"It was during my time in the Solomons that I'd been forced to attend a social event in the hotel part-owned by my soon to be appointed lawyer, Mr Bosa. It was also at that fateful gathering that I met Mrs Bosa."

Chapter 53 Ellie

Barratt seemed to be piecing the bits together. "Tell me about your relationship with Mrs Bosa" he said.

"We became lovers, Inspector. She was wildly enthusiastic, and I was a willing partner in her adultery. We'd meet secretly on her overseas shopping sprees and fuck each other's brains out. There was never any suggestion that she would leave her husband and, on my part at least, I never gave her any encouragement to do so. The only problem was, she fell in love with me. Apparently, I'm quite irresistible."

Barratt returned my smile. He appeared to be enjoying my confession as much as I was.

"If I'm being honest, Inspector, I liked Ellie a lot—but to say I was in love with her was, perhaps, a bit of a stretch. I wasn't even sure I knew what love was, at that time.

"My plan was simple. I had to disappear from Mr Bosa's circle of friends and convince him that I was dead. I'd leave him with a letter to be sent to Michael and Kate—upon the occasion of my death—encouraging them to come to the Solomons and retrieve my gold."

"Wasn't that difficult, given the fact that you were now part of Honiara's high society?"

"Oh, not really, Inspector. You see, I wasn't really part of the high society. I despised those gatherings. I attended so few that I knew I wouldn't be missed.

"Bosa was a bumbling idiot—but cunning too—so I had to make sure he did the right thing. I left instructions with him to send my letter to Michael and Kate if he hadn't heard from me by a certain date. If he didn't hear from me, he was to assume I was dead. I may have also hinted that I had a terminal disease and not long to live," I said with a guilty smile.

"I also left a briefcase at his office to pass to Michael and Kate. Inside was the one-kilogram Nazi gold bar which I had retrieved from the Japanese freighter."

"A bit dramatic," Barratt said.

"I wasn't under any illusion that if Michael and Kate thought I was alive, they would do their utmost to dob me into the authorities or, worse still, ignore me. Also, they needed hard evidence. The gold bar was all of that."

"So, you persuaded them, from the grave, to go to Honiara and recover the gold?"

"My gold, Inspector. It was always mine."

"So, what happened?"

"Ellie and I were carrying on our clandestine affair, and she was to be my partner in crime—but my plans were always to double-cross her. She'd forgive me, I was sure."

I smiled, remembering how we'd always get back together passionately after our little squabbles.

"Ellie was very materialistic—and easy to placate with a new bauble." There it was. I'd mentioned her name in the past tense. Still, Barratt hadn't reacted.

"Once the gold was recovered, it became apparent that Ellie had had her own plans to double-cross me, the Hawkins, and her husband. Fortunately, it takes one to know one—and I had anticipated something of the kind. However, I didn't think at the time that it would turn me into a kidnapper!"

Barratt looked questioningly into my eyes.

"I sort of kidnapped Rose," I said, by way of explanation.

"Sort of? You mean like being sort of pregnant?"

"Well, if you put it that way, I suppose I did kidnap her, but only as a way of reacquainting myself with the Hawkins and bringing them into my confidence. We all got along splendidly at the reunion on my yacht—well, that is, after the guns were put away. I chortled at the expression on Barratt's face. I wasn't sure if he believed me or not.

"So, what became of Ellie?" Barratt was keen to get the conversation back on track.

"In time, Inspector. Shall I continue?"

"Please."

I called out from the lounge, "David, make a fresh pot of tea, will you? There's some fruitcake in the red tin in the larder, which wouldn't hurt either.

"Inspector, that little recording device you have between us isn't going to run out of tape, is it?"

"It's a digital device, Mr Lazarus. Good for a few more hours yet."

"And I'll get a transcript of his conversation?"

"Well, we can see about that. It all depends on where we end up."

"I'd very much like that," I said.

"Ellie and I continued our affair although we had to be increasingly discreet. Unfortunately, I hadn't realised just how emotionally attached to me she was becoming.

"Michael and Wiebbe had retrieved half of the gold from the wreck before disaster struck. The Sound claimed the other half but that as they say, is another story. The gold they retrieved was eventually loaded onto *Sea Dragon.*

"Wiebbe, that's Michael and Kate's son, and Rose, that's Bosa's daughter and Ellie's stepdaughter, agreed to help me sail *Sea Dragon* down to Freo. That's what the locals call Fremantle.

On the way, we transferred the gold over to Michael and Kate's stink boat in the Abrolhos and, once safely back in Aus, we planned to divide the spoils.

"Unfortunately, Ellie had other ideas and shot me in the hallway of my own little cottage in Freo!"

If Barratt thought he couldn't be surprised any more, he was mistaken.

"It was Ellie?"

"Yes, Inspector. I knew it was her as soon as I heard her voice and smelt her perfume. Of course, there was no point in reporting that level of detail to the local cops. It was bound to get messy and even though their kind Detective Sergeant Grant always had his suspicions, he was forced to accept that it was little more than a home invasion or robbery gone wrong.

"A woman scorned, Inspector, is one thing. A woman scorned with a gun is something quite different.

"Ellie's marriage to Bosa was doomed from the very start. I couldn't imagine that I was the only fling that she had, and it wasn't long before she and Joe Bosa split, on what I understand were quite acrimonious terms. As for me, I was glad to be out of it.

"Following the recovery of the Nazi gold and my subsequent disappearance, I did return secretly to Freo from time to time. I'd long since accepted that my sailing days were over—but I was drawn, like a moth to the flame, to Fremantle Sailing Club.

There, I could watch the slow resurrection of *Sea Dragon*, monitor her refurbishment from a distance, and—every now and then—slip aboard while the work was being done. Just to check it out, you understand. Not to interfere. Not to reminisce. Just to feel the deck beneath my feet again."

"Did you reconnect with the Hawkins?" Barratt asked, his tone unreadable.

"Oh no, that ship had sailed a long time ago, but it was relatively easy to keep an eye on them, especially through the increasingly omnipotent social media."

Barratt smiled. I was sure that he was envisioning me engaging in what was widely regarded as the domain of the baby boomers. Not yet dead, I thought. Well, not yet dead again!

"I thought it best to disappear. I sold my cottage in Freo and made sure that the proceeds went to Rose's favourite orphanage in Honiara. Having heard of my own experiences, I know you'll understand why I chose to do that. I hoped—and still hope—that the money might do some good and orphans will be able to avoid the brutal environment I was subjected to, all those years ago. The pictures I see of all those children's smiling faces online gives me a little comfort—that at least I have done some good with my life."

Barratt interrupted my silent contemplation. "The gold that was transported to Australia in what, the early 2000s? What did the authorities do about that? Wasn't there duty and enquiries and the like to be sorted?"

"Inspector, you shouldn't necessarily believe all I tell you. Just the good bits.

"Your cold case review is concerning the disappearance of Ellie Bosa, is it not?"

"Yes, but what you have given me is compelling evidence to suggest that, at the very least, you are a person of interest and had a motive and opportunity to see Ellie disappear.

"Did you kill Ellie Bosa, Mr Lazarus?"

I laughed out loud. "You know, Inspector, sometimes over the last 50 years I have thought that I should have, perhaps on more than one occasion."

Barratt sat stony faced.

There was a rattle of keys in the front door as David called out from the kitchen, "Hi Mum! I'm in the kitchen."

The rustling of designer-branded shopping bags accompanied rattling of the keys and golden charm bracelets. "Take these bags, David. I'm exhausted. Where's Dad?"

"In the lounge."

"Ah, Ellie my dear," I said, "do come in. This is DCI Barratt; he's been looking for you."

END

About the Author

Born in north Yorkshire, Nigel went to school and grew up in the southeast of England.

Following graduation from the University of Hull with a joint Honours degree in Botany and Geography, he worked initially in the operating theatre of the Kent and Sussex Hospital in Tunbridge Wells, while he tried to figure out what to do with his life.

After a year he relocated to London to work for a company located just behind Westminster Abbey and later moved into international marketing and sales for a company in Berkhamsted, Hertfordshire.

He emigrated to Australia in 1990 after travelling the world with his job and deciding that Perth in Western Australia was the perfect city in which to live.

In Australia, Nigel worked for the not-for-profit sector and began writing a regular column for Have A Go News.

In 2006, he found himself working alone with time on his hands and no money in his pocket. This was when he met Chris Oakeley from the Katherine Susannah Pritchard's Writer's Group who encouraged him to 'get on with it' and live his dream of becoming a writer. *Assume Murder* was born—later to be followed by *Lazarus* and in 2025, *Black Ice.*

Nigel has a passion for natural history, geology, game fishing, and SCUBA diving and a keen interest in business and commerce from his MBA undertaken at the University of Western Australia.

Nigel is married to Wendy and together they have one child, Jack, and two beautiful grandchildren.

www.ingramcontent.com/pod-product-compliance
Lightning Source LLC
LaVergne TN
LVHW091025080826
845145LV00002B/357